## A TUBE PUNCHES FORWARD AND HITS

me in the right side, puncturing my bare skin. A new pain blossoms as the tube grows and searches inside me, like a snake with claws tearing through my body, devouring me. The gel has reached my hips when the next tube juts into me, into my chest, tearing under my ribs and upward. And then another.

I think to scream, but words won't come. My brain refuses to function beyond survival.

No power is worth this. I don't want it anymore. I want to go home. To curl into a ball and die if it will make this pain go away. I've been lied to. This is the end. I'm locked in an icy coffin, defeated in some game of the gods. A pawn in their battle for power.

When the gel reaches my chest, I can't feel the lower half of my body anymore. Another tube shoots into my neck. My fingertips tingle and lose all sensation. I struggle, but the only thing I can move is my head. The gel is at my neck. My chin. I keep my lips pressed together even as the icy chill covers my nose. My eyes. Too late. I am either going to freeze to death or drown. The gel seeps into my ears. My nose. It covers my head completely. I can't move. Can't close my eyes. Can't hold my breath any longer.

I open my mouth and suck the gel in, and the icy cold hits my throat. It burns as it travels down into my lungs. I can't cough it out. I'm going to die.

# Books by P. J. Hoover

**Game of the Gods Series**
*A Broken Truce*
*A Ruined Land*
*A Buried Spark*

**The Hidden Code** (coming Fall 2019)

**The Dying Earth Series**
*Solstice*

**The Demigod Chronicles**
*Furiously Awesome*

**Tut: My Immortal Life Series**
*Tut: The Story of My Immortal Life*
*Tut: My Epic Battle to Save the World*

**The Forgotten Worlds Trilogy**
*The Emerald Tablet*
*The Navel of the World*
*The Necropolis*

**Camp Hercules Series**
*The Curse of Hera*

# A BROKEN TRUCE

## GAME OF THE GODS
## BOOK 1

## P. J. Hoover

ROOTS IN MYTH, AUSTIN, TX

This is a work of fiction. All of the characters, organiza-
tions, and events portrayed in this novel are either products
of the author's imagination or are used fictitiously.

A BROKEN TRUCE
Game of the Gods Book 1

A Roots in Myth Book
Austin, TX
For more information, write
pjhoover@pjhoover.com
www.pjhoover.com

ISBN: 978-1-949717-06-8 (trade paperback)
ASIN: B07L611VCT (Kindle ebook)

First Trade Paperback Edition: January 2019

For Lola, for helping
me remember what it
was like

alpha

# THE PHONE IN OUR COMPUTER SCIENCE

classroom rings. I'm playing *QuestLord* on my cell phone because I've been stuck at level nine for a week. There has to be a way to get to level ten. I know I'll figure it out if I try hard enough, unless there's some kind of bug I don't know about. We're supposed to be working on our projects, but mine's been done since Monday.

At the phone call, everyone immediately stops talking. Our teacher, Mr. Shortridge answers, looks my way. I slip the phone into my pocket. My pulse quickens. I go over the past week, trying to remember what I've done to call attention to myself.

I'd got my phone taken away twice during English, but that's nothing to get worked up about. I'd made it to every class except US History on Monday, but that's because Owen sent me a text asking me to meet him after lunch so we could talk about Homecoming. He hadn't been in school, I'm guessing because of the bite on his lip. There's nothing to talk about—no excuse for his behavior—and that's what I'd planned to tell him. Then I planned to tell him I never wanted to talk to him again. I'd even brought the haptic gaming kit he'd lent me, so in no way would I be indebted to him. I'd skipped class and gone to meet him . . . and he hadn't shown. His pathetic text excuse came the next day. He said he'd fallen asleep after lunch. I don't believe him. I should have just left the gaming kit on his doorstep and been done with him forever, except it's cutting edge technology and super expensive; someone could have stolen it. Now I'm kicking myself because skipping class has to be what the phone call's about. My parents are going to be furious.

Mr. Shortridge's face whitens, and my stomach clenches because I've never seen him look so upset. Maybe the phone call's not about me skipping class after all. He places the receiver back in the cradle.

"Edie."

Dread descends on the classroom like black soil filling a grave. I seem to be under that black soil, the rest of the world slipping away.

"What is it?" I click restart on the computer in front of me because it's been frozen for the last two minutes, stuck in some funky state. It needs to be reset. The computer screen blackens as everything disappears.

"They need you down in the office."

My feet are lead as I leave the classroom. Cool air hits my face as I walk through the breezeway, winding my way to the office. I think about texting Emily, but my hands are shaking. I'm not sure what I'd say anyway. That I'm in trouble? I have no clue if I'm in trouble or not.

My cell phone vibrates with an incoming call. The vibration reminds me of the feel of the haptic gaming gloves when I'd tried them. *Unknown number.* I swipe my finger across the screen, answering it.

"Hello."

"It's starting," says the voice of a little girl, high and cute like a pixie.

"What's starting?" I say. "Who is this?"

The call goes dead.

It must've been a wrong number. I repocket the phone and keep going.

I'm almost to the office when I see the police car parked out front of the school. It's silent though the lights spin around on top, letting the world know that the police are here on official business. The hard ball in my stomach tells me that it has to do with me.

They wait for me in the counselor's office, a man and a woman cop, both holding their hats in their hands. Mrs. Brine, my junior year counselor, stands off to the side, clasping and unclasping her hands in front of her, maybe wishing she had a hat to hold so she'd have something to do with her hands. Her face is even whiter than Mr. Shortridge's had been.

The woman cop is tiny, like a doll dressed up as a police officer. Her dark hair is slicked back in a bun she wears at the base of her neck, contrasting the wild brown curls that surround my face like a wooly mammoth. She steps forward.

"Edie Monk?" she says.

I stay in the doorframe, not wanting to move any closer to whatever she's about to say.

"Yes."

She takes a deep breath. Swallows. She won't look me in the eye. It's like her eyes are fixed on my cheek instead.

"I'm sorry to have to be the one to tell you that there's been an accident," she finally says.

An accident? My mind flies to Thomas. I'd dropped him at the elementary school this morning. He'd been especially pouty, claiming he was tired. He'd snuggled against me last night, tossing and turning for hours, keeping me awake.

"What kind of accident?" I hear myself ask, like my mind

**11**

knows this is the proper response even though there couldn't possibly have been some kind of accident that concerns me. They must have the wrong person.

The woman cop looks to the man. He's holding his face stern, hard, as if he's had more practice in whatever is about to come next. He nods, and the lady cop turns back to me. Stares at my cheek again. I resist the urge to wipe at it.

"It's your parents," she says.

"They're out of town," I say. "They'll be back Friday."

She shakes her head. "They're missing, Edie. Presumed dead. Their ship went down. I'm sorry."

Her words hang there in the air, echoing silently around my mind. I search for alternate meanings.

Their ship went down? That can't be right. They can't be dead.

"They're fine," I say. "I just got an email from them last night." My parents are underwater topographers, so a big part of their job is travel at sea. Cell phone service can be spotty, so I haven't talked to them since they left, but emails always seem to go through.

"It happened this morning," the man cop says. "We got the report two hours ago."

"You're kidding, right?" I ask. If it's a joke, it's not very funny.

Mrs. Brine, the counselor, finally steps forward and tries to wrap her arms around me. "I'm so sorry, dear."

I shrug her off and step backward. "They can't be dead. It's impossible. They just haven't been found yet." The last thing I'd told Mom was to leave me alone. I hadn't even gotten out of bed to say goodbye to them.

"There was rough water," the man cop says. "The ship capsized with no warning. When the Coast Guard arrived, there were no survivors. No life boats. It was too late. The ship was in pieces."

It's like his mouth won't stop moving. Mrs. Brine shoots him daggers with her eyes, and he finally stops talking, but the damage is done.

"We've talked to your next-door neighbors, the Pralls," the woman cop starts.

I don't want to hear what she has to say about my neighbors or anything else. I run.

## I DON'T STOP AT MY LOCKER. I'M OUT

the front doors of the high school and running next door to the elementary school. I have to get to Thomas.

The lady at the front desk sees me and buzzes me in. Mrs. Brine must have let them know I was coming.

She steps forward, like she's going to offer some kind of consolation. I cut her off before she can start.

"Where's Thomas?"

"He's with the counselor," she says, pointing down the hall behind her desk.

Thomas sits in a big green chair sucking on a lollipop, his shaggy brown curls a shorter imitation of mine. His wide eyes stare around the room, taking it in, adding to the collective memories of his seven-year-old self. He smiles when he sees me, holding the lollipop in place with his teeth.

They haven't told him yet. Sickness wells up in my throat. He's too young for this.

"We need to go," I say, reaching for him.

"I don't think that's a good idea," his counselor says, holding Thomas's shoulders like she's going to keep him from me.

"Come on, Thomas," I say, taking his tiny hand in mine. "We're leaving for the day."

He pulls the lollipop out with his other hand, long enough to say, "Is it a special day?"

I nod as I try to keep tears from forming in my eyes. My parents are not dead. I refuse to believe it. They are going to be found. "It's a really special day."

"I'm going to miss recess," he says.

"We'll have recess at home." I try to hold it together. He can't know anything is wrong. Not yet.

"I think it would be better if you both stayed here," the counselor says, but she's released her grip on Thomas's shoulder, almost like she doesn't want to have to deal with this any more than I do. "We can call social serv—"

I shoot her a look that silences her. "I'll handle it. Let's go, Thomas." And I lead him from the school.

"I'm cold," he says once we're outside.

I wrap my arms around him. It's only October and we live in Florida, but there's an unexpected chill in the air. A chill that says winter will come early this year. "We'll be home soon."

"But I'm cold now."

My car is parked back at the high school; it feels miles away.

"I'll get you a blanket at home," I say. "And make you hot chocolate."

"With whip cream?" he asks.

I want to nod. I think I do nod, maybe. Dad is always the one to make hot chocolate, piled high with cinnamon sprinkled on top.

"With whipped cream," I say.

It's only when we get to my car that I realize my keys are back in school. I try the handle, but of course I locked it. I kick the side of the car, not caring if I dent the rusted frame. Today can't be happening.

"I need to get my keys," I say, resigning myself to the fact that there is no other choice. With only the two of us here, shivering in the wind, the world feels empty. We are alone. Overhead an owl hoots, its sound carrying down through the breeze, making the world seem even emptier than it already does without my parents.

"I'm tired," Thomas says. "Can I stay here?"

Thomas is seven. I'm not leaving him by himself in a parking lot.

"You can't stay here alone," I say.

"But my legs are tired."

I bend to scoop him up, but when I'm at ground level, I spot my keys, on the asphalt just under my car. I can't have dropped them here. I hang them in my locker every day. Except I must be wrong because here they are.

When I stand up and look across the parking lot, a guy with messy brown hair and dark skin wearing a blue and green plaid shirt watches me. I don't think he goes to our school, but I swear I saw him the other day in the grocery store. He'd asked me what time it was. The guy's picked the shadiest spot to stand, under a nest of low palm trees, as if he's trying to keep his presence a secret. He steps back, deeper into the shadows, and when I blink, he's no longer there. The shadows close in on the place where he just was. In that moment I want as much distance between myself and those shadows as possible. I want the sun to come out and brighten up the world. But with my parents missing, that brightness seems so far off.

The owl hoots once more, and I look away from the shadows. Once Thomas is buckled in, I shove my keys in the ignition and drive.

## MRS. PRALL WAITS FOR ME OUTSIDE

the front door. The police must have told her to expect me.

"Edie, sweetheart, I'm so sorry." Her voice cracks, and a sob catches in her throat.

I fight the sob that threatens to take hold in my own throat, studying our black front door instead. Someone's scratched the paint, carving a series of concentric circles deep enough that the metal shows underneath. Probably the kids from a couple streets over. I haven't noticed it before, but then with what happened with Owen at Homecoming, my mind's been a little out of it.

"What's she sorry about?" Thomas asks. His sucker is long gone, but he's still chewing on the lollipop stick.

I kiss the top of his head. "Nothing, Thomas." I fix my eyes on Mrs. Prall to silence her, unlock the front door, and walk inside. She must think I'm going to let her trail in after me because she steps forward. I close the door and lock it, sealing the world outside.

Only then do I let the tears come.

"What's wrong, Edie?" Thomas asks.

My keys drop to the black tile floor, falling beside my tears. Thomas takes my hand; he's not sure what to do.

"It's okay, Edie," he says, patting my hand. "I'm here."

"It's not okay." I don't know what to tell him. I wish I could pinch him and make him wake up from this nightmare. All I can picture are my parents floating in the water, face-up, looking at the sky as their lives slip away. And my last words to Mom, telling her to leave me alone.

No, I refuse to believe they're dead. My parents are survivors. They will have figured out a way out of this. They will come home.

I wipe at my face and squat down to his level, putting my arms on his shoulders.

"There was an accident," I say, and even in this horrible moment, it strikes me how identical my words are to the cop's. An accident. I know what he'll say next.

"What kind of accident?" he asks as if he's reading the same script I read only a half hour ago.

"It's Mom and Dad," I say, taking deep breaths in an attempt to get the words out without crying.

It's no use.

"What about Mom and Dad? Where are they? Are they going to be late?" He bites his lip. The lollipop stick lays discarded on the black tile next to my keys.

It's way more than being late. They've extended work trips before, by a day, maybe two. How I wish it were only that.

"They're—" I choke on my words.

"They're what, Edie?"

I shake my head. Try to pull it together. I can't say *dead*. I won't say *dead*.

"They're missing," I finally say. It's all I can accept.

It takes me forever to get my tears under control, but I have to be strong for Thomas. I manage to get up and lead Thomas to the sofa. He lies down. His head rests on my lap, and I stroke his curly brown hair, letting the strands of this new reality become my reality. Mom and Dad are missing. They could be dead. How many times had we sat in this same family room, watching a movie, eating popcorn? I freeze the image of our happiness in my mind.

Our answering machine is filled with messages. Mom's sister, Kathy, called from Colorado, saying she's booking the next flight, that she'll take care of us, that we can move to Colorado. Grandma Peg, Dad's mother, gives a long rambling excuse about how she's too sick to travel. How she wants to be with us, but it's not possible, and will we be okay? Of course we're not going to be okay. Our parents are gone. I delete each and every message. I don't return calls. I have no plans of moving to Colorado because Mom and Dad will come back and take care of us, just like always.

I pull out my cell phone and see a bunch of texts from Emily. I don't have it in me to read through them right now, especially when I see that one of the messages is asking about Owen. I didn't tell her what he'd done after the dance. I just want to pretend it never happened. Emily's text says she talked to him earlier. That he said I was mad at him. It's all so unimportant now.

There's one voicemail waiting on my cell phone.

It's from Mom.

"Something's happening, Edie," Mom says in the voicemail. In the background, sirens wail, and there's a bunch of static like the wind is blowing and she's up on deck. "The waves are rocking the boat. I've never seen anything like it before. There's no storm. Just horrible turmoil."

Her voice cuts off as screams pierce the background. A voice comes over the intercom on the ship, but I can't hear it with everything else going on.

"I think we dug too far this time, sweetheart," Mom says. "I think . . . it doesn't matter. We made a mistake. Now it's too late. You have to be strong. And whatever you do, don't trust anyone.

**19**

Nobody, Edie, seriously. You have to find it on your own, where everyone else has forgotten. You have to remember."

The sirens are blaring. They keen in the background like melodic voices, calling my parents to their death, rising and falling in pitch as my parents' future slips away.

"I love you both so much," she says. Then there's a shrill squeal, and the message ends.

That can't be all there is. Can't be the end of my parents. Their final mark on the world. A sob catches in my throat before I can stop it, and tears stream down my face. Another sob follows the first, but I try to swallow it.

"What is it?" Thomas asks. He's sitting up. Without realizing it, I've stopped rubbing his hair.

"It's Mom and Dad," I manage to say, wiping my eyes with the back of my hands. "They told me to tell you that they love you."

Thomas bites his lip and nods, but he doesn't cry.

Later, once he's finally asleep, I turn on the news. I don't want to disturb Thomas from his small sliver of escaped reality, but I have to know what they're saying about the shipwreck. See if it's become a story on the nightly news. I've searched online, but haven't found any mention so far.

The screen is split, one news guy standing on a beach, with lights illuminating him. In the background, the wind howls and water slaps against the sand. The sky glows orange. His hair blows in every direction, but he doesn't seem aware of it. On the other half of the screen stands a woman newscaster in front of what looks like a desert though it's too dark to tell. The sky glows orange behind her, too, and the wind whips her long hair in front of her face.

Inset at the bottom of the screen is another woman. She, unlike the other two, is perfectly coiffed, sitting at a desk at the news headquarters.

"Twin volcanos?" she says.

The man glances back at the water. Takes a step forward like that will separate him from whatever is behind him. The orange flickers in the sky. "We've never seen anything like this before," he says. "It grew out of nowhere, upsetting one small vessel in the nearby area."

My parents' ship. He must be reporting from Cocoa Beach, since that's where their ship went out from, though nothing on the screen identifies his location.

"We have the same thing here," the woman in the desert says. "The volcano grew in a matter of hours and doesn't show signs of stopping." Like the man, there is nothing that states where she is.

I flip to the next news channel, looking to see if I can find more information about where they might be, but all I find are stock reports and late night sitcoms with laugh tracks that make me want to pound the noise out of my brain. After checking every other news station I can think of, I switch back to the one I was watching, but there is no sign of the volcano report. The newscasters are gone. Instead, the regular news guy reports on the weather which he keeps saying is sunny and clear. Sunny and clear. I turn the TV off then back on, but I can't find anything anywhere. One minute it was there. The next minute, I can't find any report of my parents' shipwreck. And the Internet shows nothing. It's almost like it didn't happen. Like the world doesn't care.

Anger bubbles inside me, threatening to overflow. I want to throw the remote through the television. I want to rip the sofa cushions to shreds. It's not fair that my parent's death should be minimized. It's not fair that they're dead.

No, they're not dead. They're missing.

Logic. It's all I have. I grasp for it. It pushes at the anger, attempting to quell it. I can figure out what happened. Logic is my specialty. There is always a reason things happen. A cause for every effect.

I grab a notebook and a pencil off the coffee table and flip it open to a clean page, fighting the emotions that threaten to overtake me. Like I'm making a flowchart in Computer Science, I draw a rectangle and label it *"Volcano in ocean"* and underneath it I put a diamond labeled *"Cause of shipwreck?"* I know it's the cause. But if there was underwater volcanic activity, what caused that?

Mom's voicemail returns to me. *We dug too far.* On the *Yes* branch-off that is my next diamond, I write, *"Related to research?"* I'm not sure how it's related, but Mom's message seemed to imply this. I start to draw the next diamond to determine how, but my eyes are too watery. I can't see past the tears. No matter how many flowcharts I draw, my parents are still gone.

## iv

**I FLIP OFF THE TELEVISION AND PUT**
my notebook back on the table, but I don't sleep. Instead I turn
out the lights and walk through the shadows. It's especially dark
because the streetlight out front has gone off, casting our cul-de-
sac into blackness. I study the shadows, searching for movement,
but there is none.

Sitting in the hallway near the front door is the bag with the
haptic goggles and gloves Owen had lent me. I'd wanted them so
badly. Been so excited when Owen said his dad was actually on
the development team for them and that he had some at home
he could lend me. I still remember when I hooked them to my
computer for the first time. They brought video game playing to
an entirely different level. I'd used them the entire weekend. After
I got the hang of them, I'd tried some VR online games against
other people and won every single one. But I'd never felt completely immersed in the games. Even though the goggles blocked
out the rest of the world, I was always aware of it there around me.

Now I take the goggles from the bag and slip them over my

head in the darkness. Though they aren't hooked to anything, immediately my surroundings shift.

*I sit in the chair in front of my computer, at the desk in my room. Owen is here with me. We're working on his Computer Science project—or at least I am. He pushes my laptop closed and pulls at my hand, leading me to the bed. But I don't want to go to the bed. He asks every time we're together. I tell him no. Tell him I'm not ready.*

*I open my mouth to tell him this again, because with Owen I seem to need to say things multiple times. But before words can come out of my mouth, Owen presses his lips to mine, soft at first, and for a second, I think he finally gets it. I rest my hands back on the quilt Grandma Peg made. Owen tastes sweet, like he's had dessert, and I kiss him again. But as my lips part, his kisses become more forceful. He presses hard with his mouth, pushing against my lips and teeth until I taste blood mingling in with the sweetness. My hands come up.*

*"Stop," I try to say, but Owen grabs my wrists and knocks me off balance. I fall to my back, breaking our connection, but his lips are back on mine before I can hardly catch my breath. Now that his weight is on top of me, holding me down, he lets go of my wrists. I push at his shoulders to get him off me, but he's never felt so enormous before. I'm like a fly pushing against a brick wall.*

*Owen shifts his hand to my shirt and starts fumbling with the buttons, but they're tiny, and in seconds he gives up and yanks the shirt apart, sending buttons flying across my quilt. I twist and move but this only seems to make Owen more eager. He reaches inside my shirt and squeezes so hard, tears spring to my eyes. This can't be happening.*

*His hands knead my skin, and all I can think about is getting him off me. My shirt is wide open now and his hands drift lower, fumbling at the top of my jeans. I can't let him go any farther. I can't let this happen. Owen gets the button and the zipper undone and reaches his hand inside my pants. He yanks them down with both hands, but this gives me a small opportunity to break free. I try to sit up, but Owen's hand comes up and smacks me across the cheek, sending me reeling back to the bed. And though I continue to fight him, he doesn't stop.*

I yank the goggles off and throw them across the dark hallway. The vision disappears, but my head pounds. I'm shaking like everything I've just seen is real. Like all of it really happened. My cheek stings where Owen slapped me. My thighs ache. Except it wasn't real. It was only my imagination. The goggles aren't even hooked up. I'm here, in my house, alone except for Thomas who is sleeping out on the sofa in the family room. My mind is trying to cope with what Owen did at Homecoming. With my parents being gone.

I take a step, but my legs collapse from under me, and the veins in my head throb. From the shelves on the wall, Mom's doll collection stares down at me with unblinking eyes, like they're judging me. They've never bothered me before, but I hate them in that moment. It's as if they're alive and they've become witness to my weakness, my humiliation. Like they know what happened.

I turn away from the dolls but stay there, on the cold tile, late into the night until my shaking subsides and my head stops pounding.

V

## THE MORNING COMES. NEITHER THOM-

as nor I go to school. I text Emily a quick message because she's texted me twenty more times, first seeing what's wrong, then asking if I'm okay. She must've heard what happened.

"Not sure what to do," I text back, pushing last night's hallucination of Owen far from my mind. I should tell Emily what Owen did at Homecoming, but I can't bring myself to text it out, not now with everything else going on.

I plug my phone in since it's pretty much dead. Less than a minute later, it dings, telling me my text message to Emily didn't go through. To try again later. I resend it. Then my phone rings.

It's Aunt Kathy, from Colorado.

"Edie, how are you doing?" she says. She's out of breath, like she's either really nervous to be talking to me, or she's upset. Maybe both.

I pluck petals off the now-dead corsage Owen had bought me, throwing them in the bowl where I normally keep my keys. But pulling petals off isn't enough. I drop the whole thing to the floor and grind it under my foot. Hatred burns inside me. My legs ache and my cheek stings. Smashing the flower he gave me isn't going to erase Owen from my past and it's certainly not going to bring my parents back to me, but it does make me feel better.

"Fine," I say to Aunt Kathy. "Horrible. I don't want to believe it's true."

"I don't either," she says. "They were just so alive. And now . . ." Her words trail off.

"They're still alive," I say. "They'll be found soon."

"I'm sure they will be," Aunt Kathy says. But she doesn't sound convinced.

"Are you still coming?" I ask, ignoring the defeated tone of her voice.

"We're trying," she says. "But they grounded all flights out of Denver."

"Grounded flights? Until when?" Now that Aunt Kathy said she's coming, I really want her here. She's the only family Thomas and I have, besides Grandma Peg.

"I don't know, Edie," Aunt Kathy says. "There was a bomb threat at the airport."

"Can you drive?" I ask, knowing I sound like a small child but not caring.

"That's what Simon and I are thinking," Aunt Kathy says. "We'll let you know."

"I'd really like to see you," I say.

"We'll be the—" Her words cut off as the call goes dead.

I try to redial her number, but my phone isn't charging, even though it's plugged in. I try a different plug, but it doesn't make any difference, so I finally give up. She and Uncle Simon will drive here. If they leave right now, they could be here in one day, maybe two. I can make it two days with Thomas.

"I'm hungry, Edie." Thomas comes into the kitchen, rubbing his eyes. I'd let him sleep in this morning. To stay in a happy place

**27**

as long as possible.

I haven't eaten in nearly a day, but the thought of food makes me want to vomit. I feel Owen's hands all over me, climbing up my skin, under my shirt.

I squeeze Thomas into a giant hug. "What do you want me to make you?"

"Toast with no crust?" he says in a tiny little voice.

"Done."

I put bread in the toaster and press the handle down, but it doesn't light up. So I pop it up and press it down again. Same thing. It's plugged in, but maybe the breaker flipped.

I flip the switch in the kitchen on and off, on and off, but the overhead light never comes on. It's bright enough outside that I hadn't thought to turn on the light before now. This must be why my phone isn't charging. We don't have electricity.

"I'll be right back," I say, and head out to the garage. Dad showed me plenty of times what to do if the power went out. With tropical storms, power outages are nothing new.

The garage is pitch black, so I grab a flashlight and open the breaker box. None of them have popped, but to make sure, I flip every single breaker and push the reset buttons on the wall plugs, but the lights still don't come on.

"How about cereal?" I say once I come back in. This is no big deal. It's happened plenty of times before. The power company will have it back on eventually.

"Lucky Charms?" he asks.

I put the cereal in a bowl and open the fridge. Ugh. The fridge. If the power doesn't come back on soon, everything will go bad. I pour milk over the Lucky Charms and get him a spoon. Then I head back out to the garage and grab our bin of camping gear. I set it on the kitchen table and dig out a small radio and shove some batteries inside. I scan through the stations, but all I get is some religious station with a burn-in-hell sermon about the devil intermixed with hymns, so I flip it off.

"Stay here," I say to Thomas.

His eyes widen. "Where are you going?"

"Next door," I say. "To check in with the Pralls."

I head out the back, closing the door behind me just to make sure that Thomas doesn't follow, then walk around the side of the house. Once I'm at their front door, I ring the doorbell, but I don't hear it ring inside the house. Their power must be out, too. I knock on the door instead, but no one answers. I press my ear to the door, and inside, I hear the faint sound of voices. I knock again, because maybe I can use their cell phone to call the power company. But there's still no reply.

When I get back to our house, I notice the same symbol that I'd found on our front door scratched into the back door—the concentric circles with lines connecting them. It looks familiar, but I can't place where I've seen it before. I'd search online for it except we have no electricity.

Just before I head inside, I turn back, because it feels like someone is watching me. The same guy with the brown hair from the parking lot at school is there, again hidden in the shadows. There's no mistaking his complexion or the plaid shirt he's wearing. He pulls a pencil from behind his ear and writes something in a notebook before turning away.

Inside, Thomas sits in front of the TV watching a blank screen.

"What are you doing, sweetheart?" I ask.

He doesn't reply. It must be shock. It's his way of dealing with everything.

"Thomas?" I say.

He still doesn't answer.

So I sink down on the sofa next to him and put my arm around him and hold him close. Maybe I'll visit Emily after school lets out. Except then I remember that Owen lives on her street. I could run into him. Which is stupid. I'm not going to avoid my best friend and change my life because Owen's a jerk. The vision I had wasn't real. It was just stress. Regardless, I'm not leaving Thomas, and right now staying at home seems the best idea.

We've only been sitting there five minutes when the house phone rings. It's so sudden and unexpected that I jump. The power must be back on.

I run for the table where my parents have the red rotary phone. It's an antique and has the kind of ring that rattles your whole body. It rings again just as I grab the receiver.

"Hello?" I say, out of breath.

Nothing.

"Hello?"

My only answer is silence.

"Aunt Kathy?" I say. She could be calling me to tell me they're almost here.

No one answers. Either it was some power glitch or my imagination. I want to believe that I'm not making things up. I replace the receiver in the cradle but then pick it up one more time just to make sure.

"Hello?"

There is no one there.

I fall asleep back on the sofa.

*I dream of a girl, maybe nine or ten, a couple years older than Thomas. She wears a blue scarf tied as a blindfold and has two blond ponytails sprouting beneath it. Her chin and cheeks are dirty, as if she's been playing in the mud.*

*"Why are you taking so long?" she asks me.*

*I try to answer her, but the words won't come out. Then my dream shifts and Owen is near. He walks closer, but for each step I take backward he takes two forward until he's right in front of me. I open my mouth to scream but he covers my mouth with his hand and forces his body against mine. I push at him, but I'm backed against a wall.*

*"Don't fight me," he says. "I'm stronger than you. More powerful*

than you."

*I hate him. How weak he makes me feel. I try to fight, but it's no use.*

"Edie," he says, except it's not really him saying it. It's Thomas, shaking me awake.

He's sucking on a Dum Dum, and I realize I haven't reminded him to brush his teeth yet today.

"What?" I rub my eyes and sit up, focusing on being awake instead of the nightmare. Owen has no right to invade my dreams.

"The phone rang again while you were asleep," he says.

The phone call was a hallucination, fueled by my brain which has gone into some crazy paranoid mode. It explains the vision about Owen. Thomas is only trying to make me feel better.

"No it didn't, sweetie," I say, brushing the dream and Owen from my mind.

He nods. "It did. I talked to someone."

Chills run up my bare arms. "Who did you talk to?"

"A girl," Thomas says. "She told me you were going away. Are you?"

"No way. I'm staying right here with you. Aunt Kathy and Uncle Simon should be here by tomorrow or the next day." It can't be too soon.

"I thought you went away earlier, Edie," Thomas says. "I couldn't find you."

I rub his hair, brushing his thick curls from his forehead. "I was right here, next to you."

"The girl said you were leaving me," Thomas says. "That I shouldn't worry about you. That you had to go."

"Who do you think it was?" I ask. Thomas is seven. Too old for imaginary friends. It's probably a coping mechanism.

"Iva," he says. "She said her name was Iva."

I pick up the receiver because I can't stop myself. There is still no dial tone, so I hang it back up and turn the radio on, but I can't even find the religious channel this time. I pull the cover from the

**31**

radio in an attempt to figure out what's wrong, but it's a bunch of wires. Give me computer code and I'd have this thing running in minutes. It would be a simple bug fix. *IF-THEN-ELSE*. But the little wires in the radio are foreign to me.

"She said I should tell Aunt Kathy not to worry about you either," Thomas says.

"I'm not going anywhere," I say, more firmly this time.

"Good," Thomas says, and he sits in front of the blank TV once more.

I try knocking on the Prall's door four more times, but they still aren't answering. I swear I even see them moving around inside. I try some of the other neighbors, too, but it's like there's something shielding me from them. When I get back, Thomas seems surprised to see me.

"You're still here," he says.

I can't muster up any words to answer him. All I can focus on is getting through the night. In the morning, Aunt Kathy and Uncle Simon will make everything okay.

"You should get some sleep," I say.

"Iva says you'll be gone by the morning," Thomas says.

I kiss him on the forehead. "Not gonna happen."

"Can we play a game, Edie?" Thomas asks.

It's getting late, but all this talk of me going away makes me want to spend every second with Thomas.

"*Catan?*" he says.

It's one of our favorites. We used to always play together as a family. I love the strategy involved in figuring out where to place cities and settlements while trying to block other players. And though Thomas is only seven, he's amazingly good. Never good enough to beat me, but then again, I don't lose easily. That's the great thing about games. Games have defined rules which make clear paths on how to win.

"Perfect."

"Can Iva play, too?" Thomas asks.

My skin prickles. "No, Iva can't play. She's not real."

"She showed me the future," Thomas says. "I was back at school, playing with my friends. Except then Jason—you remember him; he's the kid who always has snot running down his face—he started fighting with me. I tried to call the teacher, but I couldn't find her, and then everyone else backed up and it was just me and Jason out near the swings."

"What did you do?" I ask.

"Even though I knew I shouldn't, I hit him," Thomas says. "Because he wouldn't shut up. He kept saying Mommy and Daddy were dead but I knew they weren't and he wouldn't listen."

I rub Thomas's head which is covered in sweat. It's not the future he saw. It's not even the past. He must've had a bad dream. The same kind of bad dream I had about Owen.

"I'm glad you hit him," I say.

Thomas grins. "Me, too."

I walk to the hall closet and get *Catan* out, setting up the board on the coffee table. We're halfway through the game when the phone rings.

## vi

**I STAND OVER THE PHONE, LISTENING**
to it ring.

"Are you going to get it, Edie?" Thomas asks. "It's Iva."

It's not Iva. Iva is someone he has created.

*Ring. Ring.* My fingers hover over the receiver.

Thomas is getting frantic. "Answer the phone, Edie. She's going to get mad if you ignore her. She'll make the dreams come true."

Something about the way he says it sends chills down my spine. The girl with the blue blindfold from my nightmare flashes in my mind. *Anger creases her forehead though her eyes remain covered.*

I press a finger to my lips to shush Thomas. *Ring. Ring.* I don't pick up the phone.

*Answer the phone,* a voice seems to say.

"No," I say aloud.

*Answer the phone.*

I'm not answering the phone. If I answer the phone, it's like admitting to the existence of things that make no sense. I want a world based in reality. In logic.

*Answer the phone.*

*Ring. Ring.*

I wait five more rings. Then I pick it up.

"You have to come," the voice of the little girl from my dream says. Her voice is like what I imagine the dolls in Mom's collection would sound like if they could speak. I've heard her voice before, yesterday at school. She called me then, too.

"Iva?" I barely whisper.

"It's already started," she says.

"What's started?"

"The beginning of the end," she says. "You have to come. I can show you my power." Her words sound more grown-up than her childlike voice should allow.

"I'm staying here," I say, pretending this child doesn't frighten me. She has no power. She's not even real.

"Don't fight me, Eden," she says.

"How do you know my name?" I never tell anyone my full name. It's like a secret just among our family. Mom loved the theory that the Garden of Eden might have actually been a real place on Earth, so when I was born, she named me Eden, but called me Edie. She even wrote Edie on official documents, like she only wanted our family to know my real name. *"A name hidden,"* she used to say. *"Secret, like the Garden itself."*

"I know everything," Iva says. "I know you're going on a journey."

"I'm not going anywhere," I say. Whatever her plans are, I want no part in them. All I want is to be with Thomas.

"You are," Iva says, and an image of a desert floods my mind, with a volcano at the center surrounded by four black rivers, each flowing outward from it. It's like the volcano in the news report I saw on TV. Except I hadn't seen anything. There were no volcanos, and there was no news report.

Lava flows from the volcano, mixing with the water, filling the air with steam. I have no idea where it's supposed to be. I think of my flowchart, still sitting there on the coffee table. Volcanic activity. My parents' ship capsizing. Digging too deep.

"I'm not going to wait forever," Iva says.

"Leave me alone!" I say and hang up the phone. I have no intention of going anywhere.

**AFTER CATAN, WE DIG THROUGH THE** bin of camping supplies, trying to figure out what everything is. A lot of it is rusty old junk, but at the bottom of the bin is a wooden box. Carved into it are a handful of ancient-looking symbols.

Most of them I don't recognize. One I remember from math class. The rest look like nonsense. They look like things Mom used to doodle on scraps of paper around the house. Every once in a while, I'd ask her what she was drawing, but most of the time this resulted in a ten minute long dissertation, so it became only when my curiosity got the better of me. Now, with the power off and no Internet, I have no way of knowing what they're supposed to mean.

Inside the box is a shiny golden compass. A giant owl is engraved on the cover, wings extended, and on the bottom are two letters I'm pretty sure are Greek. Mom wrote these two more than any others. Alpha and Omega. The beginning and the end she would always say. I press the button, and the spring releases, flipping the lid of the compass open. The needle spins when I orient myself. Our house faces east, toward the ocean, but the compass doesn't seem to agree. Instead of pointing north, it points west-northwest. It must be broken. When I close the cover of the compass, the engraved owl seems to watch me. I slide the compass in the front pocket of my jeans.

"Look what I found!" Thomas says.

I turn in time to see him swinging an ax around in the air over his head. My seven-year-old brother has an ax. What kind of big sister am I? He's going to kill someone.

"Oh, Thomas! Put it down. Carefully."

He's mid-swing and not in control in the least, and all my words do is distract him. The ax flies from his hands, sailing mere inches over my head and embedding itself in the wall behind me. He grimaces as he watches me nearly get scalped. My hair follicles tingle.

"I'm so sorry, Edie," Thomas says as his lower lip starts to quiver. "It was in the bin. I was trying to help."

"You need to be more careful," I snap, way too harshly. But the last couple days have every nerve in my body frazzled. The last thing I need is for something else to go wrong.

Tears fill Thomas's eyes. "I was just—" he starts.

"I don't care. Just be more careful," I say.

That was close. Too close. I walk to the wall and pull the ax free. The handle is worn and there's a split in the wood along the right side. The blade doesn't even come close to shining, but it's small and solid and balances perfectly in my hands.

"Just don't pick it up again," I say, softening slightly.

Thomas doesn't respond. He only lies down on the sofa and closes his wet eyes.

I set the ax on the coffee table and rub his head. I shouldn't have yelled, but with our parents not here, I'm responsible for him. It's my fault if something happens. He'll be over it in the morning. Everything will be better tomorrow. I'm sure of it.

## vii

**I WAKE TO THE SOUND OF POUNDING ON**
the door. Aunt Kathy and Uncle Simon are here. Finally.

I fight to open my eyes. It's like they've been glued shut. I blink
a few times to get some moisture in them, and they finally open
to slits.

Thomas has no such problem. He jumps from the sofa, ignores
me completely, and rushes to the front door, throwing it open.

"Aunt Kathy! Uncle Simon!" he yells, then launches himself at
Aunt Kathy.

She grabs him in a bear hug, and tears stream down her face.
I want so much in that moment to be a little kid again, to have
someone console me, tell me everything is going to be okay. But
with my parents gone, I have to be the grown up.

"We're here," she says to Thomas over and over. My heart fills
with warmth. Aunt Kathy will figure everything out. She and
Uncle Simon can stay here until they find my parents.

I stand and take a few steps forward, not wanting to interrupt
the hug.

"I knew you'd be here today," Thomas says, wiping at his eyes.

"We got in the car just after I talked to Edie," Aunt Kathy says. "Only stopped for the bathroom."

Uncle Simon's appearance seems to confirm this. His hair is disheveled, and he looks like he hasn't shaved in three days.

"Can we come in?" Aunt Kathy says, finally looking up from Thomas, into our house.

"Thomas, scoot back so they can get inside," I say, but everyone ignores me. It's like I haven't spoken. Thomas stays right by Aunt Kathy's side and grabs her hand, pulling her into the house. Uncle Simon follows. Once they're in, he closes the door.

"It's so empty in here," Aunt Kathy says. "Without them."

"I hate it," Thomas says. "And then Edie left, too."

At this Aunt Kathy's eyes widen. "What do you mean she left?"

"I'm right here," I say, stepping close this time, so I'm in Aunt Kathy's personal space. But she doesn't hear me. Doesn't see me. Something is very wrong.

Thomas's lip begins to quiver. "She got mad at me. Really mad. And I knew she was going to leave. She had to go somewhere. That's what Iva said. But I wish she'd waited until she wasn't mad anymore. I wish I hadn't made her mad."

"You didn't do anything," I say, trying to move close to him. But I can't get near him. It's as if something pushes me away.

"I'm sure she'll be back," Aunt Kathy says. "We'll leave her a note to come to Colorado."

My mind buckles in this moment. They're just going to leave for Colorado without me? That can't be right.

Nobody in this room sees me. I run around, trying to get them to notice me, waving my arms and screaming right in their faces. But nothing I do has any impact. It's like I've been erased from the world. I watch as they help Thomas pack his bags. I see them lock the back door. And then, when they go out the front door and lock it behind them, leaving me inside, the entire world flips upside down.

I fling the door open, running out front, but all I see is their car driving away. I scream their names, but they don't hear. They don't see me.

When their car is out of sight, I turn back toward the house. The apple tree in our front yard, the one we've had for ten years, is dead. The branches and leaves have withered. The bark looks like a strong breeze would turn it to dust. On the ground, the fruit lays rotted on the bright green grass.

I'm vaguely aware of my cell phone ringing in the back pocket of my jeans. It's been out of batteries for two days. I didn't even put it in my jeans. I left it on the kitchen counter. It plays the theme of *Twilight Zone*, my ringtone. *Doo dee doo doo, doo dee doo doo . . .*

I stare at the screen, trying to make sense of it. It's lit up, saying *Unknown Number*, impossible because it's out of juice. I swipe my thumb across the screen. Place the phone to my ear.

"What's happening?" I yell, not caring that the Pralls are in their front yard right next door. They don't even look over at me.

"You need to find them," Iva says.

"Find who?" I'm done with her games. Done with this joke that's being played on me.

"Your parents," Iva says. "I know where they are."

"You don't know anything," I say. "You're not even real."

"Maybe I'm not," Iva says. "But you'll never know if you don't come."

"Where are my parents?" I scream into the phone, letting my anger and frustration pour into my words.

"Come see me. I'll tell you," she says, and the image of the twin volcanos shoots through my mind. One in the ocean, where their ship went down, and one in the desert, far away. Lava pours down its sides, and smoke billows all around it.

"Tell me what's going on."

"I'll be waiting for you, Eden," Iva says. "You have until the fruit dies. After that, your chance is gone."

"There is no fruit," I say, but I look again to the apple tree in the middle of our yard. It's still brittle and barren except for one branch which is now filled with life. At the end of the branch hangs a golden apple.

I grasp the apple, so plump that it barely fits in my palm, and pull it from the tree. It breaks off, and when the branch jumps back, the entire tree withers and turns to dust. I stare at the golden apple, unwilling to believe it is really here because seconds ago the tree was lifeless. Then the apple begins to wither, too, shrinking away until it's nothing but dust that blows away in the wind.

This is my imagination. A manifestation of my worst fears. Maybe I will wake up and everything will go back to normal. But the sky darkens and the clouds above begin to swirl, and I realize that nothing about my reality is going to end.

# viii

## I TRY TO START MY CAR, BUT I CAN'T

get the key to turn. I kick it and curse it and try it a dozen more times, but nothing helps. So I grab some cash and pack a small bag and head toward the bus stop. The first bus that passes doesn't stop. I'm the only person waiting. But five minutes later, someone else walks up and sits on the bench next to me.

"Do you see me?" I say, not caring that it sounds dumb.

The guy, a fifty-something shaggy beach bum, says nothing.

"Hey! I'm talking to you. Do you hear me?" I wave my hand in front of his face. I poke at him. But it doesn't make a difference. As far as this guy is concerned, I am not here.

I push down the panic inside me as the bus pulls up and stops at the corner. The door opens, and the guy gets on. I try to go in after him, but the door slams in my face. I bang on the glass, but nobody sees me. Nobody hears me. My logic, normally so solid, slips away. I'm sure I'll wake up at any moment, and everything will return to normal.

I walk to Emily's cul-de-sac. Owen's cul-de-sac. As soon as her house comes in sight, I start running. She's just getting into her car. She'll see me.

"Emily!" I scream.

She doesn't answer. Doesn't look my way.

I pound on her window. "Emily! It's me, Edie. I'm right here."

But my best friend is as unaware of my existence as the rest of the world seems to be.

"Emily, please . . . ," I say, but my words trail off. There is nothing to explain what is going on around me. It's like I've slipped into an episode of *The Twilight Zone*.

Owen's house is two doors over. I glance at it and turn away, but then my eyes swivel back in its direction. There's something there. My feet carry me forward, one step at a time, until I'm on his front porch. On his front door is the same symbol scratched into the wood as on mine, the concentric circles with small lines connecting the pieces. It makes no sense that it would be on my door and his. It wasn't on Emily's door or any of my neighbors.

*IF-THEN*. If I have a weird symbol on my door and Owen does, too, then . . .

I look for the logic, but it escapes me.

The windows of his house are open, and wind blows the curtains inside.

"Owen?" I call through an open window.

There is no reply.

"Owen?"

Nothing. Maybe I should go inside and look for him, but I can't bring myself to do it. I leave the cul-de-sac and don't look back.

Once I'm across the causeway, I stop in a convenience store and grab some water and snacks. I also grab a map. I can't remember the last time I looked at a paper map. I try to pay, but the cashier ignores me. Nobody even glances my way. I leave ten dollars on the counter and walk out.

I stretch the map out in the parking lot. Where am I going? A volcano in the middle of a desert? According to the map, all the deserts are out west. Far out west. Wherever I'm going, walking is not going to cut it. I'm going to need a bike.

Out of the din of the world around me comes the hoot of an owl. I look upward but can't spot it. Yet I've heard this owl before, on the day my parents went missing. It's like a separate life than the one extending before me now, but the owl is connecting them.

My hand drifts to my front pocket, and I pull out the compass I'd discovered yesterday in my parent's camping stuff. The owl looks up at me from the cover. I flip it open and wait until the needle settles. Again, it doesn't point north. It points mostly west. The volcano flashes through my mind. *West.* I check the compass again. Turn in a circle to see how it reacts. It holds the direction, just as my mind holds the image of the volcano. The owl hoots again.

*Follow the owl,* a voice in my head seems to say. A whisper that isn't even real.

I'm losing my mind. I'm supposed to follow an owl?

*"I know where they are,"* Iva had said.

Though it makes no sense that the owl will lead me to Iva, it's the only lead I have. And the compass seems to be pointing me that way also. It's follow the owl or curl in a ball and wait to wake up. There is no choice. I'll find Iva and I'll find my parents. Then everything will become right again. Everything will go back to normal.

My next stop is the sporting goods store. It's so weird to shop among a crowded store where no one seems to see me. The world is like a dull roar around me.

I avoid everyone as I grab a pre-assembled bike from the floor along with a hiking backpack. It'll be great for supplies. I'm pretty sure I'll find places to sleep along the way, but I want a sleeping bag just in case. I grab a lantern and some glow sticks, because

I keep trying batteries in flashlights, but I can't get any of them to work. Only as I'm getting ready to leave do I allow myself a small amount of luxury. I grab a gel seat for the bike, some real biking shorts, and electric blue gym shoes. I have to walk into the back room of the store to get my size. I also grab some blue biking gloves. They should keep my hands from getting sore. They're thick and remind me of the haptic gloves Owen lent me except they don't have any wires webbed through them.

I'm almost out the door when a mannequin catches my eye. It almost seems to glow among the otherwise dim lights of the store, like it wants to be noticed. The mannequin wears a gray jacket with blue the same color as my new gym shoes along the neckline and cuffs. The sign above claims the jacket is weatherproof. I take it from the mannequin and try it on. It's a perfect fit. I zip it and tuck the compass, my phone, and some nutrition bars in the pockets, and I'm all set.

I bike as far as Disney World that first day. The little girl in me wants to sneak inside and sleep in Cinderella's castle, since no one would notice me anyway, but I can't afford the detour. Also, I'm not a little girl anymore.

ix

## I FOLLOW THE HOOTING OF THE OWL,

double-checking with the compass. They lead me the same way.
I still haven't seen the owl, but it lets me know it's there, when
my panic gets the worst. I have to believe that when I find Iva,
everything will return to normal. I'll find my parents and wake
from this nightmare I'm having.

I have no idea how far I need to go, but one day passes after
the next. I eat simply and quickly: sardines, cereal bars, and sports
drinks. But I begin to dream about food, and the dreams seem
so real. Walking down buffet lines with desserts piled high. I eat
movie theater popcorn loaded with butter. I stumble upon or-
chards with fruit so fresh and plump it's at the point of bursting.
In my fantasies, I reach for a ripe golden apple, so tempting that
I've never wanting anything so badly in my life.

*Don't eat the fruit,* a voice in my dream says. It's Mom. She
whispers as if she's afraid someone will overhear. I try to turn my
head to look for her, but in the dream, I'm unable to.

I draw my hand back, heeding her warning, and let my mind

wander into a different dream. In this one, I'm holding an empty water bottle, and I'm so thirsty. I want to drink the entire thing, but it's empty. I'm about to fill it under the sink.

*Leave it empty,* she says. So badly I want to see Mom, yet my eyes won't leave the empty bottle.

Night after night, they're always the same. Mysterious nonsense dreams that have no bearing on my real life. They don't go away.

When I get to Baton Rouge, I slow to a stop in a crowded Target parking lot. It's the middle of a busy shopping day, yet no one sees me. Before I enter, the hoot of the owl stops me, drifting down from above, always there.

*Hoot. Hoot.*

"Where are you?" I ask aloud since it doesn't matter if I talk to myself. If someone hears me, that would be a good thing.

*Hoot. Hoot.* The sound is like something from another world, echoing above the din of the shoppers.

*Hoot. Hoot.*

And there she is. I spot the owl, sitting on the red letters above the door. I think it's fake at first—one of those owls people put up to keep birds from building nests. But then it turns its head around and looks at me face-on, and the letters of the Target sign shift. The A looks like the Greek Alpha, and the bulls-eye symbol morphs into the Omega. Alpha and Omega. The beginning and the end. Just like my compass. I blink, clearing my eyes, and the letters change back to normal. But this is great. It means I have to be heading in the right direction. Or else it means I've officially gone crazy.

I lift my hand, like maybe I'm expecting the owl to fly to me and perch on my arm.

*Hoot. Hoot.* It gives a final call. Then it spreads its wings and silently flies away, over the parking lot, where it perches on an eighteen-wheeler at the edge of the lot.

That's when I hear the dog bark. My scalp prickles. There is something about this dog. Something about its bark that is different from the rest of the sounds around me. It almost echoes, like we're inside a room together and everything else is outside. Like it was meant for me to hear. I run in the direction the barking came from, rounding the corner of a large SUV.

A dog sniffs my bike, which I've parked near the edge of the lot, and runs in circles, barking. The thing probably weighs more than I do and has spiky hair like a wolf and paws that look like they could hit baseballs. Maybe it is a wolf. It's certainly big enough, and it's not wearing a collar. It catches my scent, looking up before I've made a noise, and stares directly at me.

It can see me.

I slow to a stop, not wanting to scare it.

"Hey, puppy," I call from maybe ten meters away. *Puppy* is a stretch, but it sounds friendlier than *dog*. We're not dog people at my house. Mom got bit when she was a kid so she's scared to death of them.

The dog barks in reply.

I take another step in its direction. Slowly. It barks again, but it's not baring its teeth or growling so I take one more step. I look down, not wanting it to think I'm challenging it by looking it in the eye.

The dog whines a little then sits on its haunches. Its bushy tail begins to thump on the pavement, causing little spirals of dust to rise up and drift through the air. It's a good sign, so I take another step and bend down with my hand stretched out, palm-side up.

The dog sniffs my hand and lets out another bark.

"Nails!"

The dog's head whips around.

"Nails!"

The dog, apparently Nails, jumps to its feet and starts barking so loudly that its entire front end lifts off the ground with each bark.

"Nails! Come, girl."

And off Nails goes, bounding through the parking lot, dashing between parked cars until she's out of sight.

I throw my backpack to the ground and run after her as fast as I can while navigated the moving cars. I run to the edge of the parking lot, near the eighteen-wheeler where my owl had landed. The dog barks again. I turn the corner of the giant truck and stop. The dog, Nails, sits on the ground panting, getting her ears rubbed. Next to her, doing the ear scratching, is a guy. He lifts his head and looks right at me.

His expression is hard to read from this distance because half his face is covered with a thick scar, extending from his hairline down to his neck. His shaggy hair, so black it almost looks like he's colored it with ink, covers most of his forehead and part of his eye. He looks about my age, maybe a little older; it's hard to tell. His eyes narrow when he sees me, or at least one of them does. The left eye, the side with the scar, appears to be permanently narrowed.

"Can you see me?" I ask. I've gotten used to the sound of my own voice. I've also gotten used to people not answering.

"Can you see me?" he says in reply.

I nod slowly, as a wave of emotions rolls through me. This guy can see me. Can actually see me. I am not crazy. And yet, I don't know anything about him or what's going on. It's been so long since I've interacted with anyone, and my defenses immediately go up. This guy could have a weapon or something. I mentally smack myself for standing here, completely unarmed. It's stupid. I should have grabbed a knife from Target before I went running after the dog.

I take a step back without thinking about it.

"It's okay," the guy says, with a thick accent I'm pretty sure is Cajun. "Nails doesn't bite."

He takes a step toward me but it's kind of awkward because he's got a crutch under his left arm, supporting his weigh. He uses the crutch to angle his body around. His left leg is missing from the knee down.

"Don't freak out," the guy says. "Nails is like a baby."

Baby my ass. The dog is like a tank. She could knock me over with one paw. And what kind of person names their dog Nails anyway?

"I'm not freaked out." I unclench my fists which I realize have been balled since the second I saw the guy. But I stay where I am. It's like the owl led me to this guy. Like I was meant to find him. But Mom had said not to trust anyone, and with all the freakiness going on around me, I'm tempted to listen to her.

"Are you alone?" the guy asks.

Seriously? What kind of question is that? It's the kind of question creepy people ask, that's what kind. The crutch will slow him down. I can definitely outrun him. Nails is another story.

"Not at all," I lie. "I was just inside Target getting some stuff. The rest of the people I'm with are . . ." I falter.

"Are what?" He shifts his body and relaxes on his crutch, like he's entertained by my floundering words.

I cross my arms over my waist. "They're just around this truck, back in the parking lot. I'm with my two brothers. Older brothers."

Okay, this is going nowhere. I don't have two older brothers. I don't have anyone.

"Two older brothers. For real? That's great." The half of his face without the scar lights up.

I point back in the direction I came from. "Yeah, I should probably be getting back to them or they're going to worry and come looking for me."

He steps forward, using his crutch. "I'll come with you."

Mom's voice echoes in my mind. *Don't trust anyone.*

I put my hands up. "No, that's not a good idea."

He stops. "Why?"

I bite my lip. "They don't like strangers." Ugh, this is horrible. All I'm doing is digging myself deeper. I am the worst liar in the world.

Annoyance clouds his face. "I'm not gonna hurt you."

"Right," I say. "That's what all creepy people say before they abduct and kill you. Famous last words." I take another step back, but somehow I've forgotten about the truck, and one of the giant wheels is now at my back.

"I'm not a creepy person," the guy says. "My name is Cole. Cole Tinker. And you already met Nails."

I wait. One second. Two. Ten seconds go by as I argue back and forth in my mind about the guy and his dog. Mom told me not to trust anyone, but this guy can see me. And he seems to be in the same situation I am. I should talk to him. But fear holds me back. He could be like Owen, someone I should never trust. But no, he's not Owen. And he doesn't look like a creep. Not that I know what a creep looks like. Maybe he is a creep.

Okay, this is ridiculous. I am freaking yearning to talk to someone besides myself. For two weeks all I've done is carry on one-sided conversations. And if the world has thrown me this guy, then I'm going to accept it.

"I'm Edie," I finally say. "Edie Monk."

"Nice to meet you, Edie," Cole says. "And your brothers?" With his accent he drops the "er" on brother so it comes out as "brotha."

"What about them?" Stupid lie. What was I thinking anyway? I can't manifest two guys to masquerade as my older brothers.

"What are their names?" Cole asks.

I step to the side so my back isn't pressing into the eighteen-wheeler. "I only have one brother, and his name is Thomas."

Cole motions with his head back toward Target. "He's with you?"

I take a deep breath and blow it out, letting the lie blow away with it. "No, he's in Colorado, with my aunt and uncle. And he's only seven."

Cole takes my admittance with only a nod, like he gets it. "And—okay, I know this sounds stupid—but no one can see you?"

"No one," I say. "Except you now."

"Thank god," Cole says. Relief floods his face. "I was pretty sure I'd gone crazy."

I laugh, maybe the first time I've laughed in two weeks. It feels amazing. "Me, too."

He runs a hand through his dark hair, brushing it back over the scar on his face. "I am so happy I'm not crazy."

"Maybe we're both crazy," I say. "That might explain things."

Cole shrugs. "It's better than any explanation I've come up with."

It's amazing to know that I'm not the only person in the world this is happening to.

"How old are you?" Cole says.

I think about lying again, maybe saying I'm eighteen, but there's not much point to it. It's not like I'm trying to buy cigarettes or lottery tickets.

"Sixteen," I say. "Born on New Year's Day."

Cole narrows his good eye in thought, and the one side of his mouth turns up. The other side doesn't seem able to do much of anything. "Me, too. Funny coincidence."

"For real? You're a New Year's baby?"

"Born just after midnight," Cole says. "At the peak of a full moon."

Shivers run through me. "I was born just after midnight, too. It must've been the same full moon." It's weird to have this strange connection with a guy I don't even know.

"Even funnier coincidence," Cole says.

*IF-THEN.* There is some kind of logic behind this information. If I was born just after midnight on New Year's Day sixteen years ago, then . . . what does it mean? Does it have something to do with why Cole and I seem to have slipped out of reality?

"You really think it's a coincidence?" I ask. Chills ripple through me even though the sun is blasting in the sky above.

"I don't know what to think," Cole says. "About anything."

Far above, the hoot of the owl sounds.

We both swivel our heads to the sky, and the regal bird glides over soundless in the bright sky.

"You don't normally see owls during the day," Cole says. "They're nocturnal."

With his accent, the way he says "nocturnal" almost comes out sounding like a little kid trying to use a big word, but he's using it correctly which means he knows what it means. Most owls are nocturnal.

"It's been following me." Or, more accurately, I've been following it.

"Where to?" he says.

"Out west," I say, which I know sounds completely general, but I want to appear confident, like I have a plan. A girl on a crazy road trip out west. Happens every day. I also don't want him to pry. To shoot down my loosely thought-out plan. I don't want to second-guess myself.

If Cole knows I'm being evasive, he doesn't push it. Mom's words still float around in my mind. *Don't trust anyone.*

I don't have to trust him to talk to him. But I also don't want to come off as an impersonal lunatic.

"How about you?" I ask. "Do you live here?"

"At Target?" Cole asks without cracking a grin.

I laugh before I can stop myself. "Yeah, at Target."

Cole shakes his head. "I considered it, given the one-stop shopping, but no, I'm like you. Just passing through."

"To where?"

"I'm leaving that up to Nails," he says, rubbing the giant

wolf-dog's head.

He's obviously being evasive, too, but I don't push. Maybe his mom left him a voicemail telling him not to trust anyone also.

"Well, I should get going," I say, continuing my sideways steps until I'm free from the truck. I watch Cole, to gauge his reaction. He has to be starved for human interaction like me.

"You could stay here tonight," he says, which confirms my thoughts.

"I still have twenty miles to go today," I say in a way that doesn't even convince me. But fifty miles a day has been my goal. Still, Cole seems to be in the same situation I'm in.

"We could light a fire," Cole says. "Grill some steaks."

Drool nearly slips from my mouth at the thought of a steak. He's messing with me. Target doesn't have steaks.

One night. Twenty miles. I can make it up tomorrow. And the thought of relaxing in front of a fire and speaking with a real live human makes me want to cry with joy.

I twist up my mouth as I consider my options.

"I'm seeing a yes," Cole says. He grins. Just a small smile, but it's a tiny chink in the armor he seems to have around himself.

"I haven't agreed," I say.

"But you will," he says. "I can tell these things."

Maybe he can tell. Maybe I just need this small escape from reality. One night.

*IF-THEN-ELSE.* If I stay one night, then I can make up the miles tomorrow, else I may never talk to another human again. Plus the owl had led me here, right to where Cole was. Maybe we were meant to meet.

"Fine. But I'm not building the fire."

Cole grins big enough that even the scarred side of his face lifts, giving him a lopsided yet inviting appearance. "Not to worry. Fire is my specialty."

Cole's crutch and missing leg get in the way of nothing. He

**57**

drags a pre-set-up charcoal grill out of Target and throws some briquettes into it. Since there are no steaks, I grab hamburger meat, because the idea of a fresh, loaded burger will not leave my mind. I also get s'mores makings. In an effort to be halfway creative, I grab Halloween pumpkin Peeps from the seasonal section instead of regular marshmallows.

Once the fire is ready, Cole sets the meat on the grill, getting his fingers so close to the flames that I worry they're going to burn him, but he doesn't seem fazed, so I let him take over cooking. Forty-five minutes later, our meal is ready.

"These are the burgers of the gods," Cole says, licking his fingers as he takes a second one from the grill. He piles it high with pickles and olives, then drowns it in ketchup.

"Almost better than the SPAM I had last week," I joke.

"Everything is better than the SPAM you had last week," Cole says.

"I don't know. I make some pretty mean SPAM sandwiches," I say. "You should try them."

"Maybe next time," Cole says.

Except there won't be a next time. After tonight, I am out of here.

We grill twelve burgers because I figure that whatever is left we can split up and I can bring with me for tomorrow's bike ride. Only then does it occur to me that I have no idea how Cole is traveling.

"Do you have a car?" I ask. Given the crutch and his missing leg, I'm betting against him walking or biking, wherever he's going.

"A car," Cole says, with mock disgust in his voice. "Please. I'm not going to bow to the all-time low of a car."

"So . . . you have a magic flying machine?" I suggest.

"Even better," Cole says. "I have a Jeep."

"You have a Jeep?" I admit a tiny moment of envy flows through me. I'm biking across the country, and Cole has a Jeep.

"Like I said, better than a flying machine."

"But how'd you get it to start? And what about the gas? I can't get anything with electricity to work."

"I can't either," Cole says. "So I had to basically crank the engine, old-school style. And for gas, there's a mechanism you can trip to bypass the circuits. It's illegal obviously."

"Obviously," I say. "But I doubt anyone minded."

"I don't think anyone noticed," Cole says.

It brings down our conversation, and a gap of silence enters.

"Will you pass me another burger?" Cole asks, either because he's trying to fill the silence or because he's hungry. With his accent, he drops the "r" on burger, too.

Cole tosses the burger to Nails, so I do the same with the rest of mine. I want to save room for dessert. While I get our dessert stuff organized, Cole traces something in the dirt with one of the marshmallow roasting skewers I found inside Target.

"What is that?" I ask. It's the same symbol that had been scratched in both my door and Owen's door: the concentric circles with small lines connecting them.

"It's an ancient symbol for a labyrinth," Cole says, still tracing.

"Why are you drawing it?"

"I saw it recently," he says, and continues to trace it.

"Where?"

"On my door."

The chills return, in ironic contrast to the fire that burns in front of us. "I had the same symbol traced on my door."

He stops tracing. "Seriously?"

"Seriously."

We were both born just after midnight on New Year's Day sixteen years ago. We both had a labyrinth symbol scratched into our door. We're both here now. The pieces of logic are falling in line.

"What do you think it means?" Cole asks.

"I think it must have something to do with why we're the only ones who can see each other," I say.

"How?"

"I don't know. But . . ." My hand drifts to my pocket, to the compass, because I want to tell him about that, too, but I stop before pulling it out. *Don't trust anyone.*

"But what?" he asks.

I shake my head. "Nothing. It's just weird, that's all. There's probably no connection. And anyway, isn't it about time for s'mores?"

Cole brushes his hair across his face, like he's trying to hide the scar. "Fine. S'mores. Just so you know, I am a master marshmallow roaster." He grabs a Halloween Peep and impales it on the end of the skewer, then lifts the grill from the coals so he can lower the end of the skewer closer to the burning embers. "If you hold it here, near the coals, but not touching, and rotate it around slowly, but not so slow that it catches fire, you'll end up with the perfect marshmallow."

He proceeds to roast what I have to agree is the most perfect marshmallow in existence. "Voila," he says, brandishing the finished product. But it's gooier than he's thought and slips off the skewer, falling on my arm before I can move.

I jump up and shake it off because the heat from it is burning. I yank down the zipper on my gray jacket and pull my arm out. By the time I've shrugged off the jacket, the burning marshmallow is smoldering on the asphalt.

"Oh, god, I'm sorry," Cole says, tossing the skewer aside. "Are you okay?"

No, I'm not okay. He's just dropped a hotter-than-napalm marshmallow on my arm.

Or . . . maybe I am okay. My arm feels fine.

I bend and flex my arm. "I don't think it got through the jacket."

"Seriously, I'm really sorry," Cole says. "Peeps must not roast the same as normal marshmallows. Maybe it's the sugar coating."

I don't want him to think I'm freaked out about it. "You owe me a new jacket," I say, trying to lighten the mood so he doesn't feel bad.

Cole grabs my discarded jacket up from the ground and brushes off the arm. "Actually, it looks fine." He hands it over, and I'm shocked to see that he's right. It's perfect. Not even sticky with sugar. As if the marshmallow never landed on it.

"That's weird," I say. "Maybe instead of weatherproof, they should have advertised it as flaming-marshmallow-proof."

Cole relaxes the tiniest amount when he sees I'm not going to die on the spot. "You sure you're okay."

I brush off my arm and put my jacket back on. "All good."

**WHEN IT'S TIME FOR BED, I GRAB MY** sleeping bag from my pack. It's a nice night out, and the parking lot median has thick grass that's soft like a carpet. Nails runs circles around me as if she can't wait to curl up next to me. Now that I've been around her for a few hours, her size is comforting instead of frightening. Well, maybe it's still a little frightening, but if any monsters try to attack me in the middle of the night, she'll be a nice defense.

"Where are you sleeping?" I ask Cole.

He shrugs. "Normally I sleep in my Jeep, but it's out on the street."

"You can sleep here," I say, "but you have to stay at least ten feet away."

Cole holds his hands apart as if he's measuring ten feet. Maybe he does have a sense of humor. He limps over, without putting the crutch under his arm, until he's about eight feet away.

"Is this good?"

I shake my head. "A little farther."

Another foot. "This?"

"A little bit more."

Six inches. "This?"

I let the smile that's been threatening to come out finally show. "That's good. And I hope you don't snore."

He doesn't snore. He's as silent as I am as I stare up at the night sky. Sleep doesn't come for hours. And I wonder if it doesn't come for him either. I try to spot the owl flying above, silently in the night, but I can't find her. Still, I know she's there. I can feel her. Just before I drift off to sleep, she hoots, almost in warning.

In the morning, I wake to the sound of the world quaking.

X

## "COLE!" I SHAKE HIS ARM EVEN THOUGH

he's as awake as I am.

"I feel it," he says.

"What's going on?" I stand, only to fall back to the ground. Cole is already grabbing his crutch and getting up.

"That's going on." He points behind us, from the direction I've come. The ground rumbles and rolls, and the asphalt ripples. Cars and buses drive like normal, as if they are unaware of anything unusual. But for Cole and me, it's as if we're in a world layered on top of the real world, and in our world, a full-scale earthquake has hit.

A deafening sound fills the air as the road begins splitting, right down the middle. The landscape is like a painting, and someone is tearing it in half.

"Please tell me this isn't happening."

My words can't stop the disaster that comes closer with every second that passes. If we don't move, the earth will swallow us whole. Cole starts for his Jeep, and I run toward my bike.

"No, Edie, there's no time," Cole says.

My bike is way too close to the splitting ground, but my back-pack with all my supplies leans against it. I have to get to it. I edge closer, but the crack spreads, catching the back tire of the bike. I jump backward and watch as the entire bike gets swallowed by the earth. But there's no time to mourn it because the crack in the earth keeps moving toward me.

I dare to look downward, and what I see cannot be real. Things crawl up the edges of the fissure, dead things, clawing with de-caying hands, extending rotten fingers for me. And below them, fire-breathing monsters scream furiously and bellow smoke and flames my way. It's a scene straight out of hell and beyond all belief.

"Run, Edie!" Cole calls.

Nails barks. My owl hoots in the sky.

There is no time to think. My legs pound as the crack gets closer. I'm not going to make it in time. The things in the crevasse call my name, and their fingers snap with anticipation. I push harder and lunge for the Jeep.

"There are things down there . . . ," I say.

"Come on!" Cole reaches out for me.

I grab his hand, and then I'm scrambling across the front seat of his dirty green Jeep. He and Nails jump in after me, and he shoves the Jeep into gear. Then we're flying down the road, away from the broken earth and the things that are awake beneath it.

xi

## "WHAT THE HELL WERE THOSE THINGS?"

I scream as Cole drives, staying ahead of the shaking earth behind us. The Jeep is stick shift, but Cole's rigged some kind of lever that his knee presses into so he can shift gears.

He shakes his head and swerves along other cars in the road, and I'm tossed from side to side. I clip my seatbelt so my head doesn't smack into the dashboard, and then I yank the compass from the pocket of my jacket. It points west, the direction we're heading. Cole glances over at it.

"Zombies and monsters," I say, stuffing the compass back into my pocket. "That's what I saw. Freaking zombies and monsters."

"There's no such thing as zombies and monsters," Cole says.

"Right," I say. "There's also no such thing as people not being able to see us. Or volcanos in the ocean growing overnight, swallowing my parents whole."

Everything is beyond screwed up.

"Is that what happened to them?" Cole asks.

Voicing it makes it become real all over again.

"Their ship went down," I say over the rumbling behind us. "They're presumed dead. And then the entire freaking world turned inside out."

*We dug too deep,* Mom's message had said. That's when this all started.

Cole doesn't say anything, instead focusing on the road ahead.

I push back tears that threaten to break free. Crying isn't going to help jack shit. Behind us, the quaking seems to have stopped. Maybe it's over. Far above, my owl flies, following the path of the Jeep.

Cole grabs a water bottle and uncaps it, passing it to me first. All my supplies are gone. No food. No water. All I have are the clothes I'm wearing. My throat yearns for water, but I shake my head. I don't want to have to rely on him completely.

"It's okay. I'm fine. Maybe when we stop."

He continues to hold it out. "Have some water, Edie. I promise I won't hold it against you."

I lick my lips, but I don't want to depend on him. Like he's reading my mind, he lifts the lid of a cooler between the seats to reveal six more water bottles tucked inside. It would be stupid not to take one. So I grab the water and down half of it in a single sip.

"Thanks," I say.

"Just ask if you want another one," he says. "We'll stop in Dallas and get more supplies."

I take another huge sip, letting water spill down the sides of my mouth, not wanting to think about the future, but knowing I have to. I don't want to leave Cole now that I've found him, but I also have to get to Iva.

"I told you my Jeep was better than a magic flying machine," Cole says, trying to lighten the mood.

"You were right," I say. "Thank you for being there. Without your Jeep, I could be dead."

"Consider it your Jeep, too," he says.

"Meaning what?" I ask. He hasn't told me where he's going, but he is driving the direction I'm heading.

"Meaning we travel together from here on out," Cole says. "Because I'm heading west, too."

"How do you know where I'm heading?" I say.

He taps my pocket where I've stored the compass. "I saw you looking at it."

My hand immediately covers the compass, like I should still keep it secret. But if Cole already knows, then there isn't much point. I decide to pre-empt his questions with my own.

"Why are you heading west, Cole?" I ask.

Cole rubs his forearm like he's brushing invisible dirt off. His forearms, like his shoulders, are huge, and I have this odd urge to try to wrap my hands around them to see if my fingers will touch. I keep the urge to myself.

"You won't believe me," he finally says.

"Try me."

"It sounds crazy."

"Everything about the world is crazy," I say. "One more thing won't tip the scales."

He takes a deep breath. Looks away so his eyes don't meet mine. "I got this phone call. I shouldn't have because my cell phone was dead. But the phone kept ringing. I thought it was my imagination, but it didn't stop."

My scalp prickles. "Was it a girl?"

Cole's eyes, even his scarred one, widen. "Yeah. She said her name was Iva. Told me I was going to go on a journey."

"Iva called me, too," I hear myself say. "She told me the same thing. It was after my parents went missing. I hung up on her. But she called again. And again. And then weird things started happening. Things I can't explain with logic. My brother thought I left him. But I hadn't. I was right there. He just couldn't see me. Nobody could."

"Same thing happened for me," Cole says. "Except it was my best friend, Pia, who went missing." His eyes light up when he says her name, and I immediately wonder if she is more than a friend. An odd wave of . . . jealously? . . . runs through me. I push it aside.

"I'd been crashing at Pia's house for the last few months because . . . well, just because. But one day, before school, she wasn't there when I woke up. Her parents were already gone for the day. I searched everywhere. Tried to call some friends to see if they knew where she went, but the phone was dead. So I went to school, but nobody was reacting to me. It was like I wasn't there."

"That's how it was with Thomas," I say. "He kept thinking I'd gone away."

Cole nods. "I think whatever was happening was beginning then, and it only got worse. I left school because it was totally freaking me out. No one noticed. So I went back to Pia's house and fell asleep on the sofa. And I had this bizarre dream. Pia was hanging on the side of a bridge. I managed to catch her hand, but water was blowing around everywhere. Her hands were slippery. She kept saying 'Don't let go' and I tried. I really did. But her hand slipped out of mine and she was gone. I woke to the sound of the phone ringing."

"Iva," I say. "But who is she?"

Cole shrugs. "I have no clue." He scratches at his knee just above where his leg ends. I've noticed he does this when he's thinking, like an involuntary habit. Like he wants to scratch farther down, but there's nothing left. And I wonder how he lost it. And how long it's been gone. He's kept it hidden so I can't tell if it's a fresh scar or not.

"That makes two of us," I say.

He nods. "She said that she would tell me where Pia was. That I had to come find her."

"Before the fruit died," I say.

"Before the fruit died," he echoes. "And there was this fruit tree . . ."

"With an apple," I finish. In my pocket, I trace my fingers over the etched owl on the cover of the compass.

"A golden apple," Cole says. "And I don't know where the tree is but I have to find it. It's near a volcano surrounded by four rivers. I see it when I close my eyes. I see it in my dreams. It's the answer to everything. Where I'll find Pia. Why no one else can see us. Nails is leading me. After the phone call, the next thing I know, this giant wolf dog runs up to me. I had no clue where she came from, but she kept barking. Wouldn't stop until I hit the road."

"She wasn't your dog?"

"Never saw her before," Cole says.

"She's pretty attached."

Almost like she understands me, Nails wags her tail, hitting it against the backseat.

"The owl's been leading me," I say. I pull the compass out and flip it open. "And this is, too."

Cole takes the compass and holds it out over the steering wheel, watching the needle settle.

"It's leading the way," I say. "Has been the whole time."

He flips it over and looks at the engraving on the bottom. "And these?"

"Greek letters," I say. "Alpha and omega."

"What do they mean?"

"The beginning and the end," I say.

"So we both have an animal leading us," Cole says. "And we're both heading the same way. Why do you have this compass?"

My eyes tear up before I can stop them. "My parents had it at home. I found it when I was going through their stuff."

"Why would they have it?" Cole says.

*We dug too deep.*

"I don't know," I say.

He closes the compass and hands it back to me. Our fingers brush the smallest amount, making shivers run through my entire body. With everyone ignoring me, it's been too long since I've had human contact. It wakes something up inside me.

"So are we together from here on out?" Cole finally says. His voice carries a hint of uncertainty. I can't tell if he's nervous.

"I'd like that," I say. "I'd like that a lot."

I'm no longer alone.

**XII**

## WE PULL INTO A WAL-MART PARKING

lot on the outskirts of Dallas. It's after rush hour, so the place should be packed, but there's almost no one around. The streets seem to have gotten less crowded with each mile we've driven, as if the real world is slipping away and the world that's layered on top is taking over. Nails jumps out of the Jeep and runs for an immediate pit stop. I admit to needing one myself. Nails uses the bathroom five times, on cars, on trees. She avoids the Jeep, almost like it's sacred.

"All I can think about are those burgers," Cole says. He climbs out of the Jeep, grabbing his crutch from the back where it's stowed, and walks to where I stand.

"Burgas again," I say in a mock whiney voice, but using his accent. "Can't we have something different tonight?" Now that the earthquake is behind us and the monsters crawling from the earth are fading into memory, I'm starting to relax.

Cole's half smirk is replaced by a true smile. It lights up his scarred face in a way so far he's shown to be impossible.

"Edie, you are in luck," he says, "because not only is this a Wal-Mart, it's a Super Wal-Mart, guaranteed to have the finest selection of foods available to man. And don't get me started on the variety of shopping amenities you'll find inside these walls." He places out a hand as if to take me shopping.

Laughter bubbles over, and I let out a stupid giggle and take his hand. We proceed to the Wal-Mart for what promises to be the best shopping trip ever.

In a couple hours, we're sitting around the fire, eating a ten course meal. I haven't eaten this much since . . . maybe ever. My stomach feels like it's going to burst the button of the jeans I picked up in Wal-Mart. Still, it feels great to be in non-biking clothes. While Cole started the fire, I spent over a half hour getting new socks, underwear, shoes, and I don't feel guilty about one second of it. I unzip my gray jacket as the heat from the fire reaches me.

Nails sits on the other side of the fire, chewing on a tennis ball I'd picked up in the store. She's already gone through two of them. I'll have to grab another three-pack before we leave.

"So you're from Florida?" Cole says. He's loosening up with every minute that passes. Maybe he's just not used to having other people around. Maybe he's self-conscious about his scar and missing leg. He also went shopping, though it only took him five minutes, picking out jeans and a Green Lantern T-shirt which makes it very clear that he puts lots of effort into staying in shape. His muscles bulge out of places I never knew muscles could bulge out of. I sneak glances when he's not watching.

"Cocoa Beach," I say. "Where NASA is."

The light from the fire casts shadows on Cole's face which he keeps angled so the scar isn't in the forefront. "Let me guess. You want to be an astronaut when you grow up."

"Everyone wants to be an astronaut," I say. "And I am grown up."

"So I'm right?" Cole says.

"When I was little I did," I admit. "Back when the shuttles used to fly. But once they canceled the shuttle program, the whole space travel thing kind of lost its appeal."

"So what do you want to do now?" Cole says.

Now? I want to find Iva and my parents, and figure out a way to make the world right again.

"I want to design video games," I say. "Computer programming. It's my specialty." Owen's parents had forced him to take programming in school even though he insisted he hated it. It's why he started talking to me. He asked for help on his homework, and stupid me, being flattered that he was giving me attention, gave him the help.

Okay, fine, I did his homework while he sat around texting. And he'd asked me out, and I figured it was all worth it. And so I helped him again. And then came Homecoming.

*I'm in my Homecoming dress, trying to tame my unruly curls with a rhinestone barrette in front of a mirror when he comes up behind me. I'm in the bathroom, and no one but the two of us is in here.*

*"I was just fixing my hair," I say, shocked that he's come into the girls' room.*

*He doesn't reply. Instead he lifts his arms to my shoulders, grabbing the thin straps of my dress, then yanks them down, tearing the silky brown fabric, making a sound that rips through the bathroom.*

*"Stop!" I scream, but Owen shoves one hand over my mouth and slams my head back into the mirror.*

*The world spins. I fight him, trying to push him away, but he's too strong. I twist and kick and try to scream again.*

*"If you make another sound, I'll kill you," Owen says.*

I blink, trying to remember where I am, but my head pounds. The fire is in front of me. Cole is across from me. The vision is not reality. It never happened. Owen had tried to force me to go too far, but it was never this.

"You okay?" Cole asks.

I wrap my arms around myself and shiver even though, with my jacket and the fire, I'm not cold at all. It feels so real.

"I'm fine," I say, but my hands are balled into fists, and my pounding head makes it hard to concentrate.

"You sure?" Concern fills Cole's face, but I'm not going to let fictional visions destroy my reality.

"I'm fine," I say. "So you're from New Orleans?"

He points to the sky, to the waxing sliver of a moon shadowed by inky clouds. "Crescent City. All my life."

"You've been to Mardi Gras?" My parents had visited New Orleans for Mardi Gras before I was born.

"Every year," Cole says. "Beads and floats and masks. I had a job working on a float last year. Got to toss beads down to the crowds."

"To the topless girls, right?" I myself have never been to Mardi Gras, but I've heard stories.

Cole blushes. Or maybe it's the way the coals from the fire reflect off his face. "Something like that."

"What do your parents do?" I ask.

"My dad gives cemetery tours," Cole says. "And I never knew my mom. Only my stepmom." His bitter tone makes me think there was no love lost between the two.

"Is that what you want to do when you grow up? Give cemetery tours?"

Another grin. They're becoming closer together. "I am grown up," he says.

"True," I say. We are the same age.

"I love making and fixing things," Cole says. "And maybe this is the weirdest thing in the entire world, but I want to own a junkyard. Build things from all the metal pieces and parts."

"Junkyard sculpture," I say. "Pretty niche market."

"Not just sculptures," he says, and his eyes shine in the light of the fire. "I want to create stuff. Inventions. Things that people can use."

"Sounds a lot like engineering," I say.

"Without the bullshit," he says. "I don't want to deal with school or the business world."

"If we don't figure out what's going on, then you may have gotten your wish," I say.

"We'll figure it out, Edie. Everything can be fixed."

I want to believe him, but doubt keeps getting in my way.

I fall asleep, but a scream wakes me in the middle of the night. I sit up, looking around in the darkness. The crescent moon has long since set, but Cole's outline is still visible next to me.

"Are you okay?" I whisper in case he's asleep and the scream came from someone else. But the parking lot is empty except for us.

"I'm fine," he says, wide awake. His voice is tense and alert. The scream had to be him.

"You sure?" I ask.

"Just a headache," he says. "I'll be fine."

"You're sure?"

"Just go back to bed, Edie," Cole says. Whatever he screamed about, he doesn't want to talk about it. But the headache . . . he could be having some sort of visions also, the same kind I am.

"If you need anything . . . ," I say.

"I'm fine."

**DESPITE WAKING IN THE MIDDLE OF** the night, I'm up early. Cole is already awake and packing. He wants to get through the rest of Texas in one day.

"I can help drive," I say as I roll my new sleeping bag.

"I didn't think girls could drive stick shift," Cole says with a smile playing on his lips.

I throw my empty cup at him, hitting him in the head.

Yet our truce seems too new to trust completely. And I can't get

Mom's warning out of my head. Still, I'd slept far closer to Cole than I'd needed to, pressing my back up against his as the fire slowly burned out. But I have a traveling companion! The sheer joy that thought brings me threatens to overwhelm me. And he hadn't complained as I'd scooted closer to him.

Not that I like him. I mean, I like him, but I don't *like* him. Not in that way where I hope he'll ask me to the Homecoming dance, like I had with Owen. Stupid me. I can't believe I'd ever seen anything in Owen. It's just nice to be traveling with someone. And I'm not going to compare Owen and Cole. Still, I can't imagine Cole taking me to eat fried chicken even when I tell him it's not my favorite. Or cheaping out on coffee every single time we go out. Or using me for help with his homework.

Or forcing himself on me after Homecoming. Owen had been an ass from the first time he'd talked to me. I'd fallen right into his trap.

Also Cole is heading west to find his friend, Pia. Probably girlfriend. I'd seen the way his face changed when he talked about her. He'd said she was only a friend, but I'm not stupid. Let's not forget that he'd been living at her house.

"Where do you think all the cars are?" I ask as we drive. The road hypnotizes me. I've never been west. Never seen anything like Texas. Windmills so big that they must have been built by titans decorate the flat, barren landscape. They turn in the wind far above while the same wind blows tumbleweeds across the pavement, into the path of the Jeep.

Cole slows the Jeep and glances around. There isn't anyone on the road besides us. "I don't know, Edie. Even in Dallas it wasn't very crowded. It's strange."

Strange with no logical answer. I hate when there's no logical answer.

Black clouds have been following us since Dallas, but now that we've slowed down, they descend on us and the barren landscape.

In seconds, rain drops start to hit the windshield. Cole stops under an overpass, and I help him put the top on the Jeep. It's way harder than I would have thought, and by the time we're done, the drops are heavy and coming down fast, and the wind howls.

"That was quick," I say once we're pulling back onto the highway. Within about ten seconds, we both realize what a horrible idea that is. The storm is mostly behind us, but still brutal. Rain pounds down like bullets. The drops are so hard that I worry they're going to puncture the cloth top of the Jeep. It's too loud to talk. Too dark and rainy to see anything beyond five feet ahead, which is why Cole has to slam on the brakes by the time we're able to see the two people standing in the middle of the road.

# XIII

**IT'S A GUY AND A GIRL, BOTH OF WHOM**
look about our age, and they're waving their hands at us like crazy
people. They definitely see us. The storm pounds on them, on us,
and shows no sign of stopping. But we have no idea who these
people are or why they are here or why they can see us when no
one else can. Nails runs back and forth on the backseat, whining.
She paws at the side window and barks twice.

"We have to let them in," Cole says.

He's right. We can worry about whether to trust them later.

I throw open the Jeep door, and the guy and girl rush inside.
But the Jeep is tiny, so they're relegated to sharing half the backseat since wolf dog Nails occupies the other half. I'm drenched by
the time they're finally inside. Of course, they've been standing
out in the rain and look like they're some kind of water monsters, with moisture dripping from every part of their bodies and
getting all over everything, including our sleeping bags. They say
something, but I can't hear.

Cole shoves the Jeep into gear and drives to the next overpass.

Then he cuts the engine. "We'll need to wait it out," he says, swiveling around.

The girl's face twists up in disgust, I guess because she's noticing his scar for the first time. Anger flares through me. She could try to not be so obvious about it.

Cole must be used to this kind of reaction though. His face slips back to the emotionless mask it was two days ago when we met.

The guy we've picked up, it seems, has a few more manners. "Talk about perfect timing. We were drowning out there."

"Thank the Lord you came along," the girls says with a Texas twang just like in the movies. "Though it would have been nice if you'd gotten here five minutes earlier. I'm soaked." Her disgusted face is replaced with a pouty look that makes her look adorable, even with her soaking wet hair, running makeup, and ungrateful attitude.

The girl grabs one of the ends of my sleeping bag from next to Nails and dabs below her eyes, almost like she knows her makeup is halfway down her face. "You have a big dog," she says.

She has a grasp on the obvious.

Nails does not lick her face. Instead Nails barks so loudly it shakes the vacuum inside our Jeep. She barks again. And again. And I realize it's in time with the thunder outside. The world erupts into a storm of lightning. It streaks down from the sky in jagged lines, blasting into the ground. The sky is dark gray, nearly black, except for brilliant streaks of yellow. A bolt of lightning strikes the overpass above us, and we all jump. Nails continues to bark, so loud in our crowded Jeep that I cover my ears.

Another streak of lightning hits the road above us, lighting up the dark clouds in a pyrotechnic display. Cole's eyes meet mine. We're both thinking the same thing. The entire overpass could collapse, crushing us beneath it, if we don't get moving.

The girl grabs a golden cross decorated with five red rubies that hangs around her neck and begins praying aloud. I'm certain as each lightning strike gets closer that there is no god above listening who is going to answer her prayers. Church was never my family's thing anyway. Not that we don't believe in god. Maybe we do. Maybe we don't. My parents don't think it matters one way or the other. It's certainly not going to help us now.

A giant chunk of asphalt crashes down next to us. We need to get out of here.

Cole cranks the ignition and puts the Jeep into gear. I can barely hear the guy in the backseat say something like, "Do you think that's a good idea?" Cole ignores him and drives from the fleeting safety of the overpass into the belly of the storm. His hands clench the steering wheel. For only being sixteen, he's pretty good at driving, a fact for which I am eternally grateful right now.

"Can we outdrive it?" I yell over the cacophony.

"I don't know," Cole yells back.

A blast of white lightning hits the ground behind us, sending a spray of water and debris raining down on the Jeep hood. The girl in the backseat is making nonsense sounds, crying and screaming and praying. In normal circumstances, it would annoy the heck out of me, but there is nothing normal about this. We could die any second. Behind us, something groans. I spin around in time to see one of the giant windmills falling in our direction. It's going to hit us.

"Faster!" I say, and Cole shoves his foot down on the accelerator.

"We're not going to make it!" the guy in the backseat screams. He keeps looking outside, like he thinks he can outrun the storm faster.

But Cole doesn't give up. We clear the area just as the windmill crashes behind us, shaking the ground like the earthquake of the day before.

The storm is relentless. It pounds the world. It destroys everything behind us, pushing us forward. Our Jeep shakes every time lightning strikes. Three more windmills join the one which has already fallen. Debris kicks up and pummels us. I try not to jump, but I can't help it. Nails barks the entire time. How Cole manages to drive through this is beyond me.

It feels like an eternity, but the lightning finally stops. Behind us, it looks like someone has taken a giant spoon and removed large chunks of earth. The Jeep is leaking buckets. Large holes pockmark the cloth roof.

"Nothing can stop a Jeep," Cole says.

I start laughing uncontrollably. Then I start crying. I want to be strong, but I can't help it.

Cole reaches over and puts his hand on my shoulder. And somehow it helps. I'm not in this alone.

When my stupid tears finally stop, I turn to the backseat, wiping my face even though I'm pretty sure it's not going to change my appearance which must be atrocious. Unlike me, the girl looks amazing. Her blond hair has dried into waves that frame her face, and her wet clothes are stuck to her in all the right places, making her look like some cover model at a beach photo shoot. Her V-neck shirt shows lots of bare skin and a good amount of cleavage, against which is nestled the gold and ruby cross necklace. She reaches up and brushes it every so often as if she wants to make sure it's still there.

"You guys can see us, right?" I ask. Even though by now I know they must be able to, I want confirmation.

They both nod.

"And you guys can see us, right?" the guy asks.

Cole and I nod in return. Whatever's going on, these two are part of it.

"That's Cole," I say, pointing to the driver's seat. "And I'm Edie." Like normal, I keep my full name secret.

"Abigail Ruthven," the girl says in her Texas accent.

"And I'm Hudson Brown," the guy says, winking at me in a

comically obvious flirtatious manner. He's kind of cute in that boy-next-door way, even totally drenched. Unlike Abigail, he has no accent at all.

His wink actually makes me giggle. Abigail doesn't find it quite so funny. A scowl slips onto her pretty face but just as quickly slips away. Probably neither of the guys even saw it. She's managed to get every bit of her runny makeup off . . . with my sleeping bag.

Nails bounds into the front seat with me, barking and pawing at the door.

"Can you make him stop barking?" Abigail says, wincing like she's some kind of delicate china doll that might shatter at the wrong sound. Did she not just suffer through the same storm I did?

I keep my face friendly even though, with every word out of her mouth, I can tell we have zero in common. "She," I emphasize Nails' gender, "needs to go out."

Sure enough, I can't get the door open fast enough. Once Cole stops the Jeep, Nails tears out into the calm after the storm and uses the bathroom.

"Maybe we can all get out," Abigail says. "I feel like a sardine."

Cole shakes his head. "Let's get to Pecos first. We're almost out of gas."

But before we pull away, something catches my eye. It's an enormous deer, with a giant rack of antlers, leaping over chicken wire fences, running in the barren fields next to us.

"Do you see it?" I ask, captivated by the beauty of the creature in such a lifeless landscape.

Hudson nods, and the sight of the deer seems to calm him. "I've been following it for days now."

## XIV

**PECOS IS NO METROPOLIS, BUT IT HAS**
a Wal-Mart, my new favorite shopping megastore. Still, it's like
a ghost town. I'm sure people live in Pecos, but we don't see any
of them.

"Where did all the people go?" Abigail asks.

"That," Hudson says, "is a really good question."

"Do you have a really good answer?" she asks. Her eyes are
wide and innocent, like a child's.

We all shake our heads.

Cole drops Hudson and me at the store while he and Abigail
go fill up the tank. They drive off, Abigail now riding shotgun
with Nails sitting in the back. The dog seems anxious about leaving me, but she's also not willing to let Cole go, and Abigail had
refused to shop at Wal-Mart. As they drive away, Cole says something I can't hear and Abigail giggles. I push her out of my mind.

My brand new jeans are soaked, so I ditch them and get a new
everything except for my jacket which has already dried. When
I come out of the fitting room, Hudson is just pulling an athletic

T-shirt over his head. Thankfully, he's already changed his pants.

"Feels good to be dry," he says. Hudson is tall and slender with cropped blond hair, and even though his chest and forearms are nowhere near as big as Cole's, he's still really cut, as is evidenced by the patch of stomach I'd seen, showing a six-pack covered with a shadow of dark hair.

"You look like you're ready to go for a run," I say, noting his retro-green warm-up pants and bright yellow gym shoes.

"Girls chase me all the time," he says, laughing. "I always have to be ready to run."

His carefree attitude is catching. I can't help but smile. He's really easy to talk to.

Hudson grabs a baseball cap from a nearby rack, smoothes his hair, and sets it on his head. The hat has two crossed guns and says *Don't forget the ammo.* But the two guns shift and become the Alpha and the Omega. The beginning and the end.

I snatch it from his head.

"Hey, get your own," he says playfully.

"What do you see?" I ask, holding the hat out. Except before he has a chance to look, the Alpha and the Omega morph once again until they're back to being guns. But it's like the Target sign. A message that I'm on the right path.

"I know it's a bit redneck, but we Texans like our guns," Hudson says, taking the hat back.

"It's a lot redneck," I say, making light of it so he doesn't think I'm crazy. I grab a hat also because Jeeps are solely responsible for bad hair days and my curly dark hair looks like the nest of Bigfoot. Cole and Hudson must think I'm a toad next to Abigail.

I opt for a hat with an American eagle instead of the guns. I grab a hat for Cole, too, making sure we have different colors so we don't look all twinsies. Abigail is on her own. She'd probably want a bedazzled WWJD hat, which I doubt Wal-Mart has.

I'm halfway out of the clothing department when I go back

and grab an extra hat for her so I don't look like a snarky bitch.

"Were you guys on the road long?" I ask. Now that I've opened up to Cole, I realize how disconnected I've become with other people. And Hudson and Abigail must be like me and Cole.

"Just a couple days," Hudson says. "Abigail's from Dallas, and I'm from Austin."

His answer doesn't give much away. Yet he's following a deer, the same way Cole and I are following animals. And he and Abigail see us when no one else can.

Hudson flips the hat around backward, then sideways, studying his appearance in a mirror.

"So how'd you meet Abigail?" I ask, digging to get more out of him.

"In Dallas, at the mall. She was in Neiman Marcus getting hiking boots. Who goes to Neiman Marcus for hiking boots? I told her I was leaving Texas, and she said she was, too. Of course, I don't think she was too keen on walking, but it's not like I know how to siphon gas like your boyfriend does."

My face flushes. "He's not my boyfriend."

Hudson laughs. "Yeah, okay."

"But you're right," I say before he can say anything else about it. "He'll be able to fill the tank."

"And lucky we are."

"So why'd you leave Austin?" I ask, being more direct this time.

"I got a phone call," Hudson says. "A girl telling me that I could save the world."

## COLE PULLS UP TO WAL-MART IN THE

Jeep. A grin sneaks onto my face when I see him, and the corners of his mouth turn up in return. Abigail rides shotgun. When I open the passenger door, she doesn't move. I've been ousted, so Hudson and I share the backseat with Nails which seems to thrill the dog.

Abigail and Cole are in new clothes also. I can't imagine them shopping together. I'm betting they don't have a Neiman Marcus in Pecos, Texas.

Abigail's hand touches Cole's seat back where his Green Lantern T-shirt dries. "If only we could get a new car. This one smells like wet dog."

Hudson kicks one foot up over his other knee. "Just you wait, Princess. Pretty soon, you'll smell like wet dog, too, because they're going the same way we are. Looks like you can trade in those hiking boots for flip flops."

Disappointment? Confusion? I'm not sure of the emotions that flood me. Sure, I'm happy that Hudson and Abigail are now traveling with us. But in the half hour since we've been split up, Abigail has taken over as queen of the journey and I've become nothing but a sidekick. I know my smile is completely unfriendly, but I can't pull it from my face.

Ugh, what is wrong with me? Of course I want to connect with other people.

"I got you a hat," I say, passing it to Abigail in the front seat.

She takes it with two fingers like it will contaminate her if she touches it for too long. "Wow. Thanks. It's not really my style, though." And without another word, she tosses it out the window. But she hesitates before pulling her arm back in. When she does, I do a double take. A bright blue bird with a yellow beak is perched on her finger. She brings it close to her mouth, like she's whispering in its ear, then it flies off.

"You have a bird?" I say, stating the obvious.

"It's a finch," Abigail says with complete confidence. "I found it at the mall, in the shoe department. I thought I lost it back during the storm, but it's funny because it was here waiting for me."

Four of us, each with a different animal leading us on a journey.

"When were you guys born?" I ask, ticking through my logic equation.

"New Year's Day," Hudson says at the same time that Abigail says, "January first."

Cole and I exchange a glance. So our birthdays are more than just coincidence.

"Sixteen years ago, just after midnight?" he says.

"How'd you know?" Hudson says. "My parents always said they got cheated out of a tax deduction. That I owed them."

"Daddy calls me his New Year's baby," Abigail says. "He said it was God's way of showing how special I was. That the Lord himself had smiled on me."

"We were born at the same time," Cole says.

"Funny coincidence," Hudson says.

"You really think it's a coincidence?" I ask. "And what about the door to your houses? Was there a symbol carved into it?"

Abigail's eyes widen. "How did you know that?"

The *IF-THEN-ELSE* plays in my mind. I piece through it logically even though it has no logic. "I think it's what links us together. We all have the same birthdays and all had the same symbol on our door."

"That's freaky weird," Hudson says.

"So is everything else going on," I say.

"It's all part of God's plan," Abigail says, rubbing her thumb across the rubies in her cross. "We just have to trust in Him."

I don't think so at all, but there's no reason to play devil's advocate.

Cole's silence returns. I'd love to know what's going through his mind. Okay, I kind of know. Every time Abigail opens her mouth, it's like he's put further into some kind of trance. It's the same way with Hudson. Like the fact that she's gorgeous is turning them stupid. I bet she has that effect on everyone. It makes me feel even uglier next to her.

As we drive, Abigail paints her nails. Aside from an entire

manicure set, her Target ("because Daddy would disown me if I shopped at Wal-Mart") shopping spree consisted of a yellow bra with blue polka dots, totally visible through her white shirt, a nail file ("because you never know when you'll get a chip"), and hair brushes for each of us. She tells us we can't share because of lice. I don't bother to tell her that I don't have lice and never have. I grudgingly take the hair brush, vowing never to use it, but once we're out on the interstate and driving, I break down and pull the tangles from my dark hair.

Hudson talks non-stop. In the first five minutes, we learn the entire sports history of his life. He's played organized sports since the age of four. First baseball, then soccer, then football, although, even though he was fast, he wasn't big enough to really be a contender in that. Not in Texas. Now he's all about track. He won state for the mile last year.

"Long distance, baby," Hudson says. "That's where it's at. Those short distance runners are wimps. No offense, Cole, in case that's your thing."

Silence slips into the Jeep so quickly I hardly have time to blink. One second. Two. Three. Five seconds go by before Cole responds.

"Running's not really my thing," he says.

"Yeah, sorry about that, bro," Hudson says. "I forgot. You just make missing a leg look so easy."

I don't know what to do or where to look. Hudson's utter lack of tact astounds me. I hold my breath. Abigail lets out a nervous giggle.

"It's only as hard as you let it be," Cole says.

The storm flickers in the sky behind us, always behind, as if, like the earth cracking, its sole purpose is to drive us forward. We continue driving west. Abigail talks about either beauty tips or god the entire way, almost as if she's caught in a constant struggle between which is more important in her mind. I lose myself in thinking about my parents. I know they're alive.

Finally we make it to New Mexico. And in that moment, a nervous ball forms in the pit of my stomach. Everything is about to change.

# XV

## COLE STOPS AT A ROAD SIGN IN THE

middle of nowhere. "Carlsbad, New Mexico, five miles."

"I always wanted to visit Carlsbad," Hudson says. "Check out the caverns."

"We're not going through smelly old caverns," Abigail says. "We're finding a hotel. It is way past my bedtime."

I can almost picture her putting a sleeping mask over her eyes and laying her head on a silky pillow. She probably picked up both at Target.

"Edie and I have camped the last couple of nights," Cole says.

Abigail rubs his shoulder the same way she's been doing every time she answers him. "I love how you used the past tense there. Because there is no way I am camping."

"Princess wants a hotel room," Hudson says.

I won't lie. The idea of sleeping in a bed makes happy thoughts run through my head. But I'm not about to agree with Abigail openly. Still, nobody vetoes her decision.

Carlsbad has five hotels, the nicest of which is the Comfort

Inn. The hotel is empty, so we each get our own room. Still, Abigail is not pleased.

"Daddy would cry if he knew I was staying in this place."

She has this habit of referring to her father that way. Daddy this and Daddy that. He's a preacher at a mega-church in Dallas. She's only mentioned her mother once, and when she did, she called her just that: Mother. She's also made it abundantly clear that her family has lots of money, not that it helps her current situation any more than the rest of us.

We turn in early. I try to fall asleep. I really do. I flip through the Bible that's tucked in the drawer of the nightstand because it's the only book around. I study the shadows as the thickening moon shifts across the sky. I unwrap the little bar of soap and smell it. But half hour later sleep still hasn't come. I can't stand this room.

I put my jacket on and zip it, and head out to the Jeep to get my sleeping bag, hearing my owl hoot in greeting. I lug the Bible with me and prop myself against a wheel. Maybe I should actually read the thing. I never have. *Genesis* is the first book. It's where I got my name. Adam and Eve live in the Garden of Eden. God gives them everything. All he asks is that they don't eat from the Tree of Knowledge. But yeah, they talk to a snake who convinces them that they should, so they do, because what kind of story would there be if they didn't? They'd still be stuck in that garden, sitting around naked, and nothing else would have happened in the world. So Adam and Eve leave the garden, and nobody ever sees the garden again.

It's funny because as much as my parents weren't religious people, Mom totally believed in the Garden of Eden. She used to tell me stories about it, saying that it was real, that someday she would find it and walk among the trees. *Or maybe you'll find it, Eden*, she used to tell me.

All I want to find is my parents.

I skip ahead to the part about Noah's ark because I don't want to think about my parents anymore.

"Am I bothering you?"

I look toward the voice, holding my lantern up so I can see. Cole stands there, leaning on his crutch about ten feet away. His dark hair is a mess, going every single way it possibly can. I wonder what he did with the brush Abigail gave him. Not that I want him to use it. The tousled look does him good. I kind of want to freeze this moment. Nails pushes past him and runs to me for some attention.

"Not at all," I say, tossing the Bible into the empty parking lot. Nails thinks I'm playing and chases after it.

Cole takes this as an invitation to join me, grabbing his sleeping bag from the back of the Jeep. Reassurance fills me. Things will be okay. We'll get through this.

"Were you reading anything useful?" Cole asks. He sets up his bag near mine, but doesn't zip it.

"Not really," I say. The Bible, as far as I'm concerned, is mythology.

Cole pulls out his cell phone and studies it.

"Waiting for a call?" I ask.

"Maybe," he says, slipping it back in his pocket.

"What if it's not real?" I say. "What is there is no Iva and there were no phone calls and we're all just crazy?"

"So you're calling me crazy?" Cole says.

"Only as crazy as I am."

"It's good to be crazy together." Cole rolls up the leg of his jeans so the stub of his leg shows. It's the first time I've seen it for real. There's a scar running along the bottom which means he must've had something removed, but it's an old scar, thick but faded.

He's sees me staring.

"It's pretty bad, isn't it?" he says, tucking the end of his jeans

**92**

back around it.

"Not at all." I want to pull his jeans back up, but his body language isn't offering this. "It's just you've made a point of not letting me see it before now."

"I have not," he says.

"You totally have. Even when you're sleeping, you keep it covered."

"You're imagining things," Cole says, and his tone makes it pretty clear he's done talking about his leg. "What do you think of Hudson and Abigail?"

My eyelids are starting to droop, but I smile. "I think they're crazy like us."

Cole laughs. "Good assessment." He shifts so his head is the same direction as mine and he's lying on his side, and I do the same, facing him. So close. I want to reach over and touch his face. Run my fingers down the scar. I want to tell him that I'm glad he's here with me, that I'm glad he came out to the Jeep. But then I remember that Cole has Pia waiting for him—most likely his girlfriend—so I keep my hands to myself.

"Tell me about Pia," I say. "What's she like?"

Cole glances away, watching Nails gnaw on the Bible. "She's my best friend. I've known her most of high school."

Again, he calls her a friend, not a girlfriend. But again, I see how his eyes light up when he talks about her.

"How'd you meet?" I ask.

"At school, halfway through freshman year," Cole says. "Pia started late into the year. She'd been . . . I mean, she wasn't in school for the first half."

"Why not? Was she sick?" I've heard of people having to miss months of school because they caught mono or something.

"No, nothing that simple," he says, shaking his head. "I don't know why I don't like to tell people. Pia always tells people if they ask. She says it's good to get it out. Her counselor told her so."

"Good to get what out?" I ask, not sure I want to know now.

Cole blows out a long breath. "I guess it was during eighth grade. Pia said she was getting bullied pretty bad. That friends of hers were passing around all sorts of rumors about her, saying she was a slut. Saying she kept this piece of paper at home with all the names of the guys she'd slept with written on it."

"Some friends," I say. There is no excuse for bullying.

"Tell me about it," Cole says. "So I guess during the summer, the girls mostly stopped. Pia thought everything was going to be okay. That she would start out high school and everyone would have forgotten. And then a week before classes start, she gets a text, telling her to check online. And when she looks, there's this picture of a piece of paper with a bunch of guys' names from school and the words *Ask Pia how to get your name here next.*"

I've never met her, but my heart aches for this girl.

"So what happened?" I'm afraid to ask, but I have to.

"She tried to kill herself. I guess she cut her wrists, but it didn't work. Her parents found her too soon. They took her to the hospital. She was home after a day. And less than a week later, she took every single pill she could find in her parents' medicine cabinet. It almost worked that time. They had to pump her stomach, and they kept her there for a solid week. Her parents never knew there was a problem. She never told them about the bullying. But after that, they did everything they could. Her mom quit her job so she could be home more often. They put Pia in an inpatient counseling program for a month. They switched her to a different high school—my high school, which is how we met. They found the girls who'd been tormenting her and filed charges against them."

"Wow," I say, because I'm otherwise speechless. All of a sudden this Pia girl has turned into more than a name. She's a real person with real things that happened to her.

"Yeah," Cole says. "Wow."

"She's lucky she has you," I say, and I mean this more than anything.

A voice comes out of the darkness. "Is this a private party?" Hudson says from the direction of the hotel.

I hold the lantern in his direction. He and Abigail walk toward us. Hudson has a giant bottle of something in his hand.

"Irish Whiskey," he says when he sees me looking. Guess there are no worries about being carded for alcohol.

It doesn't take Cole long to start a fire. After everything I've been through, the least of my concerns is whether I should drink alcohol or not. The first sip of whiskey immediately hits my blood, either because I'm dehydrated or because I've never had a drink before.

Abigail obviously has. She seems to fall over the edge of the religious line she walks, putting god in the background. "Too bad we don't have any mixers," she says, taking a delicate sip from the bottle. Both Hudson and Cole watch as her red lips wrap around the glass neck of the bottle. She makes the whole thing look beautiful. Sexy. I sputter and cough. Definitely not sexy.

"Mixers are for ninnies," Hudson says. "Right, Cole?"

Even Cole seems to be loosening up. "Something like that."

"So where'd you get the scar anyway," Hudson says.

It's the question I have been dying to ask but have been hesitant to. I figured Cole would bring it up if he wanted people to know.

"Nowhere," Cole says.

"Oh, come on," Hudson says, taking another drink. "You had to get it somewhere."

"It doesn't matter," Cole says.

But Hudson is persistent. "Of course it matters. Was it a fire? No, that doesn't make sense. Otherwise you'd be scared of fires and you're like the fire master. I've never seen anyone start a fire so fast. How about a wild animal attack? Of course then it would be more like scratches, and that thing covers the entire half of your face. And what about your leg? How did that happen? It looks like someone chopped—"

"Leave him alone," I say, defensively, and Cole gives me a grateful look. But he's still tense. I can't believe how freaking chatty Hudson is. Can't he take a hint? So much for the silence I thought sleeping out by the Jeep would bring.

"So about your theory," Abigail says, taking another sip. "We're all born on the same day. We all had the same symbol on our doors. Why?"

I pass on the bottle when it comes my way. My head is already spinning just from the two sips I've had. "I don't have the answers. Just more theories."

"Like what?" Hudson asks.

The logic spins around in my mind. *IF-THEN-ELSE.* If we're all born on New Year's Day and we all had the symbol on our door, then we're here right now, else . . . we'd . . .

My logic falls away.

"Cole and I are both looking for people. Me for my parents, and him for his friend, Pia."

Cole narrows his eyes at me but doesn't say a word, and I worry that he's angry I brought up Pia.

"She's your girlfriend, isn't she?" Abigail says.

Cole looks to me then quickly darts his eyes away when he sees me watching him. But my breathing has stopped as I wait for his answer.

"She's . . . it's doesn't matter," Cole says. "The point is that we're both looking for someone. And that little girl Iva says she knows where they are."

So Pia is his girlfriend. I knew it.

"And . . . ?" Hudson says.

"Are you guys looking for anyone?" I ask, forcing my breathing back to normal. I don't care if Cole has a girlfriend. She needs him.

Hudson shakes his head. "Not me. I told you that little girl called me. Told me if I traveled to some volcano, I could save the world. It was tempting, but I had this huge cross country meet coming up, so I politely declined. Then people stopped noticing me. It's like I wasn't there. I had no clue what was going on, and then Iva called again. Said I had no choice. But I did have a choice. And I chose to go find Iva."

It's a strange logic, but it fits together, given the circumstances.

"What about you?" I ask Abigail. "Why are you here?"

Her hand goes back to the cross. "I'm here because it's what God wants me to do."

"So God talked to you?" Hudson laughs, but Abigail smacks his arm.

"Don't you dare laugh. He did talk to me. He told me Iva was going to call. That I should do what she said. That it was the only path to salvation. And that I would meet someone special. My soulmate."

I can't help it. I bust out laughing. Not only is god talking to Abigail, now she's on a quest for her soulmate? It's too much. But her eyes look so sincere.

"So you think your soulmate is Cole or me?" Hudson asks.

Cole stokes the fire, keeping silent.

"It's not you or Cole," Abigail says with utter certainly in her Texas twang.

"So much for the big church wedding I always dreamed of," Hudson says.

"Then who is it?" I ask.

Abigail shakes her head. "I've never met him, but I keep having these visions of him. I know what he looks like. How he'll act. We talk. Work together. The visions feel so real."

She's having visions, too, which makes me sure this has to be another part of the logic puzzle. But what do the visions mean? Why is she having visions about her soulmate while I'm having visions about getting hurt by Owen? I'm about to ask her more, but she cuts me off.

"Hey, what's that?" Abigail's gazing out toward the desert, behind the Comfort Inn.

Hudson pats her on the head, like she's a child. "It's nothing. Have another drink."

She shrugs him away. "No really. Look over there."

I look to where she's pointing. There is something out there in the darkness. Something that is moving closer to us like a wave of blackness descending upon us. It starts at the edge of the desert and spans the horizon.

Cole jumps up to his one foot. His hand hangs dangerously near the fire, but he doesn't seem to notice.

Hudson pushes Cole's hand away from the flames. "Watch out or it's going to burn you."

But Cole isn't listening to Hudson. Whatever is coming toward us has our complete attention. The things stumble, but they're definitely walking. Their heads hang low, chins on their chest. Their arms reach out for us.

Fear grips my stomach. They're the same things I saw at the bottom of the crevasse back in Louisiana. Dead things. Things that can't be real. And yet they are.

"We need to go!" I say, and panic fills my voice. "Now!"

We run for the Jeep, leaving everything behind. Nails bounds after us, and we load into the vehicle.

"Drive!" Hudson says the second we're all inside because the things are only meters away.

"Come on, Nails!" Cole calls.

Nails barks at the intruders, loud and shrill. They don't seem to hear her. Hudson's deer bursts into view, running through the dead things, past us and off into the distance, on to the west. My owl hoots from above.

"Nails, now!"

Nails turns to Cole. Looks back to the onslaught. Then she's bounding toward the Jeep. As soon as she's inside, Cole shoves it into gear and we take off. By now the things have reached our fire. In the glow, I see their faces. Their eyes and mouths are sewn shut. They wear the finest clothes.

"What are they?" Abigail says. Her normally composed face is a wreck. She's in the front with Cole, but I don't care about who's riding shotgun right now.

"They're dead people!" Hudson says.

"Dead people can't walk," Abigail says.

He stares her down. "Then how do you explain those things? Did you see their faces?"

We all saw their faces.

Abigail begins to cry, gulping between breaths. "God never told me about this."

Cole grips both hands on the steering wheel as he veers around obstacles to get us away from the walking dead.

"Edie and I saw them the other day," Cole says. "They came up out of the ground."

"And you didn't think to tell us?" Hudson says.

"It never came up," I say.

Our conversation is cut short when one of them reaches the back of the Jeep. Arms grab for me. They scratch at my face. Pull at my hair. Paw at my jacket.

Hudson yanks me out of their reach.

"Go faster!" he says.

"There's nowhere to go," Cole says, pressing the accelerator nonetheless, which makes the Jeep run over all sorts of things that are in our way. The last thing we need is a flat tire. Then we'd truly be out of luck. But the tires hold, and Cole doesn't slow down.

"We're still heading west?" I check my compass, but instead of pointing in one direction, the needle spins. I search the sky for my owl, but in the dark, I can't find her anywhere.

"I have no idea which way we're heading," Cole says.

It's then that I smell the sulfur. And when we crest the next hill, the volcano stretches before us.

# XVI

**THE JEEP SPUTTERS AND DIES. I TURN,**
sure we're doomed, but the things behind us have stopped moving. They block the direction we came from, like their sole reason
for being here is to drive us forward. Get us to our destination.
But they're not all dead. Standing among them is a guy with
messy brown hair wearing a blue and green plaid shirt. A guy
I've seen before, the day my parents went missing and then again
outside of my house.

"Do you see him?" I ask.

"See who?" Cole says.

"That guy. He's alive." I raise my hand to point at him, but the
guy's no longer there. He's drifted back into the shadows, behind
the dead things, or he's vanished into thin air. He must be a trick
being played on me by my own mind, because there is no one
alive out there. There is only the four of us.

"Don't lose it, Edie," Hudson says.

How I'm trying not to.

"How can the sun be rising?" Abigail says.

The sun went down only hours ago, but above the volcano, it's rising again—from the west. It defies the universal laws of the world. The sun rises in the east. Sets in the west. Everything about this is wrong. Logic slips between my fingers like sand.

The sun's beams peak out from behind the giant mountain, reflecting off the lava that flows down the sides. Smoke curls from the mouth of the volcano, causing the light from the impossible sun to refract everywhere. At the base of the volcano, four rivers run, coming from all directions, meeting at one central point. Steam lifts from the water as the lava hits it, filling the sulfuric air with humidity.

Directly in front of us on the ground is a compass rose so large it looks like it was painted by giants. It's marked with the same two symbols on the back of my compass, the Alpha and Omega. And where the needle ends is a high iron fence.

This is the place Iva planted in my mind. We've reached our destination.

Blood rushes to my head. This is where Iva must be. She'll lead me to my parents. All I want to do is get out of this Jeep and run toward it. The fact that nothing about this can be real—that there is no logic—falls to the background as my parents fill my mind.

Someone's hand settles on mine. I look up to see Cole's concerned eyes watching me.

"We'll find them, Edie," he says. "We'll find them together."

"We have to go now," I say.

"We have to be careful," he says.

"But my parents . . ."

". . . are waiting for you," Cole says. He squeezes my hand. Such a small thing, but it makes me feel like everything will work out. I will find my parents. We've gotten this far.

"This might be some kind of trap," Hudson says.

"Trap or not, the Jeep's dead," Cole says. "We have to walk." Cole releases my hand and gets out of the Jeep, grabbing his crutch. Hudson and I follow, but Abigail won't get out.

She's fixed in the front seat, praying. Fast words tumble out of her mouth so quickly, they sound like nonsense. "Salvation" and "Deliver me" and "Lord" are just a few of the words I can make out. Her knuckles are white as she clutches her cross necklace.

Hudson opens her door for her. "Come on, Princess. God wants you to be here."

I get it. She's scared. But if she doesn't get out in the next two seconds, I'm leaving without her. I need to get to my parents.

Abigail doesn't budge. Her praying doesn't stop. It's like she doesn't hear Hudson. He tries again, but Abigail wants no part of it.

Hudson turns to us. "We can't leave her here."

"We have to," I say. I haven't survived the last two weeks only to stop half a mile from our destination.

Something flies through the air, moving through the open top of the Jeep and landing on the dashboard in front of Abigail. It's her blue finch. It tweets a few short notes, but it's enough to get Abigail's attention.

Her prayers stop. She unclasps her hands and lifts a finger. The finch flies to it and perches there, and Abigail's face relaxes the smallest amount.

"It'll be okay," Abigail says after a moment, wiping her eyes. Fear slips off her like water.

"Yeah," Hudson says. "It'll be okay. Now come on."

"Everything will be perfect," she says, letting Hudson help her out. "But what is this place, Edie?"

I'm not sure why she's asking me. I don't have any more idea than Cole or Hudson.

"I can't tell." I try to survey the world beyond the iron fence. There's so much steam from the lava and the water that I can't see a thing.

"As long as it's not dead things chasing us, we're good,"

Hudson says.

"I hope you're right," I say.

I still want to run forward, but caution holds me back. I spot my owl as we set out across the compass rose. She flies above, circling to make sure she doesn't get too far ahead. Nails does the same, though on the ground. She barks as she waits for us to catch up. Hudson's deer runs along the edges of the compass, toward the gates. Now that Abigail has transformed from a frightened little girl back into better-than-everyone Abigail, her finch takes flight, gliding in the same direction as the other three animals.

The dead stay where they are, back behind the Jeep, watching, guarding. There is no sign of the guy in the plaid shirt. I walk next to Cole, and Abigail walks on the other side of him, with Hudson next to her. She's probably used to being flanked by guys wherever she goes. Her transformation amazes me. She holds her head high, her back straight. Not even her impractical flip flops hinder her. We all have a reason for being here. Mine is to find my parents. Cole's is to find Pia. Abigail is here because god told her to come. And Hudson? He's going to save the world.

As we get closer, details come into view. The fence is black wrought iron that twists and curls in intricate designs. It reaches high above, almost to cloud level, but the steam still blocks most of what is beyond. All I see are vivid colors.

We cross the remainder of the compass rose and stand on the Alpha and the Omega. The beginning and the end. The symbols are mirrored in the wrought iron gates. Nails sits in the center of the gates waiting along with Hudson's deer which is off to one side. My owl perches on the top of the gate, next to Abigail's finch.

No sooner have our feet stopped on the Alpha and Omega that the gates silently swing open.

"Inside?" My voice shakes because my future is uncertain. Everything about this is crazy, from the moment my parents went missing to dead things walking the earth. I can't believe this is happening, but that doesn't stop it. It doesn't stop the fact that I have to deal with it.

Cole gives me the smallest smile, private so nobody else can see, and comfort races through me so quickly it catches me by surprise.

"Inside," he says.

Deep breath. Then another. And the four of us walk through.

The gates close with a loud boom, as if a lock is being slammed in place. Once the dull echo of the iron gates closing behind us fades, another sound reaches my ears. Music so beautiful it can't be of this world. It flows across me in a melody so sweet it makes me forget where I am, how I came to be here. The patterns of the music trick me. I close my eyes. Tilt my head so I can hear it more clearly.

In the music, I forget that the world has gone crazy.

*I'm back with my parents. With Thomas. We sit at the dinner table. Mom is putting the last bit of our meal on the table.*

*Emily has just texted me, telling me that she's sure Owen has a crush on me. That he told his best friend Joe who told his girlfriend Sara who told Emily that he was going to ask me out. I can't stop the stupid flutter of my heart. I've been crushing on Owen since he talked to me at my locker two weeks ago. It's so stupid. A guy talks to me and I fall head over heels for him?*

*I'd been trying to find my copy of <u>Brave New World</u> because it was the day we were going to be talking about it in class. I'd marked some of my favorite parts. But the stupid thing wasn't in my locker. I know I'd brought it to school.*

*I'd slammed the locker closed, and there he was, leaning against the locker almost like he'd been watching me.*

*"You're upset with the locker?" he'd said.*

*I give myself credit. It only took me a few seconds to process the fact that he was talking to me. He hadn't spoken a word to me in my life before this day.*

"It's a book. I can't find it." I glance at my watch, because, though I'm happy Owen is talking to me, I have to get to class or I'll be late.

I start walking. Oddly enough, Owen joins me.

"Where are you heading?" he asks.

"Computer Science." I almost add the AP part but don't want to sound like I'm bragging. Even at that, it's so basic, I could teach the class.

"I have that fifth period," Owen says.

"You like computers?"

"Hate them," he says. "I suck at computer programming, but my parents made me sign up. My dad works in video game design."

"I'm really good at programming," I say, but then I try to laugh at the end so it doesn't sound boastful. And how cool that his dad actually works on video games. Maybe he could get me set up as an alpha-tester.

"That's what I hear," Owen says. "Oh, and look. Here you are."

That had been it. The entire extent of our conversation. And now Emily is telling me that he likes me? Still, it had been all I thought about through dinner.

"How's school?" Mom asks. She's wearing a green shirt with the black silhouette of a tree on it. From the tree hangs a single piece of fruit.

I shrug. "I was thinking about checking into computer classes at the university." FIT is spitting distance from us, but my parents have been reluctant to let me sign up for anything because of my age. I'm sixteen now. That has to be old enough.

"Maybe for spring semester," Dad says. "You'll be seventeen then."

I don't think one year makes much difference, but I don't want to argue at the table. Our family dinners are so few and far between.

"You guys are traveling tomorrow?"

Mom nods. "Until Thursday."

"I don't want you to go," Thomas whines. He whines every time they go away.

*Mom rubs his head. "It's only a few days. And Edie will take good care of you."*

The patterns in the music shift, stirring me from my memory. I'm back in the real world, and the front of my head pounds like with my visions of Owen. But this was real. A sliver of my life from before. Not like the other visions which are my fears manifested.

The memory makes reality that much worse. I'd been completely wrong about Owen, thinking he was actually a nice guy. And my parents, so alive in my memories, are missing. I have to find them.

My headache fades to gray, and I step forward, through the smoke and humidity and into a garden. My friends are nowhere to be found. Fruit hangs low on trees all around me, trees that reach so high, their branches rest on the wrought iron fence I've just come through. Apples and pomegranates and nectarines. Grapes droop low on vines that twist around the iron fence. Flowers blossom and birds sing, flitting between the branches.

The music draws me forward. It embraces me and makes me feel like I am a part of this place. Like I could belong here. Live here. I never want to leave. I continue walking, not knowing or caring where Cole, Hudson, or Abigail is.

Deep in the forest of fruit trees I go. I unzip my jacket and let the warm air caress me. I step over roots and bend under branches. The fruit tempts me. I can almost taste the juice on my lips. But every time I'm about to reach forward and pluck a piece to eat, my owl hoots from above, stirring my mind enough to get me back on track.

I come upon a clearing, blanketed with grass so green it makes me want nothing more than to lie down on it. To look up at the sky. To dream of the days when things were better. But nothing can be better than this place. At the center of the clearing is a solitary tree, an apple tree, with plump fruit on nearly all the branches. It reminds me of our apple tree back home, except that one was dead, and this tree is so alive. The branches hold golden apples that shine in the sun. I reach my hand up, not thinking about what I'm doing.

*Don't eat the fruit,* Mom's voice says in my dreams.

I hesitate then draw my hand back as the memory of my dream fades away. Behind the tree something begins to show through the shifting mist, like a staircase carved into rock.

"Golden apples," someone says.

I whip around to see Cole walking toward me. His crutch sinks softly into the thick grass with each step.

"Don't touch them," I say, positioning myself between him and the tree. Mom had warned me about the fruit for some reason.

"I won't," he says, but juice runs from the side of his mouth, trickling down his chin. He could have eaten some of the fruit before I got here.

"Where are Hudson and Abigail?" I ask.

He wipes at his chin and looks back in the direction he came. "They ran toward the cave."

"What cave?" I ask, glancing back at the staircase. The mist is moving again, covering it.

"The cave where the music is coming from," Cole says.

Our conversation is cut short by Abigail's scream.

## XVII

**THE SCREAM CLEARS THE CONFUSION**
on Cole's face. He starts back in the direction he came, but with his crutch in the grass, he's moving slowly. Abigail could be in trouble, and even though I feel like the staircase is where we need to go, I hurry after Cole as fast as I can. It seems like forever, but we finally burst out of the trees.

In front of us is a cave so black on the inside that it almost looks like it's been painted on the side of the hill. No, not hill. Volcano. Through this garden, we've reached the volcano. Music drifts from the mouth of the cave, so evocative that the memories it stirred up before threaten to take over me again. Memories of a past I want back so much that I ache inside. I want my family.

The music sinks deeper into me. It tells me all the wonderful things I can do. It reassures me. It tells me that I can make everything better.

My owl hoots, shaking my mind. The music screams in response. Mom's voice from my dream replays. *Don't eat the fruit.*

*"Eat the fruit,"* the music tells me.

I'm not going to eat the fruit.

*"Eat the fruit,"* it says, more urgent this time.

I will not eat the fruit. And I'm not here for these memories. They're nothing but deception cloaked as something irresistible. Like Owen and his lies. I want no part of it.

The music shifts, turns ugly. It tells me to go away. That I am no longer welcome here. That I have invaded this place. It screams like the sirens blaring in the background on my parents' ship when it capsized.

"Do you hear that?" I ask Cole, but he's not even aware I've spoken. He walks forward, toward the cave, like he's in a trance.

"Don't go in, Cole," I say, but he either doesn't hear me or he ignores me.

The music pulls him. And for every inch that it does so, it pushes me away. The cave seems to grow sharp, jagged teeth, jutting both upward and down, like it truly is the mouth of a monster and Cole is about to enter. I run for him but trip on a rock I swear wasn't there two seconds ago.

"Come back," I call, but I don't think he hears because he's already too far in. Nails stands at the mouth of the cave, barking incessantly.

*"Turn away,"* the music sings to me as I watch Cole disappear into the blackness.

"Not without my friends," I say aloud.

I run for the cave, but the closer I get, the farther away it seems, like I'm running on a giant treadmill. I quicken my pace, but it only makes the distance between me and my destination increase. I'm never going to get there.

"Go back," the voices sing.

I'm not going back. I close my eyes and continue running, and when I reopen them, I am in front of the mouth of the cave. Instead of drawing me in as it drew Cole, it repulses me. Something evil lives within. My nerves prickle with its energy. The song floats just inside the cave, echoing off its stone walls. I have to go after my friends, but something tells me that if I do, I will die.

The song comes at me, like ripples across the water, like fairies floating through the air, laughing and taunting. The melody flows like frosting on a cupcake, swirling in patterns and coated in sugar. The music tells me to stay away. To leave this place. That I don't belong here. That I will fail at everything I try.

I'm not a failure.

It tells me that I am not loved. Never have been. That all my friends are dead.

But they're not dead. And I have to help them.

I cover my ears and try to take a step forward, but the grass at the mouth of the cave holds me. I tear my right foot from the ground, then the left. One agonizingly slow step after another, I get closer to the mouth of the cave. Nails continues to bark. She snaps at the evil that lies within but doesn't enter, as if she's afraid.

*"Be afraid,"* the voices sing to me. Their song is sweet like honey and yet filled with poison.

"Cole!" I scream, hoping he can hear me. Hoping he knows that I'm coming.

I grit my teeth, focus on my steps. I have to get to them. One step leads to the next, and the next, and I am inside the mouth of the cave. Pure blackness lies in front of me.

*"Leave now,"* the voices sing.

*"You aren't welcome here."*

*"You will never see them again."*

It's a chorus of voices, pushing me backward.

*"They are all dead to you."*

*"They ate the fruit."*

There it is. The reason the voices are pushing me away. I wanted to eat the fruit, yet a warning in a dream of Mom told me not to. But Cole had eaten it. I'd seen the juice running down his chin. Abigail and Hudson must have also.

**111**

Nails barks from beside me, stirring me from the music I've fallen into.

"We'll find them," I say. "Together we'll figure out where they are and we'll get them back." Maybe if I say it aloud, I'll believe it.

Nails barks twice in reply, almost like she understands. Then we both move into the darkness.

# XVIII

**I CAN'T SEE ANYTHING. DRUMS BEGIN**
to beat as the melody increases. *Boom. Boom. Boom. Boom.* They
push memories through my mind, but I force them away. How
much I want to get lost in memories of my parents, of happier
times, but I don't have that luxury right now. I can't fall under
their hypnotic spell. The song blends with the drums like a caress
on the wind.

I stumble and fall against a stone wall I hadn't known was right
in front of me. There's no way I can find anything in here. I wave
my hand in front of my face but can't see it. I should have grabbed
some matches. There had been some at the hotel. That was only
hours ago, but it feels like a lifetime.

I shove my hands into my pockets to make sure I didn't mag-
ically put some in there, but instead of matches, I find the compass. It has led me this far. Maybe it can lead me the rest of the
way. I pull it out and flip it open. Immediately the dial illuminates, not enough to light the chamber around me, but enough
that the needle is visible. It points to the right.

"Let's go find them, girl," I say to Nails, happy to feel her padding along beside me as I set out, following the compass in the dark. The hoot of the owl sounds out from somewhere in the cave. The singing fills the cave, louder, stronger.

*"You'll be sorry,"* the voices sing. *"You'll never leave."*

I will leave. I will find Cole, Hudson, and Abigail, and get out of this place.

The compass leads me. In the dark, ghost shadows bounce in the corners of my vision, but every time I think I see something, I turn and there is only blackness. This place is messing with my mind.

*"Too late,"* the voices sing.

I follow the compass. The melody follows me. When I find its source, I will find my friends. And when I find my friends, I will free them from the spell they're under.

*"Death waits for you,"* the voices sing.

The air inside the cave turns fetid, and the walls narrow with each step. I hunch over so I don't hit my head. The ceiling above is cold, wet stone that drips moisture onto my shoulders and hair. I make the mistake of tilting my head upward, and water falls into my eyes, stinging badly enough that I squeeze my eyes closed to flush it. When I reopen my eyes, instead of darkness, the tunnel around me has taken on an eerie green glow. I press my palm onto the stone wall beside me, and when I pull my hand back, it, too, glows green, like I've fallen into some echo of the real world.

The singing continues, and each step I take, it is filled with hatred and venom. It tells me that I am nothing. That I will die just like everyone. That it is too late.

I continue forward until Nails and I enter a vast cavern. The ceiling glows far above me, and around me, green rocks jut up like plants, spanning the perimeter and filling every crack and crevice. A Greek temple fills the center of the cavern, with six pillars that reach high above. It has to be manmade, but how someone could build something so vast in this remote cave is beyond me. Nothing about this place makes sense. Through the spaces between the pillars comes thick fog.

The compass needle holds steady, pointing at the entrance to the temple.

"Ready?" I say to Nails as I tuck the compass back into my pocket.

She barks in reply.

I move forward, and the fog pushes me back. It surrounds me, and I suck it in, coughing as it fills my lungs with its rank odor. I trip on a rock and stumble, scraping my hands, but I get up and push through.

The inside of the temple is vast, with pipes lining the walls. My eyes trail along the pipes to where they connect to a giant pipe organ way bigger than any I've seen before. Scattered around the rest of the room are all sorts of other musical instruments.

Cole stands in the center of the room. His eyes are opened, but he's balanced on his one leg, completely immobile as if he's made of stone. I can't see the rise and fall of his chest. Abigail and Hudson are there too along with two other people I don't recognize, a guy and girl, both with dark skin and bleached hair, that look enough alike that they could be brother and sister.

I rush to Cole, but when I get within five feet of him, I'm repelled, flying backward where I land on my butt. The world spins around me.

"You can't get in," the voices sing in perfect synchronization with the beating of the drums. "He is ours. They all are. They ate the fruit." This time the voices are truly here, in this room with me. And the way they rise and fall, I'm again reminded of my parent's shipwreck, of the alarms wailing in the background, as if maybe they weren't alarms at all, but instead these same voices singing my parents to a watery grave.

Something from the right lunges at me. I barely have time to

**115**

jump out of the way. It's a woman with claws extended and razor-sharp teeth. Her hair hangs in wet strings over her pale green shoulders. She's not wearing any clothes to speak of though leaves and bark are pasted on her skin. She hisses and lunges again, and I evade, scooting around the room. My hands scramble for some kind of weapon. I find nothing but solid stone.

On her third try she manages to grab my forearm. Her claw fingernails dig into me, but instantly she shrieks and lets go as if she's been burned. Smoke curls off her hands.

I glance down quickly. She didn't tear the fabric of my jacket. Where she grabbed, the jacket gives off smoke, but there's no time to think about it because two more demon women shift out of illusion and materialize in the temple. One moves next to Cole, draping her arms around him like she's dancing with a statue, and the other stands by the guy I don't know, doing the same.

"Get away from him!"

The woman licks her lips and smiles, exposing her fanged teeth. She presses her palm flat against Cole's stomach. He shudders and winces in pain. He's still alive.

"Stop!"

I run for him without thinking and wind up flat on my butt again.

"The fruit was not theirs to take," the first woman sings. "They took what didn't belong to them, and now they must pay."

I struggle to get past her, but she guards me. She won't touch me, and her hands still smoke, but her claws are extended. Before I can stop her, she swipes out and scratches my face.

My hand goes to the cut automatically and comes back bloody. My cheek stings, and the woman starts laughing. She swipes at the other cheek. I fall backward, and heat moves through me, from my cheek down my neck, up to the top of my head. The room starts to spin.

"You are not meant to succeed," the woman sings. "This is all a trap."

I can't speak. Can't reply. This can't be a trap. I am supposed to find my parents. My face feels frozen. Paralyzed. My neck won't move. The warmth continues to spread.

My jacket. There is something about my jacket. I can still move my arms and body, so I tear it off. And before she can stop me, I throw it over her head.

She starts screaming. Smoke comes in giant waves from under the fabric. This gets the attention of the other two demon women. They stop pawing at Cole and the other guy and come at me. My head swims, but I focus. Nails bounds forward and pounces on one of the women. She flies backward and Nails tears into her. The first woman is no longer moving, so I grab my jacket from her and throw it over the third woman at the same time my owl swoops into the temple and dives at her, claws extended toward her eyes. She begins to smoke and scream. The entire top half of the first woman has melted, leaving only her bare stomach and legs, covered with smoking bark and leaves.

When the third woman stops moving, I pull my jacket off her, averting my eyes from what she's become. The woman Nails attacked is in pieces. I collapse to the floor.

The statues that are my frozen friends release. Cole falls because he hasn't been balancing his own weight. I reach out to help him, but darkness overtakes me.

# XIX

# I WAKE UP TO A GIANT DOG KISS. NAILS

slobbers on me, and when my eyes open, her tail starts thudding against my leg. Cole is behind her and tries to hold her back, but she's persistent.

"Was I out long?" I'm still in the nest of the sirens. The world glows green around me. My owl rests on a pillar far above.

"Only a couple minutes," Cole says.

My hands go to my face. I can move my neck and eyes again, and the warmth is gone. Where the scratches were only moments before, the skin is now smooth.

"How did my face heal?"

"It healed on its own," Cole says.

"You don't remember it?" Abigail says. "We all watched. I prayed for your healing." Her eyes are wide and earnest, and I try to decide which person Abigail really is: the devout one who is concerned with god and the good of others, or the one who cares only about how beautiful she looks each day. Maybe it doesn't matter. Maybe she's just Abigail.

"I don't remember," I say.

"How did you resist them?" Hudson asks. "That music . . ." He shakes his head as if the memory of it threatens to entrance him all over again.

How did I resist it? It was like I was able to see reality beyond fantasy.

"The fruit," I say. "You all ate it, didn't you?"

"I tried not to," Cole says. "I knew I shouldn't but I couldn't stop myself."

"You saved us!" Abigail says, and she throws her arms around me. "Thank you so much, Edie. You are my hero."

"Creepy bone pile, dead ahead," Hudson says, pointing to the opposite wall from the massive pipe organ.

Skulls are stacked up in a pyramid, balancing perfectly like some piece of art. Hundreds of them. Thousands. They've yellowed and rotted with age, the ones on the bottom so far gone that they look like they will collapse at any moment. And next to the pile of bones is an equally high pile of treasures. Gold and silver glitter in the eerie green glow of the room. Tools. Hairbrushes. Suitcases that look modern.

"There have to be thousands of them," Hudson says.

"Maybe they've been doing this for a while," Cole says. He stumbles because he doesn't have his crutch.

I move next to him and put my arm around him. "Here, lean on me."

He shrugs me off, instead holding onto the wall. "I got it, Edie," he says, which he totally doesn't. He has to hop on one leg, and the floor is slippery with moisture.

"Suit yourself," I say. Why does he have to be so stubborn anyway?

He makes it over to the pile of stuff and grabs his crutch which rests on top.

"How the hell do we get out of here?" someone says, and I

remember the girl and guy who are in here with us. It's the girl talking. She's got bleached braids that come to just below her ears and dark skin that is marred by two thin scars running along either of her cheeks. They can't be accidental, because the guy she's with has the same scars, the same bleached hair, though his hair's really short. They're both about the same height, well over my five-four stature, and solid.

"There was a staircase by the tree," I say as my memories clear. "I know the way."

We don't waste time. The memory of the sirens is too fresh. I use the compass to lead us out of the cave and back to the tree. The fruit calls to us again, but we push past it, through the mist, and start up the stairs, taking the black granite steps two at a time. They go on forever. Fifty. Sixty. Eighty. At two hundred steps, we reach the top. We're high above the garden, panting from the exertion.

The sky above is midnight blue, but the moon and stars are nowhere to be found. The only thing I see is the volcano. We stand on the side of it, on a small ledge that looks out across a vast emptiness. The stairway we just climbed is blocked by a flow of lava. The side of the volcano is too steep to descend.

We're trapped.

My phone begins to ring, playing the theme song from *The Twilight Zone*, but it's not just my phone. It's everyone's. Six cell phones, long out of batteries, chiming in harmonic disharmony. My hand instinctively goes to my pocket, but I hold it there.

"Who's gonna get it first?" Hudson says. We're all poised, ready to answer.

"My sister," the new guy says. "Nobody beats Taylor to anything."

Sure enough, the girl who must be Taylor, whips out her cell phone and answers it. Mine continues ringing, so I pull it out. Swipe it on.

"It's the alpha and the omega, the beginning and the end," Iva says in her pixie voice.

"Where are my parents?" I demand. I played her games. I followed the compass. Here I am. Now I intend to find my parents.

"You have to sacrifice yourself to enter," she says.

"Enter where?" We're on a ledge in the middle of nowhere. But as she speaks, the lava illuminates the rock wall we stand against. Etched into it are symbols. The same symbols that had been carved into the wooden box where I found the compass, back in my parents' camping supplies.

This is the place the compass has been leading me.

I can't read the symbols, but almost like reading isn't necessary, I feel their meaning inside me. They're like an illusion, coming together into something that is real. One word forms in my mind.

*God.* In different languages. Different cultures. *God.*

"The Home of the Gods," Iva says, and the phone line goes dead.

delta

## XX

**MY OWL SWOOPS DOWN AND LANDS ON**
my shoulder. She hardly weighs a thing. Her feathers brush
against my cheek, and comfort fills me like I haven't known since
the dreaded phone call in Computer Science class. I'm in serious
need of that comfort because I have no idea how to get into the
volcano, and I don't know where my parents are.

"Home of the Gods?" Taylor says. "That's stupid. There are no
gods."

Her words echo the doubts in my mind. I'm not sure at all that
god exists. If he does exist, then he's to blame for everything that's
happened.

"Don't say that," Abigail says, and her face is the color of the
ash billowing out of the volcano. "You'll go to Hell."

"I already live in Hell," Taylor says.

The ground begins to rock under us, great, upheaval shaking. I
fall to the ground on the small shelf and cover my head with my
hands as rocks rain down. Fire spews from the mouth of the volcano, and thunder fills the sky. The quake goes on for well over a

minute, monstrous rumbling so loud that my bones vibrate. Only when the thunder and the shaking of the ground subside, do I dare to look up.

"Don't say another word," Hudson says, pointing directly at Taylor.

She steps forward and clenches her hands like she's going to challenge Hudson to a death match.

"You're not really trying to blame that on 'the gods' just because of these freaking symbols, are you?" Taylor says.

"Just don't tempt faith," Hudson says, stepping back, avoiding the confrontation. He may be a track superstar, but his get-along-with-everyone attitude makes me think he's not a fighter.

Taylor obviously is. "Faith!" She laughs. "Don't get me started. Where was faith when our brother Jack got shot? And how about when my dad died? Please tell me because I'd love to know."

The guy next to her who has to be her brother puts a hand on her shoulder. She scowls at it, but the anger in her eyes reduces to a simmer.

"We need shelter," Cole says.

Abigail holds her hands around her middle and shivers even though, with the lava flowing around us, it's the farthest thing from cold.

"She said we had to sacrifice ourselves to enter," Abigail says. "What does that mean?"

"I don't know, but we aren't the first ones here," Cole says. "Check out the rocks."

There on the rock wall is a handprint. It's so dark that it blends into the side, making it almost invisible. But at the correct angle, there is no denying it. No denying them. It's not the only one.

The rock wall is covered with at least ten more handprints. Nails sniffs at the lowest one and barks. My owl hoots and flies off my shoulder, landing on the rocks above the symbols. *God. Home of the Gods.* There is no sign of Hudson's deer or Abigail's finch, and if Taylor and her brother had animal guides, they're nowhere to be found either.

"It looks like blood," Hudson says. He reaches a finger out and swipes at it. His finger comes back covered.

Abigail gasps. "That's gross."

"It's the way in," I say. "It's how we sacrifice ourselves. With blood."

Taylor pulls out a knife and draws the blade across the palm of her left hand. Bright red blood springs to the surface.

"Ugh, that's awful," Abigail says.

Taylor ignores her. The two of them seem as different as thunder and rainbows. Taylor smears the blood all over her palm with her finger then does the same to her brother. He winces when her blade cuts into his skin—he's not as tough as she is—but in seconds it's over.

"Adam and I go first," Taylor says, and as one, they press their bloody hands on the rock wall.

They vanish. That's all there is to it. They're just gone.

"I'm not cutting myself," Abigail says.

Cole pulls a pocketknife from his jeans. "Then you can stay out here."

Her wily female charms are useless here on the edge of the volcano. Cole slices the knife first into his own hand, then Hudson, and then it's my turn.

I hold my hand out steady even though my heart is pounding. Cole gives me a quick smile before digging the knife in. It hurts like crap. But I have to get inside if I want answers. If I want to find my parents.

"Last chance," Cole says to Abigail.

She's torn. She looks down the rocky cliff, at the pools of lava and the steam rising from the rivers below, then at our hands, now covered in blood, and shakes her head. "There has to be another way in."

"Suit yourself," Cole says, pocketing the knife.

Hudson, Cole, and I press our hands to the side of the rock wall. The world collapses and reforms.

## XXI

**I'M ON A SANDY BEACH. THE SUN BEATS**
down overhead. There is no sign of the volcano. No cave with sirens. Just the sun, sand, and gentle waves ebbing and flowing on the shore.

There is also no Cole or Hudson. Only the little girl I know is Iva.

"You nearly didn't make it," she says. Her blond ponytails sprout out from below her blue blindfold. She wears black stretchy pants, a blue shirt the same color as the blindfold with sequins spelling out the words *"There will be Drama,"* and blue and white checked little-kid Vans.

"Where am I?"

"You're here, with me," Iva says.

"What does that even mean? Who are you? And where are my parents?" I ask.

Iva sits down cross-legged and starts digging in the sand. "How did you get past the sirens, Eden?"

A warning in a dream from my mom not to eat the fruit? That's as crazy as everything else going on. But if Iva doesn't know, I'm not going to tell her.

"I covered my ears," I say.

Iva purses her lips as she considers this. "Hmmm . . . You had help." Even with her blindfold on, she reaches a hand into the pocket of my jacket before I can stop her and pulls out the compass. "And this. This is interesting. Where did you get it?"

"I found it," I say, wanting to grab it back from her. It's my only connection to my parents.

"Found it where?" she asks.

My parents must have wanted me to find it. And I'm willing to bet they didn't want me to tell Iva. *Don't trust anyone,* Mom had said.

"Where are my parents?" I ask.

"Oh, tell me," Iva says. "Pretty please?"

"I don't remember," I say, protecting my secret. Wherever my parents got the compass, if Iva doesn't know about it, there must be a good reason.

Iva claps her hands together, and the compass disappears. "Fine, Eden. But no more advantages."

"Advantages for what?"

"Why did you ignore my phone calls?" Iva says, disregarding my question.

"There was no power," I say. "You couldn't have called me. The phone calls weren't real."

Iva looks at me, like she can see despite the blindfold. "I don't need your kind of power."

"What other kind of power is there?" I ask.

"The power of the gods," she says.

"Yeah, right," I say, feeling like Taylor as the words come from my mouth. But power of the gods sounds like a bunch of baloney.

Iva gets up from the sand castle she's started building and walks to a couple chairs under a nearby cabana. She plunks down in one, and immediately a drink appears in her hand, complete with an umbrella and a cherry.

"Don't worry," she says as if she can see me looking at her through her blindfold. "It's a Shirley Temple."

My throat is parched, and in that moment, I want a Shirley Temple more than anything in the world. Like magic, one appears in the drink holder of the chair opposite hers. But I refuse to give her the satisfaction of taking a sip.

"How did you do this?" I ask, waving at the beach, the drinks, the world in general.

"I told you. Power of the gods."

"Which is what?" I say, wanting to take a sip of the drink, resisting.

Iva twirls the umbrella in her drink. "It's like this energy, right? It runs through the universe. It fuels everything. Matter. Solar systems. Life as we know it. But now is the time of change."

"What kind of change?"

The corners of Iva's mouth turn down. "The old gods are dying, which is a good thing because they're a bunch of idiots. They've run things into ruin. They've created messes beyond anything I could have possibly imagined. Which is why you're here."

"I'm here to find my parents." It's why I've traveled halfway across the country.

"No," Iva says. "That's why you think you're here. The real reason you're here is different."

"No, it's not."

"Yes, it is."

"Why do you think I'm here?"

"To save the world," Iva says. "Haven't you figured that out yet?"

This is past the point of being ridiculous. Her games are enough. "Tell me where my parents are."

Iva shakes her head. "I'm getting there, Eden. First you have to help me salvage this situation. It's a mess. Has been for years. But if you can help me, which I'm sure you can, then you get to spend forever with your family in a utopia of your own creation. Easy, right?"

"You're lying," I say.

"I wouldn't lie," she says. "I have no reason to."

"Then tell me where they are."

"First, I need your help," she says.

"Help with what?"

"I'll make it easy," Iva says. "The gods are all fighting. Did I mention that most of them are idiots?"

I nod so she continues.

"A lot of them are also dead. But don't be sad," she says like she's worried about my feelings. "They've been fading for centuries. The ones that are left aren't going to be around much longer. Their time is nearly up. And listen close, because here is where you come in."

I'm not the least bit convinced I believe in her gods, but I'll listen if it will help me get my life back to normal. "How?"

"Once they're all dead, who do you think will take over?" Iva asks.

"No one?" I say. "Why do you need gods in the first place?"

Iva throws up her hands in disgust. "Did I not mention the energy? The entire universe runs on it. No gods. No one to control the power. Everything slips away, and you know what's going to be left behind?"

"Nothing?" I say.

"Exactly!" Iva says. "The power needs to be harnessed so everything can start fresh."

"You can harness it," I say. "You don't need me."

Iva shakes her head and her ponytails bounce from side to side. "That's just it, Eden. I can't."

"Why not?" It seems like a simple solution to me.

"Because I am the power," Iva says.

"No you're not. You're a little girl."

"That's how you see me," Iva says. "What your mind creates to accept the truth."

"Which is what? That you aren't really a little girl?" I say. "You're actually some universal power?"

Iva beams like I've finally gotten it. "Exactly! I'm the power, and gods are needed to control the power. I'm the child, and they need to help me do the right things. They need to guide me. I can't do it myself, no matter how much I might want to."

Her comparison makes sense, in some peculiar way. Seeing Thomas grow up, I more than understand how out-of-control kids can be.

"Okay, let's just say that what you're telling me is true," I say. "You want me to take over for these dead gods?"

Iva puts up her hands. "Slow down, Eden. You're getting ahead of yourself. You're not my only egg in the basket. And as sad but true as it may be, not everyone's good enough to harness the power. It takes the exact right person."

"So that's why Cole and the others are—?" I start.

"Yes, yes, yes," Iva says. "That's why everyone is here. You were all picked for this from the moment you were born."

"On New Year's Day," I say.

"Cute, right?" Iva says. "I love creating connected events that look like coincidences. Calculated plans that look like accidents. So here you all are. One of you will rule the world. Control the power. It will run through their veins. They'll be able to do anything."

Goosebumps pop up on my skin. "Anything like what?"

"Funny you should ask," Iva says. "Remember how we talked about your parents?"

All I remember is Iva avoiding my questions.

"Where are they?"

"Their ship capsized," Iva says.

"And you said they weren't dead," I say. "So where are they?"

Iva wags her finger at me. "I never said they weren't dead. I said I knew where they were. And if you control the power . . ."

*The world shifts, and I'm out in the middle of the ocean, floating in the air. Power runs through me like I've never imagined. Never believed possible. Below me a ship rocks on the waves: The USS Arcadia, my parents' underwater topography vessel. There's some big piece of equipment extending off the side with a wire rope uncoiling as it's lowered. It stops and a motor begins to buzz. But no sooner than it's started, a giant wave surfaces, springing out of nowhere. This is it! This is the moment when my parents ship goes down. As the wave grows, I know there is no hope for them. No hope unless . . .*

*Each of my fingers tingles from the power. I only have one thought. Stop the wave. Save my parents.*

*I could do it. So easily in that moment. I could make the wave go away. Keep my parents alive. Turn everything back to how it was before any of this started.*

I grasp for the power, but as quickly as it happened, I'm back in the cabana, breathless from the experience.

"See, you know what you want to do," Iva says, once the world has shifted back. "You can start there and only make things better. You can start before there. Or after. You can do whatever you want."

Before there. Before my parents died.

*I'm back on the beach. After the Homecoming dance. Owen leans toward me, ready to press his lips against mine. Except I can read the thoughts running through his mind. He isn't going to stop with a kiss. He has no intention of doing so. He's going to keep going and he's not going to stop. I shift my mind until I'm back at the dance. Back in the bathroom with Emily. I could go back to this point. Leave right now. Make what happened on the beach disappear. Become irrelevant.*

*Use the power, Edie. Take control.*

I have never wanted to use something so much. It's like Iva's pushing a drug on me. I've never used drugs. Never plan to. And yet this . . . this power . . . I want to own the control it gives me more than I've ever wanted anything in my life. It's like a part of me I never knew existed, and yet now that I've felt it, I am empty without it.

"Pretty cool, right?" Iva says.

"One more time?" I ask, hating that I am asking, but not being able to stop myself.

"One more time," she says.

So I think about my house back in Florida. Sitting at my kitchen table with my parents and Thomas, finishing up a game of *Catan*.

*Thomas laughs as he rolls the dice. Mom writes crazy symbols on a piece of paper, translating our names into different languages while she waits for her turn. She's on Dad's name right now—Wayne— spelling it in Greek and Russian and even ancient Egyptian. Dad sings along to some classic rock song called* In-a-Gadda-Da-Vida *that they both love.*

*I reach out because it's my turn to roll, but when I toss the dice, the world shifts and I'm in a throne room. A golden throne sits at the top of a platform with steps leading up to it. Light surrounds it, beckoning me forward. I take one step, then another until I am at the throne. And when I sit in it, the rush of the power is so great that I can't imagine living one more second of my life without it.*

"You liked it, didn't you? Iva says, tearing me from the throne and the power.

I reach for the world again, for the power than ran through me, but just as it feels like it is within my grasp, it slips away.

"Bring it back," I say. I can still hear the song Dad was singing in my mind.

"I can't."

"Can't or won't?"

"Won't," Iva says. "But maybe you'll be able to. It will be yours to do anything at all with."

Restore my family. Change my past. Never start dating Owen in the first place. But changing the past won't erase it. It will still be there in my mind, haunting me.

"I don't want it," I say. "It's not real."

Iva tsk-tsks me, like I've failed some test. "Of course it's real, Eden. But I'm not going to force you. If you don't want it, then someone else will be happy to control it. Like I said, there are others."

*Immediately I'm thrown back into the world. Except the sun no longer shines in the sky. Dark clouds descend upon the earth. The landscape is barren. The trees stand like a skeleton forest. The ocean is black, and dead things float on the surface: fish, seaweed, people. I move from forest to beach to mountain, until I look out at what may be the last vestiges of humans alive.*

*As I watch, the ground begins to shakes. And the mountains . . . they begin to crumple in on themselves, like a force underneath the earth is sucking them in with a straw. Dust fills the air, mixing with the dark clouds. People run, coughing as they inhale the dust. Mothers grab for children, except the children fall to the ground gasping for air. Their parents fall next to then, one by one, as the clouds reach them.*

*With each person that falls, hope fades away. Each person represented a chance for the world to survive. Each death represents failure. My failure.*

*At the end of the graveyard of people stands Thomas, sucking on a lollipop, tears filling his eyes.*

*You never came, Edie, he says. You left me forever.*

*I reach for him to tell him that no, I'm here. I've come to save him. But it's too late. He falls beside the others.*

*And then . . .*

*. . . from the black clouds, from the shattered remains of the earth, comes something new. Something horrible. A black egg, so glossy and*

*dark, it seems to draw all remaining light into itself. Not one egg. Many, covering the earth. They push to the surface and grow, pulling dust and decay inside. They swallow bodies, both alive and dead. And when they stop growing, they begin to crack. And I know that whatever is inside these eggs, what is about to be born into the world, will fill it with hatred and despair. It is the complete end of hope. And the start of something wholly evil.*

"You can't do that," I say when the vision clears.

"I didn't do it," Iva says. "Whoever got the power did."

"But you are the power. You can stop them." What I'd seen was not just the death of my little brother. It was the end of the world.

"I can't stop them," Iva says. "But you can."

"How? How do I stop them?" I can't let that future ever come. The despair was visceral. I felt every single person die, heard their screams in my head. And the evil of what was to come . . . It haunts me.

"Easy," Iva says, like this is just one more item being added to my to-do list. "You get to the power first."

Get to the power first. More than anything else in the entire world, I need to make that happen. It's not just about my parents. It's about everything. I'm going to save the entire world. I have to do it. It is the real reason I'm here.

"What do I have to do?" I ask.

## XXÏÏ

**IVA AND THE BEACH VANISH, AND I** find myself strapped to a hospital bed. Cords are connected to me everywhere, linking me to a monitor that's blinking. Aside from the beeping noises the machine makes every time I shift even the slightest amount, the room is silent.

I scan the area to my right. This doesn't look like any hospital I've ever seen. A white board covers one wall, completely filled with sketches and chunks of computer code. My language. Rectangles are drawn around *CASE* statements and diamonds enclose *IF-THEN-ELSE* clauses. But they've all been drawn stacked against each other such that the whole thing looks like some kind of study of geometry. At the top of the board in blue dry-erase marker are the words *KLAM STEW*.

"This won't take long, I promise," a voice says from the left.

I turn my head away from the white board. There's a guy about my age sitting at a giant desk that is so messy, no part of the surface shows. His hair is a dark mop of waves that doesn't look like it's seen a hairbrush or a pair of scissors since he hit puberty, and his dark skin is smooth, unmarked by acne or facial hair. He's wearing a green and blue plaid button-up shirt with a white lab coat overtop and chews on the end of a blue dry-erase marker. I've seen him somewhere before, but the second I try to remember where, the information slips away, like there's a fog obscuring part of my mind. It can't have been in the last couple weeks. Maybe he's from school. No, I would remember that. But he is my age, so I don't think he works with my parents or anything. The harder I try to remember, the less I can.

"Where am I?" I struggle against the straps that hold me which makes the monitor next to me go crazy.

"Prep room," he says, wheeling back on his chair and spinning around. "Just hang on for ten more seconds."

Ten more seconds. I count them down, studying the tubes connected to me; they look like they've been embedded in my skin which will make it hard if I try to escape. When I escape.

"Prep for what?"

The guy walks over and pushes a button on the monitor so it stops blinking. The tubes pull out of my skin, not leaving a single mark, and the straps release. I sit up immediately and try to piece out where I've seen this guy.

"There. We got all the information we need. Easy, right?"

"For you, maybe."

"You're Eden Monk, right?"

"I'm guessing you already know the answer to that," I say. Interesting that he knows my real name when I can't remember who the heck he is.

He cracks a grin, which does the dual job of making him look nerdier and actually kind of cute at the same time. And so freaking familiar. It's almost there. I almost have it.

"'Course I know," he says. "Just making sure you remember."

"Why wouldn't I?" Unless I've been drugged. Maybe that's why I can't remember where I've seen this guy before. I run a quick scan of my memories and they all seem intact.

"Sometimes the brain has defenses," he says. "I'm Zachary by the way. Zachary Gomez."

His name doesn't ring any bells.

"Great, Zachary. Why'd you hook me up to the monitor?"

"We had to check a few things. Make sure you're strong enough."

"Did I pass?" I ask, flexing my fingers and toes. I'm strong enough to save the world. I don't need a bunch of monitors to tell me so.

He punches a few buttons on the monitor and silences it. "Yeah, you passed."

"So what do I do now?" I'm ready to go, Whatever Iva has in mind, I am more than up to the challenge.

Zachary Gomez shrugs. "If you're ready, we can go ahead and start."

A wave of hesitation hits me out of nowhere. I know nothing about what waits for me ahead. Nothing about what I am supposed to do. But I'm willing to bet that Zachary Gomez does.

"What's up with all the code on the whiteboard?" I hop off the hospital bed and walk over to examine the writing. There may be information I can use here.

Zachary hurries over after me. I lift my finger to the board and he cringes, like he thinks I'm going to erase it.

"Just some bug fixes," he says.

"For what?" The code has things like:

```
IF ((cur_zone==PI) & (debug)) THEN
    exit_en=true;
```

"What zones and exits is it talking about?" I ask. Maybe it's the exit out of this place which would be good information to have.

Zachary places his hands on my shoulders and pulls me back

**140**

so I'm not so close to the board.

"Parts of a game world I'm designing," he says. "See the world is divided into twenty-three zones. Well, actually, it's twenty-eight, but five are hidden. I mean, not hidden. They work just like the others. Crap. I'm not supposed to mention that part, so just pretend I didn't say anything, okay? Anyway, it's user-controlled, but there have been some problems with one of the zones, and I've been trying to piece it out."

I step forward again, keeping my hands clasped behind my back so he doesn't freak out. "You design video games?"

"Not all by myself," Zachary says. "I'm part of a team. Best video game ever."

"What makes it the best?"

"Because it's never been done before," Zachary says. "The most massive video game ever undertaken. Ultra MMO. It's taken us sixteen years working day and night to get this thing complete, and let me tell you, it is sweet. Totally worth the effort."

If he's been working on this game for sixteen years, he must've started working on the game the day he was born because he looks no older than me.

"How do you play?"

"That's confidential. You shouldn't even be looking at this stuff." Zachary grabs the eraser and, in a single swipe, clears enough of the board that most of the code is gone. I scan the rest before he erases everything. On the top left of the board is a set of circles, grouped together like flowers. A smaller circle forms the center of each group, and larger circles surround it, forming the petals, some of which are shared between more than one cluster. There are sixteen of these clusters, but Zachary swipes at the figure with the eraser and they're gone, too.

"What's Klam Stew?"

He erases the words at the top of the whiteboard. "My cafeteria lunch choice. Way better than the Beef Stroganoff."

**141**

It's ludicrous that Zachary Gomez would write his lunch choice on a whiteboard. He's not in Kindergarten. And with the way he erased it along with everything else, it must mean something.

"Fine. Don't tell me." I'll figure it out on my own.

"You're a coder too, right?" he asks.

My muscles tense up because it's bad enough that he knows my full name. Now he knows what I'm good at? "Maybe. Why do you think so?"

He runs a hand through his mop of dark curls. "Look, I just want to start out by saying that I am not a stalker. Not at all. Watching you was my assignment. It's not like I asked for the job."

"You've been watching me?"

The fog in my mind clears, and when I grasp for the memories, this time I am able to hold onto them. That's why Zachary Gomez looks familiar. I have seen him, the day my parents went missing, outside the school. Then later, outside my house. Also not too long beforehand at the grocery when I'd run out to grab milk for Thomas. Someone had asked me what time it was. Someone who looked a lot like Zachary Gomez. And then there were the dead people. He was standing with them, at the edges of the compass rose.

"I had to," Zachary says.

"Um . . . ," I say, clearly waiting for an explanation.

"Each of you had to be watched," Zachary says. "And for the record, what the hell were you doing with that Owen guy? Guy's a total creep. You actually went to Homecoming dance with him?"

At the mention of Homecoming, my stomach clenches and bile rises in my throat. Owen's betrayal is raw. I push away my memories of the dance and of my visions.

"I don't appreciate you spying on me," I say.

"Take it up with the management," Zachary says. "And now

that I can actually talk to you—by the way, I wasn't supposed to talk to you at the grocery, so just don't mention that—I just want to say that you are a brilliant programmer."

Fine, so he knows my sweet spot. I soften the tiniest bit. At least he can recognize genius when he sees it.

"Seriously, Eden Monk, aside from me, I've never seen such talent. I'd love to work with you sometime on the programming team."

"What do you mean, the programming team?"

Zachary Gomez shrugs. "You know. There's the programming team, and then there's you guys. You'd have been brilliant working on the project with us."

If I didn't know better, I'd say Zachary Gomez has a crush on me. His eyes are wide, almost in fanboy admiration, and he is sincere about every word that comes out of his mouth.

If there are teams, then maybe I should have been put on the programming team, because Zachary's right. I am brilliant with computer code. But with the power of the gods, with what it could do to destroy the world, I have to have it. I am going to make everything better. Save my parents. Save everyone from the fate that will befall them if the wrong person gets to it first. It's what I was meant to do, and maybe, if teams were chosen, it's why I'm not on the programming team. Because no matter how much I love programming—no matter how good I am at it—I can't see sitting here programming when I could be out there saving the world.

"Thanks, Zachary Gomez," I say, using his full name since he seems to enjoy using mine. "Why is there a programming team anyway?"

Zachary shrugs like it's no big deal. "Normal things, you know. To control the lights and temperature and run statistical analysis. Stuff like that."

"So you're like a glorified janitor." It makes me doubly thankful

I didn't get stuck on the programming team. My coding skills are far beyond turning the lights off at five o'clock.

"A very smart glorified janitor," Zachary says. "Like genius level. A lot like you, actually."

"And we're both pretty modest, too," I say. In another life, Zachary and I could have been good friends. "So how long until lunch? When do you get your clam soup?"

"What?"

"Your lunch choice."

"Oh yeah, right," he says, shuffling papers around on his scattered desk. With as many things as are piled on top, I have no clue how he can find anything. But in the center, on top of everything else, is a large piece of paper that looks like some kind of aged parchment. It curls up at the ends and would probably crack in half if I lifted it. It's covered with the same circle pattern from the white board, the smaller circles in middle of the larger ones like flowers, all interconnected.

I pick it up, trying to be careful so I don't hurt the parchment. "This is amazing," I say, gushing over it. "What is it?"

Zachary can't help but fall into my line of flattery. I get it. It's why hackers want to be caught a lot of the time. They want their brilliance to be recognized. Zachary leans close so he can whisper in my ear. "It's the computer game. All of it. The zones I designed are the ones in pods zero, one, and two."

"That many?"

He takes the paper from me and begins to roll it, so maybe it's not as fragile as I thought. "I know. It's a lot. But that's because I'm really good at what I do."

"You must be to be given that much responsibility."

Zachary doesn't fall into my flattery trap quite so easily. "Look, Eden Monk. I know you're trying to get information, but you're not going to get it from me, even if you are cute. I'm sorry."

I make my eyes wide, trying to play off the cute thing. "Not even one small piece? Something? Anything so I have an edge?"

Zachary flicks his eyes from one side of the room to the other, then leans close. "One thing," he says.

I hold still and wait.

"Klam stew isn't my lunch choice. But don't mention it to anyone or my ass will be in deep shit."

"What is it then?" I whisper back, barely audible.

"A cheat code," he says. "But keep it to yourself."

Klam stew is a cheat code. I don't know what it's for, but I file it away for future use.

"Thanks, Zachary Gomez," I say.

"You're welcome," he says. "And good luck, Eden Monk. I believe in you."

Zachary Gomez leads me to a giant steel door. Through it lies my future. The future of the world. The power still tingles inside me. I am going to reach that power first. I am going to save my parents. I turn the knob and walk through the door.

chaos

# xxiii

## "DON'T MOVE," IVA'S VOICE SAYS.

"Where am I?" My voice echoes in the space around me. Only seconds ago, I was in the lab with Zachary. I turn, but the door I just came through is gone. There's no sign of Zachary Gomez. There's no sign of anything.

Iva doesn't reply.

Blackness stretches on to infinity around me. I can't see the walls, the ceiling, the floor. Underneath my feet, white light casts upward, illuminating the void where I've arrived.

As my eyes adjust to the dark, I see that there are others here with me, laid out in a grid of columns of light, each exposed in this cavern of black. I spot Cole two pods over and back, balancing on his one leg. He's searching the room, and when his eyes find me, his face relaxes. Then his eyes slowly trace the lines of my body. Holy mother, I am buck naked! Everyone is. How did that happen? When did that happen? My face must be bright red.

I glance away from Cole, though he still watches me, and find Abigail. She must've found some way to enter the volcano. Some advantage I don't know about. I also spot Hudson. Taylor and Adam.

And . . .

Owen.

He's here.

My worst suspicions become confirmed. The symbol on his door had been no coincidence. In the span of five seconds, every part of our relationship replays in my mind. He'd used me. He'd tried to force himself on me. He'd humiliated me.

And then there are the visions where he hurts me. They feel so real. In the seconds that pass, his hands tear at my clothes, dig into my skin. They violate me, and as much as I fight, as much as I tell him to stop, he never does.

No, the visions aren't real. They are not real. Owen may be a complete jerk, but he didn't actually rape me. He might have stopped on his own.

Who am I fooling?

*Owen is on top of me on the beach, pressing on me. I fight, but he refuses to listen. He grabs my wrists. Holds them back. I kick and punch and twist, but my movements are futile. He grabs at my clothes . . . He doesn't stop . . .*

No. I'd stopped him. But why does the vision make it feel like I hadn't?

Owen's eyes on me intensifies my nakedness, making me want to cover myself. I harden my face and glare at him, feeding off the hatred that flows from me like a river.

*His hands are on me, groping, violating. He ignores my pleas for him to stop. He smiles as I cry out in pain.*

I squeeze my eyes shut. It's not a real memory. Here. Now. This is real. This is what I have to deal with, not some hallucination.

Please don't tell me that he's actually someone who could wield the power. All Owen cares about is himself. He'd ruin everything.

The world Iva showed me fills my mind. I'd wondered who

could create such a thing. Who could destroy everything?

*Owen could.*

I have to stop him.

I look away from Owen to the others. There's a guy nearby with skin so pale he could be an albino. A giant grizzly bear tattoo covers his arms, shoulders, and bare chest down to his stomach. The shading and lines are inked deep and bold against his nearly translucent skin. Mom has a tattoo on the inside of her wrist—one of the strange symbols she's always drawing—but she made it super clear that I wasn't to go near a tattoo parlor until I lived on my own.

The tattoo guy sees me looking and nods. Not friendly, like he wants to be best pals or something, but more of a good luck gesture. I nod back in reply. I'll take any luck I can get. Any allies I can find. Anyone to help me fight Owen.

I try to lift my foot, but it won't move. It's like it's been glued to the floor. Like the column of light holds it in place.

*"I told you not to move,"* Iva's voice says in my head. Her voice may not even be real for all I know. I could be making all of this up.

Some of the others struggle, too, trying to move from their lights, but nobody, not even Hudson with his super track skills, has made any headway.

"Where are we?" I yell, but my voice echoes back, like it's bouncing off an invisible force field. I lift my hands to reach outward, but resistance hits me when I stretch beyond the length of my arm.

Someone flips a switch. White lines illuminate across the room in a giant grid, exposing the confines of our space. The lines stretch from the floor up the walls and onto the ceiling above. Each column of light where we stand is situated at an intersection of two grid lines.

"Countdown beginning," Iva says, and this time her voice

sounds like it is not in my head but echoing around the entire room. "Entering virtual reality stasis in ten, nine, eight . . ."

Virtual reality stasis? Nobody said anything about VR. I'm here for the power she was talking about. I don't see what virtual reality has to do with that. I press my palms against the force field, but my feet are locked. My body trapped.

". . . seven, six, five . . ."

Panic rises in me. I need to get out of here. Find my parents. I don't have time for this. I never agreed to this. This whole thing is a mistake.

". . . four, three . . ."

Or is it a mistake? This may be the way to the power. The memory of it running through me returns. With that power I can do anything. Bring my parents back from a sure death. Give Earth a future. The right future. I'm the only person who can do it. The only one who will make things right. Anyone else with that power will be a disaster. Owen with the power of the gods will destroy the world.

I need the power. More than anything I know this. With the power, I will make everything right.

". . . two, one . . ."

I brace myself. I dig for bravery, but it feels like an act because I'm not that brave.

*You're weak, like in the visions,* I think.

I hate that my thought might be true.

Thick gel swirls around my feet in a circular pattern as if contained by the very force field that holds me. I take each breath, one at a time. I have to do this. When the gel reaches my ankles, shock runs through me. Ice shards drive into my bare skin. So cold. So very cold.

Deep breath. It will pass. I will adjust. But the cold is too much, and by the time it reaches my knees, I'm gasping from the pain that rolls through me. It has to stop. I can't take one more second of this, but it's relentless.

When it hits mid-thigh, my mind enters a delirium. This can't go on. Not one more second.

A tube punches forward and hits me in the right side, puncturing my bare skin. A new pain blossoms as the tube grows and searches inside me, like a snake with claws tearing through my body, devouring me. The gel has reached my hips when the next tube juts into me, into my chest, tearing under my ribs and upward. And then another.

I think to scream, but words won't come. My brain refuses to function beyond survival.

No power is worth this. I don't want it anymore. I want to go home. To curl into a ball and die if it will make this pain go away. I've been lied to. This is the end. I'm locked in an icy coffin, defeated in some game of the gods. A pawn in their battle for power.

When the gel reaches my chest, I can't feel the lower half of my body anymore. Another tube shoots into my neck. My fingertips tingle and lose all sensation. I struggle, but the only thing I can move is my head. The gel is at my neck. My chin. I keep my lips pressed together even as the icy chill covers my nose. My eyes. Too late. I am either going to freeze to death or drown. The gel seeps into my ears. My nose. It covers my head completely. I can't move. Can't close my eyes. Can't hold my breath any longer.

I open my mouth and suck the gel in, and the icy cold hits my throat. It burns as it travels down into my lungs. I can't cough it out. I'm going to die.

I suck in again and the world eases away from me.

## XXIV

**WARMTH . . . PRICKLES IN MY BLOOD**
vessels as my skin acclimates. I'm floating. I ebb back and forth
gently, like waves carry me in an ocean. My hands drift at my
sides, brushing against my bare hips with the rocking.

The gel. The cold.

I'd been frozen.

But the warmth continues to increase, like water in a tea ket-
tle. I let my mind drift along with my body. Memories from my
past flow through me. Memories I can make a reality again by
using the power Iva taunts me with. I can see my parents again.
I can bring them back to life. I can chat with Emily and think
about where I should go to college. I can eat pizza and watch
*Star Trek*. I can play *Mario Kart* until I unlock every course and
customization.

My eyes fly open. All I see are lines crossing back and forth
around me.

*"Initial stasis complete,"* says the voice of Iva, though it sounds
like a computer. *"Beginning sensor attachment."*

I flinch as needles prick into the ends of each of my fingers. I wiggle them around and feel the drag, like something's been attached. Other spots on my body the same thing happens. The bottoms of my feet. Along my torso. Inside my ears. My nose. My cheeks and lips. I barely feel the sensors but I know they are there, attaching me to a machine. I can't see the others, but I have to imagine that the same thing that is happening to me is happening to the rest of them. Virtual reality stasis. I used to fantasize that I would invent flawless VR and get worldwide acclaim among scientists. It's why I was so excited to try out the haptic goggles and gloves that Owen had lent me. But those were just silly dreams. This is real.

Something lowers over my eyes, prying them open and pressing against the lenses, and the entire world flickers.

*"Stasis complete,"* Iva says.

## XXV

# I STAND IN THE CENTER OF A ROOM

with metallic gray walls, the same color as the clothes I wear. I'm dressed in gunmetal gray pants that hug my legs, a matching tank top, and black boots that lace halfway up my calves. A belt is slung low around my waist equipped with all sorts of pouches and hooks. On the right side is a hunting knife longer than my forearm that looks like it could effortlessly flay the skin from a man. On the left are binoculars. I place them to my eyes, but all I see is blackness. There's also a metal water bottle clipped to the back of the belt.

"Where am I?" I ask, willing to bet that, wherever Iva is, she's listening.

*"About to enter the labyrinth,"* she says, her voice in my mind.

The labyrinth. Like the symbol scratched on my door. On all of our doors. The labyrinth must be the virtual reality world.

My hands reach to my face, looking for the tubes and sensors. I run them the length of my torso. I know the tubes are there. I felt them go in. Felt needles going into each of my fingers. But when

I wiggle my fingers around now, there are no tubes and there is no gel encasing me. I am solid, standing in this room. I touch my face again. Take a deep breath. This is real air that I am breathing. Fresh, clean air. Not anything like what I imagined VR to be like.

*"You get one item,"* Iva says.

"One item for what?"

*"To help you reach the end first. What do you want most?"*

My mind immediately tries to piece out the most logical item. If this really is virtual reality, I shouldn't have to worry about eating or drinking. But if that's the case, then why do I have the water bottle? I shake it, but it's empty. A weapon seems more logical.

"What is the labyrinth like?" I ask.

*"Each part of it is different,"* Iva says. *"You need to be ready for anything."*

"So what should I pick?" I ask.

*"Whatever you want,"* Iva says, and she giggles, reminding me that she's like a psychotic little girl and I am trapped in her game.

"My owl," I say without hesitation. The owl guided me this far. She can lead me to the end.

*"The animal guides aren't allowed in the simulation,"* Iva says. *"Pick something else."*

"The compass," I say. It had led me through the den of the sirens.

*"Not that either,"* Iva says. *"You should have never had that in the first place."*

"You said I could pick whatever I wanted."

*"So I lied,"* Iva says. *"We get to play by my rules. Pick something different."*

I can't have my owl, and I can't have my parents' compass. What else is there? I go over all the items I can think of, but nothing feels right. It's only when my gray jacket comes to mind that I know it's what I must choose. It protected me from fire, from scrapes. It killed the sirens. Hopefully it can protect me now.

The jacket appears at a thought. I slip it on, zipping it up mid-chest so just the top of my dark gray tank top shows underneath. My choice is made.

*"And the bottle,"* Iva says. *"Fill it with whatever you want."*

"Like water?" I ask.

Another giggle. *"It doesn't have to be so boring. Anything is possible."*

I uncap the bottle and piece through the puzzle. What else would I put in a water bottle? Soda? Juice?

*You can do better than that,* Zachary Gomez seems to say in my mind, though I know it is just my memory of him. But he's right. Those things are equally as mundane. I can do better than that.

If anything is possible, I need to figure out what would help me most. My goal is to get to the end first. Find the power. And get out of here. Maybe something to guide me, like a map. Or a way I can leave a trail, like breadcrumbs, so I don't backtrack. I have no idea what this labyrinth is going to bring. Maybe a way to tell me if anyone is near me. Or some way to communicate. To find Cole.

*Leave it empty,* Mom's voice from my dream replays in my mind.

I'd trusted her voice and not eaten the fruit. But if I leave it empty, I may lose an advantage.

*Leave it empty.*

I have to trust her now. God, I miss her. I have to get her back.

"Nothing," I say, capping the water bottle and hooking it back to my belt.

*"Interesting,"* Iva says. *"No one else did that."*

I'm either really stupid, or I know something that nobody else does. Probably the former. But maybe someone is helping me, someone Iva knows nothing about. She hadn't known how I got the compass, which means that, no matter how smart and in control Iva appears to be, she doesn't know everything.

"Is that it?" I ask. I'm itching to get to the end.

*"That's it,"* Iva says. *"Now it begins."*

## XXVI

**THE ROOM VANISHES AROUND ME, OR I**
vanish from it, and reappear in a circular room of white. I'm all
alone, but within moments, Cole appears—just appears, like a
button is pushed and there he is—across the room. He's dressed
the same way I am, except for my jacket—but what's missing is
his crutch. Instead, from the bottom of his knee is a prosthetic,
the same gunmetal gray as our clothing. It must be the item he
chose. He catches me looking and grins. For all we know, we're
about to die, and he's picking this moment to grin at me?

Before I think it through, I cover the distance and hug him.
Seeing him here makes me think that at least there is some bit of
normal left in this world.

He kind of half hugs me back which is really awkward. Maybe
he's not the hugging type. Or maybe he's thinking about Pia.

"Hey, you're here," I say, stepping back from the hug.

"Same as you," he says, crossing his arms like he doesn't want
to accidentally touch me again.

"Sorry about the hug," I say. "I was just happy to see you."

His eyes meet mine. "Don't be sorry, okay?"

"Okay. I'm not sorry then." Cole is my friend—at least I think he is—and I should be able to give him a friendly hug if I want to. His hair is still crazy, even here in this VR world, going every way possible. I kind of want to run my hands through it to tame it, but I figure the hug was enough. The gray tank top shows a huge amount of his muscular build.

Cole sees me staring at his chest, and I quickly look back to his face.

I hesitate one beat. Then two. Then, "Did you talk to Iva?"

Cole nods. Even now the memory of the power thrums inside me. I want it back.

"And?"

"I never felt anything like it," he says.

Neither had I. It's what I need to not only save my parents but to ensure the future of the world. But what about Cole? Iva had to have shown him the same things she'd shown me. He's going to want the power, too, not only to save Pia, but for the same reasons I am. And how about Hudson? And Abigail? Taylor and Adam? They'll all want it.

And Owen.

My muscles tense. He's going to show up here. I'll have to face him. But he can't be the one to get the power. He would be the destroyer of the world.

Hudson appears next. He spots Cole and me but holds back, like he's drawing an invisible line between us.

It's because of the power. He wants to reach it first. But these are my friends, not my competitors. And Hudson wouldn't destroy the world. Or maybe he would. I have no way of knowing. Everything depends on me finding the power first.

Someone else appears, and my breath catches, sure it's going to be Owen. I don't want to see him. Don't want to have to talk to him. Why of everyone possible, does Owen have to be one of the chosen few?

But it's Taylor, followed immediately by her brother, Adam. Taylor has a giant bow across her back and a quiver full of arrows, like she is ready to hunt. I have an empty water bottle and a jacket. I only hope it's enough.

Abigail appears next. Like Hudson, she keeps her distance yet moves to the center of the room as if she wants everyone to see her. She is beautiful and confident and looks like she is capable of conquering the world with her beauty. Cole, Hudson, and Adam all stare at her openly.

The tattooed guy I'd seen in the VR pod room shows up next, followed by an Asian girl with long hair woven into a braid that hangs over her shoulder. She's so tiny that she can't be much taller than Thomas. Her face is hard, without even a hint of a smile. Next is a guy with curly dark hair who stumbles no sooner than he appears in the room. He moves like he's drunk, which his bloodshot eyes hint is a definitely possibility.

I jump every time someone new appears, sure Owen will be next.

Two skinny guys, twins by the looks of it, with matching sandy blond mops of hair show up. They take one look at Abigail and nearly fall over in their gawking. The fact that every guy in the world is in love with Abigail makes me feel like a hideous ogre. Next is a tall Amazon of a girl with bright red hair who probably has a future in the WNBA.

Dread fills my stomach as kids continue to appear. Owen is coming. I'm sure of it.

"You okay, Edie?" Cole asks.

"Fine," I say, taking deep breaths to calm myself. "What do you think's going to happen next?" Taylor and Adam eye us warily as they talk in hushed tones, and Hudson's eyes bounce from one of us to the next, as if he's sizing each of us up.

Cole whispers as he answers. "I don't know. We should stick

together. We'll figure out what to do. Maybe we can both have the power."

His words are the happiest things I've heard, because with all these people in this room, I officially have an ally. If I don't trust Cole, then I am totally on my own.

My heart stops when Owen finally appears. His eyes find mine, and he gives me a half smile, like he's gauging my reaction. My face is incapable of pushing past my memories and visions and smiling in return.

Owen runs his hands through his spikey blond hair and walks over. I take a step back without thinking about it, so I'm next to Cole.

"Edie! I can't believe you're here," Owen says.

My hatred for him bubbles inside me.

"I can't believe you're here either," I say. My body's tense. I want to get away from him.

"This is so cool, don't you think?" he says.

"No, I don't think so at all," I say. I don't find it the least bit cool that my parents are dead and that my only way to get them back is to play some stupid game of the gods.

Owen maybe realizes he's said something not quite right. "I don't mean that it's cool all the crazy stuff we've gone through. Just that this is a huge opportunity to make a stronger world."

A world controlled by him.

From next to me, Cole clears his throat. I turn so I'm kind of angled toward him. "This is Cole by the way. We traveled together."

Owen's upper lip curls up in disgust, and I despise him even more in that moment.

Cole, like always, ignores the reaction to the scar on his face. "You and Edie knew each other before?" Cole asks.

Owen's face relaxes and slips into a sly grin. "Oh yeah. We knew each other well."

**163**

I feel his hands pawing at my body. With his words is the promise of what he would do to me, given the chance. He'd make the visions real. He'd destroy me. Then he would continue on while I was left to pick up the pieces of my life.

My hatred is so full and complete that it takes my breath away.

"We went out a couple times," I say, easing out of the hideous moment. Then Abigail walks up, saving me from having to think about or talk about my past with Owen.

"Hello, gorgeous," Owen says, running his eyes over Abigail's body like he's undressing her right there in the middle of the room.

Abigail duly blushes and giggles. "Who is your friend, Edie?"

He's no friend of mine, and she can have him.

"This is Owen," I say. "Owen, Abigail."

"Nice to meet you, Abigail," Owen says, like he's Mister Manners.

Abigail may not be so impressed if she saw him pulling my panties down at Homecoming.

"How did you get through the wall?" Cole asks Abigail.

Abigail's eyes widen and fill with sincerity. "I prayed to our Lord, and he opened the door. He always listens to me."

"Lucky you," I say, thankful that she doesn't actually have some real advantage.

Abigail wastes no time with her female charms. She grabs Owen's forearms and looks him directly in the eyes. "This may sound totally crazy, but the Lord also sends me dreams. Visions. And I've seen you in them. I close my eyes and there you are. And now . . . I can't believe it. You're real."

Abigail's been having visions about Owen? They can't be anything similar to mine, given the way she's acting.

Oh god. Abigail thinks Owen is her soulmate.

Owen is beyond flattered, and when Abigail leads him a couple steps away and whispers in his ear, his eyes widen and he smiles.

Owen doesn't bother me. I can't let him.

"You dated him?" Cole asks. His face is impassive, because it's not like he would be jealous. He's here for his girlfriend, Pia, after all. Still, I want to put Homecoming and everything to do with Owen as far behind me as possible.

*His hands press into the sides of my head, so hard that tears spring to my eyes.*

No. That didn't happen. My head throbs.

"We worked on homework together a few times." I don't want to admit to Cole that I actually liked him. If there is one person on this earth that I would have been happy to never see again, it is Owen, and now, of all things, he has to be here?

"Nice guy?" Cole asks.

"No."

Cole opens his mouth, like he's about to ask more, but a screen appears on an area of the curved wall, and words begin to scroll downward. They're written in obscure letters, strange symbols like the sign on the side of the volcano.

"Stick to the path," Iva's voice says, reading what I am assuming must be the words on the screen. "Assume *everything* you see is trying to kill you. Assume *everyone* you see is trying to kill you, because everyone wants the power as much as you do."

I want the power, but I'm not going to kill over it. And Cole won't try to kill me. I'm pretty sure Hudson won't either. Abigail wouldn't know how. She might chip a nail, and unless she picked a nail file as her one essential item, she won't risk it. Taylor and Adam . . . I know nothing about them. I put them on the list of people I can't trust along with the others who I don't know.

And then there is Owen.

*He reaches his hands for my neck. He squeezes tight, pressing his fingers into my veins, cutting off my breath. I struggle but this only makes him grip tighter.*

My head pounds as the vision slips away, but I'm left with one thing in its departure. The Owen in my visions would definitely try to kill me. He'd kill any one of us. It's like I've been given the visions as a warning.

Iva continues talking. "If you die inside the virtual reality landscape, you die outside of it, too. There are no second chances."

No second chances.

I need to make sure I don't need one. I need to watch my back.

"Your goal is to get to the end first. At the end you will find the power. Only one of you can have it. Only one of you can leave. For everyone else, if you're still alive when someone else gets to the power, the exit will be sealed. You'll be trapped in the virtual reality landscape forever."

I have no idea what will happen to my parents if I'm not the one to get to the power.

*Get there first,* I think. *Don't let others reach the end before you.*

My feelings are mirrored on the faces around me.

In the center of the room, a wide golden urn appears. I scoot forward so I can see the contents. It's filled with small tiles the color of bone, each with a different number painted in black.

"Choose a tile," Iva says.

Hudson doesn't hesitate. He's next to the bowl with his hand inside before anyone else can react. He grabs a tile and immediately vanishes. I have no idea what number he got or where he went.

Owen is next, but Abigail runs after him. They choose tiles and are erased from the room. One by one, each person takes a tile. Taylor and Adam grab a single tile, and they disappear together.

There are only a handful of tiles left, and there are only a handful of us. The drunk guy, the skinny twins. The red-headed Amazon girl. If I am going to get to the end first, I can't be last to start.

"I'll find you," I say to Cole, and rush to the bowl, plunging my hand inside. I grab the first tile I come in contact with, and I am gone.

labyrinth

# XXVII

# I SPIN SLOWLY, ASSESSING MY NEW

situation. The room is solid white and circular, like the room I just came from, with no doors or windows. I walk the perimeter, looking for the way out.

"Pod six. Pick your zone," Iva's voice says in a sing-song tone, though she's nowhere to be found. No one is. I'm the only one here. In the center of the room, where the golden urn was in the previous room, a white pedestal appears, coming to about my waist. It's flat on the top, with four symbols made of dimly glowing light. I'm pretty sure they're Greek letters. Why hadn't I paid more attention when Mom was trying to teach me what they all were?

"What zone?" I ask, but no answer is given.

I run my hand along the top of the pedestal. The letters glow brightly, and Iva's voice sings out with each one.

"Eta."

"Psi."

"Beta."

"Omicron."

I move my hand over the top this until I've committed all four sounds and symbols to memory, then I hold my hand over the Eta.

"Zone Eta. Is that your choice?" It's Iva's voice, but it sounds more computer generated, like those phone calls that are recordings made to sound like real people. In addition to the Eta lighting up on the pedestal, on the wall in line with the symbol, the outline of an arched door appears with the same Eta symbol above it.

"What is Zone Eta?" I ask.

Iva doesn't respond. Either her computer voice is not programmed to give me this information or it's ignoring me.

I lift my hand and the outlined Eta door vanishes. I move to the next.

Four symbols. Four doorways. I have no idea of knowing what is beyond any of them. But I do know that if I stay in this room, I will never exit the labyrinth. I need to be the first to the end. I need to stay alive. And I need to get my parents back.

I finally decide on Eta. It looks like an H, but the way Iva says it reminds me of my name. Eta. Eden. Both have the *E* sound. It's the best logic I can come up with. I place my hand over the symbol.

"Zone Eta. Is that your choice?" The outline of the doorway appears again.

"That's my choice," I say, tempering the butterflies that flit around in my stomach.

The door slides open, exposing grayness beyond. I check my knife. My empty water bottle. My binoculars. I zip my jacket higher up on my chest. I'm as ready as I will ever be.

I step through and enter a new world.

From far ahead, a scream rings out, breaking the silence around me. It could be a cry for help.

Or it could be a trick. Each of us wants the power. How far will

**172**

we be willing to go to get it?

I hold my position, waiting to see if the scream comes again, but there's nothing except an eerie silence that seeps into the space around me.

I'm in some sort of cathedral. The floor is polished stone, and the ceiling is so far above that it gives the impression of almost being out in the open. Beams of light extend through stained glass windows and cast colored light across the stone floor.

The doorway that I came through is gone, replaced by the cathedral behind me equal in size to what spans ahead. However I got here, I won't be leaving the same way. The cathedral is covered in cobwebs, stretching from staircase banisters to rafters to the stained glass windows. I brush them out of my way. Aside from the cobwebs, the cathedral is empty and stretches on forever. Tentatively, I walk forward to see what I can find out about Zone Eta. My heavy boots pound on the slate floor no matter how silent I try to be, echoing through the vast space around me. Cobwebs cover the walls and ceiling, catching in my hair as I duck underneath them. The emptiness is overwhelming, confirming just how alone I really am. I have to get out of here. Have to find the exit before something bad happens.

*Assume everything you see is trying to kill you.*

Iva's warning quickens my steps.

The feeling that I'm being watched pushes inside my mind. No, not watched. Hunted. I hurry down a hallway until I come to a room filled with church pews that look like they've been layered in white cloth. As I get closer, I realize that it's not white cloth at all. It's the cobwebs. They're so thick that only small pieces of the wooden seats underneath show through.

Something clatters in the distance, and the sound carries to me, filling the empty space around me.

I'm not alone.

*Assume everyone you see is trying to kill you.*

I slowly look around, trying to find an exit. Tapestries cover the walls. Nothing moves. But I'd heard something.

Graffiti covers the altar near the front of the cathedral, but it's masked by the silky threads so I can't read what it says. I take a step toward the altar. Maybe whatever's written up there will give me some hint about what I'm meant to do now. Someone could have been here before me and left a message. Maybe they're still here.

My scalp prickles, making me sure, again, that I'm being watched. I listen but don't hear a sound, don't see anything, so I dare to take another step and then another until I've reached the front of the cathedral. I climb the stone steps to the altar and pull back the cobwebs.

# THE POWER IS A LIE

I reach a finger out and touch the letters, and my finger comes back red and wet. This message is fresh, and it's been written in blood.

If the power is a lie, then this has all been a trap.

I smear the letters with my palm. I will not believe them.

Minutes pass. Then an hour. My surroundings become more ornate. Chandeliers hang from the rafters high above, littered with more cobwebs. The tapestries increase in size and color. Some reach as high as the ceiling, far overhead, and some are small like a tiny window to another place. Each has an elaborate scene spun in the foreground, with vibrant backgrounds full of details.

I move to a tapestry to get a closer look. It's a man and a golden

**174**

throne—the same throne from my vision where I'd felt the power of the gods. Seeing it here now, I want the power that much more. I want to sit in the throne and harness it.

The throne sits unattended, and the man lies on the palace floor nearby with a woman—no, not a woman; it's the tall red-headed girl who is one of us. They're locked in an embrace, while, unaware, around them, chaos rules the earth. In the background, cities burn. Storms rage. The people in the tapestry don't notice. They're insignificant. But the throne . . . it tempts me. I imagine eating from the tree with the golden apples and sitting in that throne. Ruling the world. Taming the chaos.

The next tapestry is similar, but this time, instead of the red-headed girl, it's Hudson. He's playing cards with a different man while the world is being destroyed. Again, the throne is there, and again it is empty. Each tapestry I come to, in addition to showing one of my competitors, shows the failure of the person who should be sitting in the throne. The neglect of the world. Of the universe. When I have the power, I will make sure the world is safe.

My heart stops when I see the next tapestry. It's the largest one in the entire room, hanging from the rafters above and draped on the ground. On one side of the tapestry is a beautiful girl sitting in front of a weaving loom. Her dark hair flows in waves around her shoulders, and her lips are pressed tightly in concentration. Her hands work the loom—they almost seem to move—and her fingers bleed with the effort. On the other side of the tapestry, in front of an identical loom, is me.

I am exactly the same as I appear right now down to the gunmetal clothing and the gray jacket that I wear. I'm sitting back, laughing, not working, and around the backdrop, the world is falling into shadow. I am unaware. Uncaring. In the tapestry, on the loom in front of me, is one word written in symbols that shift around and take form in my mind. *Unworthy.*

*I sit across from the girl, knowing my skills are superior, knowing I don't need to try. But she continues to boast, sure she is better than me. I have nothing to prove to her. And when the hour of weaving is done, and our looms are judged, the gods fly into a rage. She has used her hour to diminish the gods. To point out their weaknesses. And when they demand her life, I plead on her behalf. She is a stupid girl who's made a stupid mistake. I am able to get her life spared but at a cost. And she hates me for it.*

I snap my eyes away from the tapestry, pressing my fingers to my temples, massaging away the pain. The memory is a trick. A mind game designed to make me feel inferior, but I won't let it work. I am worthy to wield the power. I'm not the person that the tapestry portrays me to be. I'm not the weak person Owen makes me feel like I am.

Hatred I don't understand fills the chamber around me. It's hatred on par with my feelings for Owen, like a seed planted deep in this cathedral which has only now blossomed.

I need to move past this place. I'm not safe here. This place is filled with vengeance.

I spin around just as something jabs me in the stomach, doubling me over and causing my vision to blur. My eyesight moves in and out of focus, but something hairy and enormous with fangs and so many eyeballs that I can't count them stands in front of me. A spider? Or is it a girl? I can't focus enough to tell. Pain ripples from my stomach all through my body. I can't stand up straight. Can't hardly move. I want to vomit, but my body won't comply. Then the thing in front of me, a spider with the face of the girl in the tapestry, reaches four legs out toward me and begins to spin me, covering me in her silk.

## XXVIII

A KNIFE. I NEED MY KNIFE. IT'S A thought that runs through my head as the spider immobilizes me.

"Stop," I try to say, but it's muffled by the spider silk that covers my mouth.

The spider hisses in response.

"Mmmm . . ." My words are indistinguishable. I'm completely covered in the silk. The spider tips me upside down and hangs me from the rafters that run far overhead, supporting the monstrous ceiling. Then she licks the entire length of my body. I didn't think spiders even had tongues. A scream like the one I heard before pierces the silence around us, and the spider retracts from me and scurries away.

Silence returns. Moments tick by. I'm aware that I should be poisoned. That the spider injected me with something when she bit me. Poison to paralyze me if I remember correctly from Biology class. First I'll be paralyzed then she'll devour me alive. But each second that passes, my head clears as whatever fog was placed there evaporates, and everything inside me seems to be working fine.

Far below, on the ground, are footsteps. I'm tempted to call out a muffled cry for help, because if there is someone down there, then maybe they could cut me free. Except if I call out, the spider will hear and she'll know I'm not paralyzed. I battle back and forth, weighing the options. Calling out for help will bring the spider back to me, and it will also bring the spider to whoever is walking down there. Not calling out could make me her next meal. I'm still working through the decision as the footsteps fade away.

I move my body just barely as I hang there so I sway and turn, scanning the chamber for the spider. I don't see her at first, but movement catches my eye. She's off in the corner gnawing on one of the many things hanging like me from the ceiling. Panic hits. They could be my friends. Hudson or Abigail. Or what if the spider trapped Cole? If only I could be lucky enough that one of them is Owen. He, of all of us, deserves to be digested by a mutant spider.

A pale hand hangs from the cocoon the spider's eating. On that hand is a detailed grizzly bear claw tattoo. A tattoo identical to the one I'd seen on the albino guy in the stasis chamber. He can't have been here long, couldn't have arrived much before me. But from the way the spider has her fangs embedded in him, I can only assume he's dead.

Dead.

Iva's words return to me. If we die in the virtual reality world, we die in the real world, too.

If I don't get out of here, I will be dead. I don't have long before she'll come back to me.

My hands are pressed to my sides, wrapped so tightly in the silk that I can barely wiggle my fingers. I stay still until my body stops swaying. I don't want to call any attention to myself if I can help it. I need to reach my knife. I wiggle my fingers again. And

**178**

again. And each time I'm able to move them a bit more. Half an inch at a time. The knife hangs over my right hip. I try to move my elbow, looking for give.

The spider's head snaps my way. I've been found out. She must've seen me moving because the next thing I know she jumps for me. Her fangs extend and sink into my belly again, knocking all the wind out of me. I grunt from the pain of her assault, but I can't double over because I'm hanging upside down. I wait for the poison to flow through my system. Maybe she didn't bite me hard enough last time, but this time there was no missing. When she shifts forward again, I realize that the poison should have already knocked me out.

It didn't.

I let my body go completely limp and stay as still as I can. My body swings gently from side to side. I appear lifeless.

She hisses then she scurries off, back to her meal.

## XXIX

**THE SPIDER GIRL WATCHES ME WITH**
four of her eyes. My fingers are nearly to my belt. But every small
movement I make causes the silk to sway. I am not poisoned. Not
paralyzed. But if I don't get the knife, I will be dead. The spider
will get her revenge and eat me. Then my parents really will be
gone.

The spider's meal is filling, because each slurp she makes, the
eyes that watch me drift more and more until she retracts herself
on the thread that holds her and returns to the rafters above. The
wooden beam wobbles as her weight is suspended from it and I
realize that they aren't rafters at all. They are thick silk extensions
of her web, spanning out from the center of the cathedral. We,
her prey, hang from her web, saved for later. The spider casts me
one more glance. I hold perfectly still. Then she curls her legs up
under herself and sleeps.

I look back to what's left of her meal, but as I'm watching, the
body of her victim fades away until the silk threads fall limp as if
nothing was ever there.

Oh, god, I will really and truly die if I don't get out of here.

I pull up on my arm, straining against the silk. It sends a ripple through the entire web, but the spider doesn't stir. The tips of my fingers brush my right hip. The silk has so little give, but with the tattooed guy's empty cocoon hanging from the web as my motivation, I struggle until my fingers touch the end of the knife. My movements are tiny, but my shell still sways from side to side. If the spider wakes, it will all be over. I pull the knife out of its sheath with my thumb and forefinger and begin to saw through the silk. With so little room, the first few strands take forever to give, but eventually they break, freeing up more space until I've broken through and my arm is free.

I reach across and free my left arm next. The silk is sticky and clings to my jacket and hands. With my left hand I reach up, grabbing the silk thread that holds my weight and right myself. Then I free the rest of my body.

I'm suspended ten feet from the ground. It's a long drop but not impossible. The spider still sleeps, and now that I'm free, I scan the other cocoons. The one with the tattooed guy is empty as are two others nearby. But the one nearest me is fresh, like I was. I reach out with a leg to hook the silk holding it, and once my leg has hold, I jump across the distance between it and me.

It shakes as if I've woken whoever is inside, and at the movement, the spider's eyes fly open. She's awake.

With my knife, I saw through the strand of silk that holds the cocoon in the air, and we drop, landing on the hard ground far below.

"Umph!" comes a voice from inside. Whoever is in there is definitely awake.

The spider hisses, and she spins a thread and lowers herself to the ground. She's still far from me. I saw through the middle area of the cocoon I've freed, exposing the arms and torso, then I start on the legs.

"Mmmm," comes the voice from the cocoon.

"I'm hurrying," I say, keeping my eyes on the spider. The first leg is free. Then the second. Except there is no second leg. There's a metal prosthetic.

It's Cole!

I yank him to his feet, even as he tears the silk from his face and eyes. The spider is only ten feet away.

"She's coming!" I scream.

He's bleary-eyed but waking up more with each second that passes. And when his eyes lock on the spider, he comes fully alert. He grabs his water bottle from behind his back and uncaps it. A ball of fire bursts from it and hits the spider and the web around her, causing the web to burst into flames.

He filled his water bottle with fire balls!

The spider begins to shriek, but we don't stick around to listen. Instead we run. My knife clatters to the ground, but I don't waste time picking it up.

"Do you know the way out?" I ask.

"I hoped you did," Cole says.

What I do know is that the way out is not toward the spider. The only thing waiting for us in that direction is death.

"The door I came through vanished," I say.

"Me, too," Cole says.

Think. There has to be a way to get out of this zone. If there is a way in, then it only stands to reason.

"This is a giant computer simulation, right?" I say.

"She can still kill us," Cole says. "You saw what she did to Kevin."

"The guy with the tattoo?" I say.

Cole nods.

"So we try not to die," I say. "And we look for an exit. We got in here by using the Greek letter. So look for the same Eta symbol. If we find it, maybe it will activate the door."

**182**

The spider is screeching behind us. She wasn't moving at first, but now her cries get closer. Whatever damage the fire did, it's not enough.

"You check the columns," I say. "I'll check the walls."

There is no point in the labyrinth having more than one zone if we can't get around between them. I run to the tapestries and yank them from the wall, one by one, looking for the Eta. But the walls behind are smooth stone, like the floor.

I fling the tapestry I'm holding to the ground. Maybe I'm looking in the wrong place. Maybe the tapestries themselves have the symbol. I scan them, one after another, looking for Eta. And though there are plenty of other Greek letters woven into the scenes, I can't find Eta.

Smoke fills the air as the web burns. The spider tears toward us, moving from one silken strand to another, weaving as she goes. She'll be here in no time.

I turn back to Cole. "Please tell me you found it."

His face tells me all I need to know.

I reach for my knife, but I dropped it back when the spider started chasing us. At the same time, I remember the binoculars. We must have them for some reason.

The spider shows no sign of slowing down. The flames only seem to enrage her. Cole and I scoot to the center of the large cathedral room. Light pours through the stained glass windows above, casting colors everywhere. I unclip the binoculars and hold them to my eyes. Immediately I see the resemblance between them and the haptic goggles back at my house in Florida. They add a layer over the already existing world, like an augmented reality. Perfectly shaped, about a hundred yards away, is an Eta floating in the air. The exit.

"Run, Cole." I grab his arm and we take off, me holding the binoculars so I can see where we're going.

The spider is nearly on us. Her fangs drip venom. She is ready

**183**

to pounce.

"Exit," I scream as we come upon the floating Greek letter, and at my words an outline of a doorway appears.

"Zone Eta. Are you sure you want to leave?" Iva's voice says.

"Yes!" I scream, and the door slides open.

The spider hisses as Cole and I leap through.

The door to Zone Eta slides closed behind us, muffling the spider's cries for revenge.

"Thank god for you, Edie," Cole says. And the next thing I know he grabs me in a hug I never would have thought him capable of based on my attempted hug earlier. I completely hug him back. Then he moves forward, almost like he's going to kiss me. I freeze, unsure of the emotions that pour through me. Wanting him to kiss me. Anticipating it. Not sure about anything.

Cole pulls back.

"Sorry about that," he says, stepping out of my reach. "It must've been the venom still in my system."

I hold my face steady, so he won't be able to read my emotions. I'm not quite sure what they are anyway.

"Sorry about what?" I say. Pieces of spider silk still hang from my curly hair. I tear them off and toss them to the white floor below. We're in another circular white room like the one I started in.

"Nothing," he says. "Forget about it."

I have a burning desire to tell him that I wish he had kissed me. That there is nothing for him to be sorry about. But I hold my tongue. Maybe he really is sorry he almost kissed me.

"No problem," I say.

He angles his body so the scarred side of his face is turned away.

"Really?" I say.

"Really what?"

"Have we not gotten past that yet?"

"Past what?" he says.

"This." I angle my body, like him, so the entire side is hidden from him. "You try to pretend that it's no big deal, your face and your leg. And yet you keep them hidden. All the time. Try to act like you don't care."

"I don't care," he says.

"Then why are you trying to hide yourself from me? I just saved you from a freaking man-eating spider for god's sake."

"I'm not trying to hide myself," he says.

"Then turn to me." I cross my arms and wait.

"Oh, come on, Edie," he says. "This is ridiculous."

"Just turn to me. It's that easy."

"We need to go," Cole says.

"I'm not leaving," I say. "Not until you do it."

Cole rolls his eyes. "Fine." He turns his body and face completely toward me. "Is this better?"

I step forward without a word. Reach my hand up. And I trace it along his face, directly over the scar that covers half of it, trailing it along his cheek and over his eyelid and onto his lips. One side of his face is perfect. And one side of his face is flawed beyond repair.

I press my palm against his cheek. "How did it happen?"

Cole steps back. "I don't really want to talk about it, okay?"

I lower my hand. "Yeah, okay." Except I wish he would tell me, because even if Cole does get out of this labyrinth, there is no way he'll be free. He's haunted by something else.

## XXX

**WE DON'T TALK ABOUT THE ALMOST**
kiss.

"You know that makes twice that I've saved your life," I say, referring to the cave of the sirens.

"Maybe," Cole says. "But I gave you a ride in my Jeep."

Ah, the Jeep. And the time when it was just the two of us.

"Did you ever see Nails?" I ask.

Cole hardens his face. "No. I haven't seen her since we crossed over. But she'll turn up. Everything will be okay."

I imagine my owl flying around the labyrinth, protecting me. Except my owl is not allowed here. She's in the real world. I am in a virtual world. I have to protect myself.

"So your water bottle . . . ," I say.

". . . is filled with fire," Cole says. "What did you pick?"

"Nothing."

"Oh come on. Tell me," Cole says.

"I picked nothing. That's what I picked."

"You're kidding," Cole says. "You must've picked something

that makes you impervious to spider venom because that spider knocked the shit out of me."

The spider had bitten me twice, and neither time had done anything. I look down at my jacket. There is not a scratch on it. But underneath, my stomach is tender, and a giant purple bruise blossoms.

"She got me," I say.

"Not like she got me," Cole says. He lifts his torn gray shirt, exposing his very nice abs along with not only a bruise but two puncture marks from the spider's fangs.

"I thought maybe she missed me the first time," I say. "But the jacket must've protected me." It's like back in the real world. The fire hadn't burned me. The road hadn't scraped me. The jacket had killed the sirens. The jacket seems to be invincible both in the real world and here in the virtual world.

"You think they make that jacket in my size?" Cole asks.

I shake my head. "I'll tell you what. Next time you get yourself captured and I need to save your butt, I'll let you borrow my jacket."

Cole grins, and it's amazing.

"Deal, Edie," he says.

Awkward silence slips in, but Iva's voice interrupts it. "Which zone are you picking next?" she asks, and the white pedestal appears in the center of the room.

"Why did you pick Eta last time?" I ask.

Cole shrugs. "It was sort of like the first letter of your name. I mean it looks like an H, but it sounded like an E."

"Seriously?" I say. We'd thought that much alike?

"Seriously," Cole says, flushing.

"Time to pick," Iva says.

"Which one this time?" I run my hand over the four letters on top of the pedestal. Iva translates them, and again I commit them to memory.

"Lambda."

"Phi."

"Eta."

"Kappa."

Except the Eta isn't lighting up. We can't go back the way we came, which in this case, is a good thing.

"It's not the same pod I started in," I say. "The letters are different."

"It's different for me, too," Cole says. "I started in the same pod as Kevin."

The guy with the grizzly bear tattoo. Dead.

"He ran ahead," Cole says. "I suggested we stick together, but he ignored me."

"And the spider got him first," I say.

"You need to pick or I'll pick for you," Iva's voice says.

Cole looks at me. "Your call."

"Kappa," I say. It's as good as any of the others.

I press the Kappa symbol and the corresponding outline of a door glows on the circular wall. Above it is the same symbol.

"Zone Kappa. Are you sure?" Iva says.

"We're sure," I say.

The door slides opens, and we walk through.

## xxxi

**WE STAND IN THE MIDDLE OF A PATH**
lined with tree trunks covered in thick gray bark that are so wide
around it would take ten of me to encircle one of them. Their
branches are pure black and heavy with leaves colored in fluores-
cents. Electric greens. Poppy reds. Yellows the color of lemons.

"A forest?" I reach my hand between the trees, but I yank it
back when something jabs the end of my middle finger, as if in
warning to keep away. "Ouch!"

"What happened?"

"Something bit me." I press my finger to my mouth. It's throbbing at the very end, like a bee sting.

Cole acts like he's going to stick his hand through also, but I
yank it back.

"Not a good idea," I say. "They're alive."

"But they're not animals," Cole says. "They're just oak trees."

I may know my video games, but I'm no tree expert. "How can
you tell?"

He runs his hand over the side of the nearest trunk. "The gray bark. The shape of the leaves." Then he squats down, coming back up with an acorn the size of his fist. "Big oak trees, but still oak trees."

I wouldn't have thought it possible for trees to get this big, but then again, we are in a computer simulation.

Cole moves to pass the acorn to me but winces and drops it instead.

"Are you okay?" I ask.

He presses a hand to his forehead, like he has a headache. Like how I get the headaches after the visions of Owen.

"I'm fine."

"You sure?" He is having visions just like me, though I'm willing to bet his visions are way different than mine.

"I'm sure."

We jump back as a neon green stem sprouts up through the soil under our feet. The acorn has burrowed into the ground, and it's already growing. In under a minute, the baby tree is taller than I am.

"Let's hope there are no squirrels around," Cole says.

If the acorns and trees are this big, squirrels would have to be gargantuan.

The path we're on extends not only forward but backward where the door to the pod was just a minute ago. I pull the binoculars from my belt, but when I look through them, the scene is unchanged. There is no Greek Kappa symbol visible.

"Maybe we have to be close to the exit to see it?" I say, reattaching the binoculars to my belt.

Cole tries his binoculars but must not see the exit either. "It'll turn up," he says.

I only hope we find the exit before something in this zone tries to kill us.

The black branches of the trees drape low over the path with moss and sharp sticks jutting downward, scratching at our faces

**190**

and hair. Unlike the zone of the spider, there is no light here. Cole uncaps his water bottle, letting loose the glow of the fire inside. His hand shakes, making shadows bounce around like animals skittering between the trees.

From ahead, a sound drifts through the air, reaching my ears.

"Shhh . . . ," I say. "Do you hear that?"

We stop moving and listen. Laughter. Talking. Someone is here with us.

"Put it out," I say, and Cole caps the water bottle, casting us into darkness. I hold his arm, and we stand motionless in the pitch black. Far ahead, light filters between the trees. It's barely visible, like a crescent moon peeking through dark curtains. It's where the voices are coming from.

I tug on Cole's arm, and we move forward in the direction of the light.

"Who do you think it is?" I whisper.

"Maybe Hudson? Or Abigail?" Cole says.

Or Owen. The thought of running into him makes my stomach clench into a ball so tight it's hard to breathe. I don't want to run into Owen here or anywhere.

"What?" Cole whispers.

"What what?"

"You're clenching my arm."

I ease up. "Sorry," I whisper back, praying I won't have another vision about him.

"What are you worried about?" Cole asks, his voice barely audible. Whoever is up there, we don't want to announce our presence.

"I'm not worried about anything," I say.

"You can tell me," Cole says.

As we inch closer, the light gets brighter, but the oak trees shield us.

Could I tell Cole? Should I? But what would he think of me

**191**

if I did? He might think I'd actually let Owen do those things to me. That I'd let him have his way and that I was lying about it.

"It's nothing," I say. "Promise."

"Whatever."

"I swear," I lie. The thought that Owen waits for me beyond the trees makes me want to turn and run.

Cole grabs both of my hands and looks me directly in the eye. It's funny how used to his face I've become in such a short time. How familiar he is.

"Look," Cole says. "I don't know who else we can trust, but know that you can trust me. Always."

"And you can trust me," I say. "Always."

We stay just like that, unmoving, in a silent moment that feels more profound than our almost kiss. It pulls us together.

"It's just Owen," I say before I change my mind.

"What about him?"

Deep breath. "He scares me. That's all."

Cole's eyes narrow. "Did he hurt you, Edie?"

I shake my head. "No. Not really. I just . . . I think that he could. That he would."

"Why do you think that? What did he do?"

"He . . . we went to Homecoming. He tried to . . . you know. But I stopped him. I swear I did. That's all that happened. I promise."

"Edie . . . ," Cole says.

"That was it. I swear."

"I won't let him hurt you." Cole's voice is gruff and serious, as if given the chance he would pull Owen's arms from his sockets. "I won't let him near you."

How much I want to believe that. But I also don't want to have to test it. I never want to see Owen again.

A peel of laughter snaps us back to reality.

"We should see what's going on," I say, ready to leave the conversation about Owen behind.

"I'm here for you, Edie," Cole says. "Okay?"

"Yeah, okay."

The laughter comes again, louder this time.

"Are you ready?" I ask.

"Only if you are," Cole says.

"I'm ready."

We turn the corner and step forward into the light.

A girl's voice says, "One more step and I'll kill you."

# xxxii

**IT SOUNDS A LOT LIKE TAYLOR, BUT I**
can't swivel my head to see who's talking because something
presses up against it.

"We're not going to hurt anyone," I say.

"Shut it," the girl says.

"Dude, call your sister off," a guy says. From the sound of his
voice and the way his words are slurring, I'd guess it's the guy who
looked drunk earlier.

Sister. This must be Taylor and Adam.

"Dominic's right," Adam says. "You need to chill. Let them at
least talk before you kill them."

Dominic must be the drunk one.

"Seriously," Cole says. "We're not going to hurt anyone."

"Missing leg or not," Dominic says. "I bet this guy could rip
your throat out with his bare hands."

I can't imagine Cole ripping anyone's throat out.

"We just want to talk," I say. "Lower your weapons."

"I don't trust you," Taylor breathes in my ear. "With your shifty gray eyes and your attitude like you're better than the rest of us. It was the first thing I noticed about you."

"Are you kidding?" I say, swiveling enough so I can see her. "You and Adam would both be dead now if it weren't for me. The sirens would have killed you."

"We'd have gotten free," Taylor says, and her voice is full of enough confidence that I almost believe her.

"I'd like to have seen that," I say.

"Truce," Cole says. His word hangs in the air. And with it, images drift into my mind. Wars being put aside. Rival armies celebrating together. The word has some kind of power here in the labyrinth, and once he has spoken it, it's like a calm descends on us. The word will be respected.

"Truce for one night," Cole says. "We'll be gone in the morning."

I don't see why Taylor has to be so hostile. I did save her life. And it's not like I've gotten in her way so far. And yet . . . I assume that I will reach the end first. I know I can do it. And maybe everyone has the same thought. I might not be willing to kill to get the power, but others could be.

The fire highlights the thin scars running across Taylor's cheeks. Two in a row on both sides. They're so perfectly symmetric that I'm sure they've been put there intentionally. The lower ones look old, but the upper scars look fresh, like they've only just healed over in the last few weeks.

"Truce for one night," Taylor says and pulls away. She's holding her bow with the arrow still nocked. And though she's granted us a truce, distrust ripples off her in waves.

The three of them have built a campfire in the middle of the path, using black thorny branches as the fuel. Shadows from the flames bounce around between the trees. Taylor returns to the fire, sitting next to her brother Adam. On the other side of Adam is Dominic.

**195**

"Care for a drink?" he says, holding out a bottle.

"You filled your bottle with alcohol?" I ask. Maybe Kappa, the forest zone, is a magical, happy, party zone, and I chose a dud before with a killer spider instead.

Dominic's face eases into a lazy grin. "Anything we wanted, right?"

I take the bottle and sniff it. Honey and vanilla. Sharp yet sweet at the same time, it lures me in with promises of relaxation and fun.

False promises. I hand it back.

"It's magical alcohol," Dominic says, passing the bottle to Adam who takes a sip under Taylor's eagle eye.

"That's what you picked to help you get out of the labyrinth?" I say.

Dominic shrugs. "It helps with most any situation."

Cole and I sit, me next to Dominic and Cole next to Taylor. She reaches over and squeezes Cole's bicep. He doesn't pull away.

"How did you get so muscly?" Taylor says. "You lift weights?"

Seeing her hands on his skin doesn't give me warm fuzzies inside, but I keep my mouth shut. One look at Taylor here, in the wild, makes me sure she will put an arrow between my eyes if I don't watch myself.

Cole shrugs. "Off and on," he says, but he doesn't elaborate.

"Yeah, well they're nice," Taylor says.

Cole glances to me then quickly looks away when he sees that I'm watching. "Thanks," he mumbles.

"Stop pawing at him," Dominic says.

"Jealous?" Taylor asks, and she rubs Cole's upper arm for effect, trailing her hand up and over his shoulder and onto his chest where she rests it.

Cole gently lifts her hand away and places it on her lap.

"So I showed you mine," Dominic says, avoiding answering her question. Maybe he is jealous. "Time for you to show us yours."

I'll give Dominic this. His slurred words don't irritate me like kids from school when they get drunk. He reminds me more of an over-needy puppy, begging for attention.

"What do you want me to show you?" My tone is lighthearted. Unlike Taylor, I'm not here to pick a fight. And truly, the more allies I can make, the better my chances of getting out alive.

"Not sure what you're talking about," Cole says, and annoyance creeps into his voice. Maybe he doesn't see the puppy comparison.

"What'd you choose to bring with you?" Dominic says, as if it's the most obvious thing in the world. "Either of you two pick anything interesting?"

I expect Cole to sink back into his normal defensive shell. Instead, he uncaps his water bottle and shows the flames roaring inside, making everyone except him jump backward.

"I got fire," Cole says.

If I didn't know better, I'd say he's showing off.

"Fire!" Taylor laughs and pretends to bow down to him. "All hail the fire god."

"All hail!" Adam says.

Taylor holds her bow up. "With this, I can shoot that stupid Iva between the eyeballs when I see her. And I filled the bottle with poison for the tips, just to make it faster." She rubs the bow in a loving gesture.

"So don't screw with my sister," Adam says, bumping her with his shoulder.

"I wouldn't dare," Cole says. His response almost sounds like flirtation. And I wonder why it is that he's willing to flirt with Taylor but not with me. Not that I'm saying I want Cole to flirt with me. But I wonder what Pia would say if she saw him flirting. And I wonder how serious they were.

"You were pointing a poisoned arrow at me?" I ask. If she'd slipped up, I could have died, and we'd never be having this conversation.

**197**

Taylor shrugs. "Chill out. I didn't puncture your skin."

Easy for her to say.

"How about you, lovely?" Dominic says. "What did you bring into the labyrinth with you?"

"I got this jacket. It keeps me warm." I leave it at that. Its protective properties are my own business. And I don't want to mention my empty water bottle. More and more, as everyone's sharing all the useful things they have, it feels like a mistake.

"Because she's cold as ice," Cole says.

They all burst out laughing. My eyes meet his in the firelight. He covered for me. Kept my secret.

"No wonder you two are together. You're hot and she's cold." Taylor laughs and leans back on her hands. Maybe she's accepting us after all. Our truce could last longer than one night.

"What about you?" I ask Adam. "Are you good at shooting things like your sister?"

Adam takes a drink from Dominic's bottle before answering. "Nope, I'm the smart one. I filled mine with light, something that's come in useful so far. Have you seen this place? Dark freaky trees. Acorns that grow in turbo mode."

"Enough, bro," Taylor says. "We need more wood on the fire."

She snaps a low branch from the nearest oak tree and tosses it on the flames. The tree groans in response, almost as if it's sentient.

"Is that a good idea?" I ask.

But Taylor isn't listening. Instead, she's bent over, pressing her palm to her forehead and grimacing. Adam is at her side in seconds, but she doesn't seem to notice he's there. It's a good ten seconds before she rights herself and her eyes refocus.

"You okay, Tay?" Adam asks.

Taylor looks so weak in that moment. So not like the girl who just threatened to kill me. She turns to Adam with eyes wide, like she's seen a phantom.

"Don't leave me, Adam," she says, still holding her hand to her forehead. The motion is familiar, like what I've done after my visions, making me wonder if she's having visions, too.

Regardless, I'm sure as hell not going to ask her. She might take it as a challenge and slit my throat.

"I'm here," Adam says. "And I'm not going anywhere."

Taylor grips his arm. "Promise me. Don't you dare leave my side."

"Taylor, I won't," Adam says. "We're sticking together, through this place, all the way to the end."

"Speaking of this place," Dominic says, breaking the intensity of the moment. "What have you two found out about it?"

Cole and I relay the story of the spider. Taylor regains her composure, and the distrust in her eyes returns. It seems the three of them were able to avoid the spider's lair, coming from a different direction. Cole tells them about Kevin starting in the same pod as he did and about his fate. The horrific images of the spider sucking the life from him fill my mind. I try to push them away.

"What about you guys?" I ask. "You three have been together this whole time?"

"Taylor and I grabbed the same chip," Adam says. "Maybe because we're twins it worked. This is the first zone we came to, but we have no clue how to get out."

I glance to Cole who meets my eyes. Do we tell them about the binoculars? If the truce ends tomorrow morning, then possibly it's information we should keep to ourselves.

"And you?" I ask Dominic, avoiding the subject for the time being.

"I ended up in the same pod as a psycho," Dominic says.

He has to be talking about Owen. The veins in my temples throb. I focus on his words, trying to keep another vision from slipping in. Even now, I feel Owen's hands on me, hurting me as I try to break free. I sneak a glance. Cole watches me.

"Who was it?" I ask, trying to sound casual.

"This guy named Owen." Dominic takes a long drink from the bottle and wipes his brow as if the mere memory of Owen will make him fall over on the spot and die. But Dominic's terror is real. If anything he's actually trying to minimize it.

I don't let my face give anything away.

"He was with that really pretty girl," Dominic says. "You had to have noticed her. We all wound up in the same pod. I tried to be friendly, but Owen didn't want any part of me being around. Maybe he was worried I'd try to move in on the girl, but she seemed way into him. And way into God. She wouldn't stop praying. So Owen pulls his knife out and tells me that if he sees me again, he'll kill me. Needless to say, I picked the first zone my hand landed on and got the hell out of there. Ended up here."

"Don't ever trust him," I say, breaking my silence. "I knew him before. He doesn't think about anyone but himself. I'm sure all he wants is to get the power."

"We all want the power," Taylor says. "Too bad Adam and I are the only ones who are going to."

"You can't both get it," Cole says, still studying me.

I try to act normal, like Owen doesn't make my skin crawl.

"Try to stop us," Adam says.

I will try to stop them . . . when I get the power myself. But I wonder if it is possible, two people getting the power. Maybe they can, since they are twins, like with the selection chips. Or maybe that was a trick to lull them into false security.

"Have you seen Owen since?" I ask Dominic.

"We haven't seen anyone," Taylor says. "But we did hear footsteps a few hours ago. I searched for whoever it was, but there was no sign of anyone. But if this Owen or anybody for that matter shows up . . ." She trails off. There is no reason to finish the sentence.

If Owen does show up, he will not ask for a truce.

## XXXiii

### I ATTEMPT TO SLEEP. IT'S POINTLESS.

Dominic is still drinking when my eyes snap open. I wonder if he's slept at all.

"Mimosa?" he asks.

I blink my eyes to get some moisture in them. If I slept an hour, I'd be surprised. I'd heard Cole's breathing, uneven like mine, but I hadn't said anything to see if he was awake because I hadn't wanted the others to hear.

"I just woke up," I say. It doesn't qualify as morning. There is no sun and there is no moon and everything is cast in shadow. The fire still burns though it's down to embers.

Dominic takes a long sip from his bottle. Drinking in the morning must not bother him. Drinking any time of the day or night probably doesn't bother him either.

"You guys figure out how we get to the end?" Adam asks, stretching as he comes awake. "Another hour in this stupid forest and I'm going to kill someone."

A gust of wind howls through the thick branches, making

the trees groan the same way they had last night when Taylor snapped branches off for the fire. Smoke billows off the fire, sending a burst of sparks toward the base of the trees.

"We follow the yellow brick road," Dominic says.

Taylor glares at him. She, like Dominic, doesn't look like she's slept at all. They sit far apart from each other. It's obvious that no love is lost between the two of them.

"We don't know how to get to the end," Cole says. "But good luck figuring it out."

That's right. The lame excuse for night has passed. The truce has ended. It's time for us to leave.

Taylor eyes him up and down, but it doesn't feel so flirtatious now. More like she's assessing him for his capabilities. His muscles. His strong hands. Her eyes settle on his prosthetic.

"You think you'll slow us down?" she asks bluntly.

Adam slaps her on the arm. "That's rude, Tay."

"Rude or not," she says. "We need to find the end of the labyrinth and get out of here. This place gives me the creeps."

The trees seem to press inward, as if they've taken her words as a challenge. Something in the corner of my eye moves, but when I turn to look, it's only the swaying of the branches in the wind.

"Doesn't matter if I will or won't," Cole says. "We'll leave you guys to your bickering." He straightens his belt and looks my way, almost as if he's seeing what my plans are.

"Right," I say, backing him up. "Nice seeing you all. Stay alive."

"Oh, come on," Adam says. "We should stay together. At least for a little while. It's safer that way."

Unspoken is the threat of the others. Any of them could try to kill us at any time. Owen has already threatened Dominic. And Owen has threatened me.

*He hits me, and before I have a chance to recover, he shoves me to the sandy ground and presses himself against me. I can't move under his weight. He tears at my clothes. His fingers invade me.*

*"When this is over, I'm going to kill you,"* he whispers in my ear.

I gasp as I'm pulled from the vision, stumbling on the rough ground. My head pounds, but I resist putting my hands to it, hoping that no one has noticed.

Taylor studies me, but she doesn't say a word. Cole's face, on the other hand, is filled with anger.

I smile wanly, hoping to tell him I'm okay. He doesn't look convinced, but in the moment he's smart enough not to say anything.

I can't let Owen bother me like this.

"Don't do us any favors," Cole says to Taylor.

"Except for not killing you, I assume," Dominic says.

Dominic has a point. Staying with these three will at least keep them on our radar.

"You want to extend truce?" I ask. "What do we get out of it?"

Taylor grips her bow. "How about if you join us, I don't kill you?"

I kind of love and hate her attitude at the same time. I give an almost imperceptible nod to Cole who nods in reply.

"We'll stick around," I say. "Extended truce."

"Extended truce," Taylor says and puts out her hand to shake. The deal is sealed.

"Now how do we get out of this god-forsaken forest?" Dominic asks.

So Cole and I tell them about the binoculars. I'm still not seeing the exit, but now there are five of us to look.

We set off down the path, weaving between the branches of the enormous oak trees. In some places, there is so little room to pass that we walk single file and they still scrape at my arms. My jacket keeps me protected though, whereas the others have multiple scratches. Taylor almost seems to have a vendetta against the trees, snapping branches and tossing them on the ground, as if she's taking revenge on them for the situation she's in.

There is no way to tell the passage of time. Since Cole isn't sure how much fire is left in his water bottle, we use only the glow coming from Adam's water bottle to light the way. Taylor and Adam take the lead, followed by Dominic, with Cole and me in the rear. The fact that they trust us enough to keep us behind them makes me want to trust them more, but not too much. Years of playing first-person shooter games has taught me that unearned trust is a huge mistake. Anyone can kill you, even people on your own team.

We walk for hours, checking with the binoculars every five minutes or so. Though the path is narrow, it's still clear, not marked with a yellow brick road, but well worn, as if others have walked this way before us. But the simulation only started what—less than twenty-four hours ago? It could have been programmed that way, to mimic something in the real world, or someone could have come before us and left their tracks. Taylor had said they'd heard footsteps.

Another hour, and the path of trees widens until it spills out into a clearing about the size of my backyard in Florida. Beyond the clearing is a true forest with layers of trees and roots that grow so fully out of the ground that they're as tall as I am. I look up, hoping to see some glimpse of the sky, but the gray trees grow so thick that if there is a sky above, it's completely blotted out by the black branches and neon leaves. My head spins from the immensity, and I look away.

"Anyone been this way before?" Taylor asks. She raises her bow, ready to shoot whatever may cross her path.

Cole and I shake our heads, but before Dominic can answer, he jumps, dropping his alcohol-filled water bottle which rolls to the tree line and bumps into a thick root. "Did you see that?"

"See what?" I ask.

"Eyes. In the dark." He looks to his bottle but doesn't appear to have the nerve to go near it. So much for liquid courage.

"What kind of eyes?" Cole says.

"Faces," Dominic says. "Horrible faces with sharp teeth and demon eyes."

A scraping sound tears through the darkness, like wood grinding against wood. It's followed by another and then a groaning like something is bending a branch that will snap back at any moment.

"They want to kill us," Dominic says.

Adam takes a step closer to the trees. "I don't see anything."

Taylor is next to Adam in a second, yanking him back. "I told you not to leave my side."

He shrugs her off. "I'm fine."

"I'm serious, Adam," Taylor says. "Stay back."

"I swear I saw them," Dominic says.

"Well, there's nothing there now," Taylor says, but she seems apprehensive, as if she doesn't completely believe herself.

Dominic eyes the bottle again.

"Leave it, Dominic," Taylor says, but it's too late. He lunges toward the tree line, grabbing for the bottle.

Taylor is after him in a flash, trying to stop him. Dominic makes it to the bottle and yanks it back from the base of the trees. He turns around, a victorious smile crossing his face.

"You stupid idiot," Taylor says, shoving him back toward the group. "You put us all in danger when you do stuff like that."

"Relax," Dominic says, uncapping the bottle and taking a long drink. "We're all fine, aren't we?"

"This time," Taylor says, but she speaks too soon, because just as the words leave her mouth, something long and spindly extends from the trees, like grasping fingers. It wraps itself around her shoulders and yanks her from sight.

# XXXIV

**"TAYLOR!" ADAM SCREAMS. HE RUNS** for the spot where she was.

Dominic jumps out of the way, scurrying back to Cole and me. "What the hell was that?"

"We need to get her back," Adam says.

Cole is already pulling his knife from his belt. "We'll find her," he says, scanning the tree line.

Adam's light illuminates the spaces between the trees, but all that shines back at us is more trees. "Taylor!" he calls.

The trees grind and moan. Then I see faces, too. They're just like Dominic described, mouths open, teeth sharp. Demons, hidden among the trees. Part of the trees. I blink and they're gone.

"Taylor!"

"She'll be fine," Dominic says, caressing his water bottle. "She's a tough girl."

This is too much. Adam grabs Dominic by the front of the shirt. "You keep your mouth shut, you stupid drunk. You're the whole reason she's gone. We should have turned you away when you came running because there is no room for cowards."

Dominic's eyes are wide. He looks to me, but he can't possibly be thinking I'll defend him. I hold my face even.

"Let go of me," Dominic says.

Adam doesn't move.

"Now," Dominic says.

Adam twists the shirt then shoves Dominic backward. He lands hard on his butt and spits out a string of words that don't need repeating. But Adam has already turned away.

"Taylor! Come back."

"We need to go after her," I say, stepping forward to where he and Cole stand.

"We can't go in there," Dominic says. "There are things alive in there. We'll die if we do."

"Then stay here," Adam says. "Because I'm going after my sister."

Dominic refuses to go, so we tell him that we'll come back to this same spot. At least I tell him this. Adam doesn't speak another word to him.

"I'll wait right here," Dominic says, sinking to the ground. At least he has the sense to wait to uncap his bottle until Adam turns away.

We push our way between the trees. Adam's light brightens a tiny diameter around us, only enough to make sure we don't trip on the rocks or smaller tree roots. The larger roots we either have to scale or go around, neither of which makes it any easier.

"Did you see where she went?" Cole asks quietly as if he doesn't want the trees to hear.

I shake my head. "I saw them take her. That's it."

"We have to find her," Adam says, panting between words. "She's probably scared to death. Taylor . . . she tries to act so brave. But deep down—god, please don't tell her I told you this—deep down, she's one of the most frightened people I know. It's like she uses her fear to propel her forward into action. Like she can't cope without it."

Taylor doesn't come off the least bit scared . . . except when she told Adam not to leave her side. Then she'd seemed frightened to death.

"We'll find her, Adam," I say.

"She can't be dead. I would die without her." On the last part, his voice cracks. He clears his throat quickly to cover it.

We're far enough in that we can't see the tree line anymore. Can't see Dominic. When I think about him sitting back there in the clearing, drinking, it makes me want to punch him. I kick a tree root instead, and something twists around my foot. I jump, yanking my foot out of the way.

"The roots are moving." I edge away from the giant root in front of me. On the ground, the roots of the trees twist around, like fingers, groping. The trees are alive. The entire labyrinth is alive.

I turn and come face to hideous face with one of the trees. The mouth gapes open. The teeth extend as if she's going to eat me. The other trees are all the same, as if women have somehow been captured inside the trees, become one with them.

*She is ours,* the trees seem to say.

"She's not yours!" Adam screams.

*She will become one of us,* they say.

"No she won't!" He yanks on a branch of the nearest tree.

It howls in response, a true shriek as if the woman trapped inside is in horrific pain. I tear my eyes from the faces and look upward, to the spiny black branches which twist and turn. And there, amid their artful dance, is Taylor, bound at the wrists and ankles with vines and branches. She struggles, but her efforts are futile against the tough wood. Her mouth is gagged with another branch, cutting so tightly across her face that she can't even grunt.

"Taylor!" Adam lunges for the nearest tree, as if to climb it.

Neon green lightning the same color as the leaves of the tree streaks through the air, shocking him.

Taylor's eyes are wide.

Adam tries again, at a different tree, but the same thing happens, this time sparking bright orange lightning.

"I can't get near it," he says. Despair fills his voice.

Maybe he can't get near it, but I can. I loop the ends of my jacket around my hands and start to climb, swinging as I move because I can't use my legs or feet. Only my upper body can touch. Only they are protected. I wish my owl was here to help me. To carry me up through the tree branches. But the owl isn't allowed here. It's back in the real world, and this world, though deadly, is only an illusion.

Green lightning blasts around me, but it can't pass through my jacket. Each spot my jacket touches on the tree hisses and withers, the same way the sirens had, as if it's dying. But the lightning assault continues. Smoke fills my eyes as it strikes again and again. I push through, climbing branch after branch until I reach Taylor. I wrap one arm around a branch, and using the other arm, being careful not to touch anything with my bare skin, I pry the branches from her mouth and wrists and feet. Taylor drops from the tree. I jump down after her.

Adam rushes over to Taylor. She's hit the ground hard, but there wasn't anything I could do about that.

"Taylor, are you okay?" He cradles her, holding her head and shoulder off the hard rocks and roots she's landed on.

"Mmmmm . . . ," she responds. It's not much, but it does mean she's alive.

"I'm right here," Adam says. "I have you."

Taylor's eyes blink a few times then open, settling on her brother. They fill with such warmth that it makes me miss my brother Thomas a million times more in that moment. He hadn't even missed me. But there's no time to think about it. The branches reach for us. We run.

Branches scrape at my back, my neck. They rake through my hair. I run hard, making sure to keep Cole in my sights. With the prosthetic, he could trip more easily, and I'm not going to leave him here to die if that happens. He keeps turning to me, maybe to wonder why I'm not going faster, but I pretend not to notice.

We burst through the tree line, and the spindly fingers of the branches follow, trying one last time to ensnare us. But we're too fast, flying to the center of the clearing. We're free of the trees.

We fall to the ground, panting. That had been way too close.

"How'd I get free?" Taylor asks. I'm exhausted, but Taylor looks like she's been beaten. Her dark face is ashen and giant swatches of her bleached hair have been ripped out.

"In the forest," Adam says. "Edie saved you."

Adam helps Taylor to her feet. She wobbles at first, but then she straightens herself. "Thanks, Edie. Maybe I misjudged you."

Confirming that she didn't trust me before.

"Maybe," I say.

"I won't make that mistake again," she says, and though the moment passes, I now believe we are in this together.

"I'm going to kill Dominic," Taylor says. Disgust creeps onto her face. "Where is he?"

I scan the clearing. There is no sign of him.

"Maybe he left," Cole says. "Went back down the path we came from."

"He ran like the coward he is," Adam says. "And good riddance. He'll never make it out of here alive. Something will kill him while he's passed out drunk. Stupid thing, filling his bottle with alcohol."

"You didn't think it was so stupid last night," Taylor says.

Adam presses his lips together. "That was before his stupidity almost got you killed."

"We should go," Cole says, eying the branches around us.

"Go where?" Taylor asks. "Because I'm not seeing a way out."

She's right. The path that we came from is gone. There is only the clearing where we stand surrounded by the trees.

Adam steps closer to his sister. "We're not going back in the forest."

"We have to," Taylor says. "There's no other way."

"No," Adam says. "The trees almost killed you last time. We're not risking it again."

"Oh, come on," Taylor says. "Give me a little more credit. Now we know what to expect. We'll be more careful."

The trees inch closer, narrowing our safety zone.

"We need to find the symbol that brought us here. K for Kappa," I say, scanning everywhere with the binoculars. Maybe it's on one of the trees.

Again, the trees move. We step together.

"So where the hell is it?" Taylor demands, her attitude fully returned.

Adam rests a hand on his sister's arm. "Relax, Tay, she just saved your life. Remember?"

"Sorry, I'm just a little tense." Taylor says. "But the trees must be hiding the exit. And I'm going to find it."

She nocks an arrow, draws back, and lets it fly. It sails through the air and embeds itself with a solid *thunk* into the base of one of the gray oak trees.

The trees groan and twist before our eyes.

"I don't think you should have done that," Cole says, scooting closer to me.

The trees give up their subtle stalking and go into attack mode. They scrape across the ground. Branches and leaves rain down on us.

"Anything?" Cole asks.

"There!" I say, spotting the Kappa on one of the enormous tree roots, the opposite way of where Taylor had been taken. We take

**211**

off, ducking to escape the assault. Branches spear down, narrowly missing us as we flee. We're almost to the tree root. As we approach it, the Kappa glows through the binoculars.

"What about Dominic?" Cole says. There is still no sign of him.

"He's probably dead by now," Taylor says. "Killed by the trees."

Right or wrong, I know we're not waiting around for him to return.

"Exit," I say, and the letter begins to glow. On the massive tree root, an outline of a doorway appears.

"Are you sure you want to leave?" Iva's voice says.

"Yes, we want to leave!" I say, and the door slides open.

We run through the doorway, but just before it seals behind us, something flies from the darkness of the forest. It spins, end over end. Then it hits Adam square in the back.

The doorway seals shut, and Adam drops to the ground.

## XXXV

**TAYLOR SCREAMS AND FALLS TO THE** ground, next to her brother.

"Please, no!" She grabs Adam and holds his body. He can't even keep his head up.

"Be careful, Tay." Adam can barely get the words out. They're so faint, I hardly hear.

Cole slams his fists on the wall where the door was, but it's gone.

Adam meets my eyes, almost like he wants to say something, then his head rolls back.

"No! Don't leave me!" Taylor wails as she rocks back and forth. Adam's arms hang limply at his sides, and there is blood. Lots and lots of blood. And even as Taylor holds him, Adam's body begins to fade away, slipping from between her fingers until it's nothing but a memory.

"Please no, please no, please no."

Taylor's words go unanswered. Adam, like Kevin, is dead.

"Dominic?" I whisper to Cole so Taylor can't hear me. She's

absorbed in grief. Her face is covered with tears. And watching her cry, I can't help the tears that spring to my eyes.

"It had to be," Cole says, but too loudly.

Taylor whips her head around at our words. "That bastard is going to pay, because when I find him I'm going to carve his eyeballs from his head with my fingernails and smash them under my heels."

The labyrinth, for all its vast zones, seems to shrink around me. Is Dominic truly a killer? A drunk, that's for sure. But could he actually kill someone?

"What if it wasn't him?" I ask.

"It was him," Taylor says. "We just saw him. Who else could it be?"

"You yourself said you heard footsteps," I say. "Maybe it was someone else. Maybe Owen. He threatened Dominic."

"Edie knew him from home," Cole says. His voice is filled with bitterness.

Now that I've dug myself into this hole, all I want to do is get out of it. I don't want to dredge up my past with Owen. He's nothing but a jerk.

*And a killer,* a voice from somewhere in the back of my mind says.

"Could he kill someone?" Taylor asks.

"Yes," I say without hesitation because the memories are filling my mind. Images of him hitting me. Raping me. And maybe those things never happened, but I believe deep down in my heart that he's the kind of person who would act them out, given the chance. "He could and he would. And if there is one thing I know it's that we can't let him get to the end before us. He can't get the power, because if he does, the entire world will die. It's what Iva showed me. What my visions are trying to warn me about. He won't try to save humanity. He'll destroy it."

Silence.

"You're having visions, too?" Cole says.

So he has been having visions, like me. If I have visions about Owen trying to rape and kill me, what does Cole have visions about?

"Yeah, since this all started," I say. "And no, before you ask, I don't want to talk about them. They're not real anyway."

"They are real," Taylor says, wiping at her eyes. "For the last month I've been having them. I watch Adam die again and again. I try to save him. I never can. And now look."

"But that doesn't make sense," I say. "They can't be real."

"Then explain this to me," Taylor says. "If the visions aren't real, then why is my brother dead?"

I look to Cole. Are his visions real like Taylor's or are they like mine? Nightmares of my worst fears.

"So we don't trust Owen or Dominic," Cole says, avoiding my gaze. "And we stick together. Reach the end before either of them."

Taylor can't argue with his logic. The three of us are now officially a team.

"One thing before we leave," Taylor says.

"What?" Cole asks.

She pulls one of her arrows from the quiver and snaps it in half, leaving two jagged wooden ends. With one hand she runs her hands along the thin scars on her right cheek. Two parallel lines. With the other hand, she takes the broken wooden end of the arrow shaft and draws it along between the two lines, cutting deep. Bright red blood springs to the surface of her skin. When she finishes on the right, she moves to the left until blood drips down both sides of her face, trailing to her chin and dripping on her shoulders.

"For Adam," she says, then she tosses the broken arrow away.

## XXXVI

**THE POD WE'RE IN HAS A PEDESTAL IN**
the center, just like the others, with three choices that Iva names.

"Gamma."

"Kappa."

"Pi."

As the Greek letters become more familiar, the labyrinth begins to form a picture in my mind. Round pods with multiple zones clustered around. It mimics what I've seen in real life.

"That's it!" I say.

"What's it?" Taylor says. The blood still trickles down her cheeks. She doesn't wipe it away, wearing it instead like a red badge of mourning.

"The labyrinth. It's not just a VR world." I walk to the pedestal to scan the Greek letters. When I run my hand over them, the Gamma and Pi light up, but the Kappa doesn't since we just came from it.

"What do you mean, not just a VR world?" Taylor says. With Adam's death, it's like all the energy has been sucked out of her.

"What else would it be?"

"A video game," I say. "That kid Zachary Gomez in the prep room . . . He's one of the designers. There were pictures of it on the board. On his desk. It's a giant computer game."

"So what?" Taylor says. "It's a game. What difference does that make? We're still stuck in it."

"Games have rules," I say. "There are ways to win." Like *Catan.* If I plan my strategy carefully and follow the rules, I almost never lose.

"So what are the rules, genius girl?" Taylor says. The fresh cuts have erased all grief from her face and replaced it with cold determination.

"What makes you think I know?" I say.

"Because you seem to know everything," Taylor says. "Which letter should we pick to reach the end?"

In a flash, our alliance is gone. I'm on the opposite side of the playing field from Taylor. In that moment my mind tells me that she is an opponent. That I need to reach the end of the maze before she does. That she will not only kill Owen or Dominic, she will kill me. She has nothing to lose now that Adam is gone. Her only source of compassion had been brutally murdered right in front of her eyes.

I push the thought away. We have to work together if we're going to get there first.

"Edie doesn't know the way out," Cole says, coming to my defense. "You think we'd still be trapped here if she did?"

"Maybe," Taylor says.

"That's ridiculous." I try to erase the image of Taylor as my enemy, but this place makes it hard.

"Which zone are you going to pick?" Iva's voice says as I move my hand over the three letters.

"Pi," I say. It's the most common Greek letter in math. The one every kid learns. It may be the way out. Or it may be another death trap waiting to claim us.

"Zone Pi. Are you sure?" Iva asks.

"We're sure," Cole says.

The outline glows and the door slides open. I can't see beyond the door, but we step through anyway, me in the lead and Taylor in the rear. When the pod door slides closed behind us, we're cast into complete darkness.

Cole uncaps his water bottle, exposing the fire, and the world lights up around us. Except there is nothing around us.

"Hello?" a guy's voice calls through the darkness.

"Hello?" I call back, just as Taylor hits me on the shoulder.

"Shhh . . . ," she whispers. "It could be a trap."

It's too late for that.

The voice calls back. "Edie, is that you?"

I recognize the voice from our journey to this place. "Hudson?"

Wherever he is, Hudson must see the light from Cole's bottle because he comes running and reaches us before Taylor can even remove the scowl from her face.

"I figured you guys were dead," Hudson says, then he gives me a hug that is almost too quick to be considered a real hug.

"Why would you think that?" Cole says, and suspicion layers his face. Needless to say, he and Hudson do not hug.

Hudson takes a step back, eyeing the blood on Taylor's face as he does so. "Just this place. Everywhere I turn, things are trying to kill me."

"Things like what?" I ask, and the memory of the spider's lair comes back to me. The sounds I'd heard while I was wrapped in her silk. Sounds that could have been another person trying not to get caught. Another person who maybe had seen me or Cole get captured but hadn't done anything about it.

Hudson runs a hand through his cropped blond hair. "You name it. I've been to ten of these zones so far, and every one of them is deadly. Except this one. This one is empty."

Ten zones? Hudson is fast, but that's incredible. And ten zones means Hudson has a good chance of finding the end first. But he can't have already found it or else he wouldn't be here right now.

"Where did you guys meet up?" Hudson asks.

"Zone Kappa," Taylor says. "The forest zone."

"Scary trees," Hudson says. "Watch out or they'll grab you when you aren't looking."

So he's been to Zone Kappa. The question running through my mind is when was he in the forest zone? If it was the same time we were, then his footsteps could have been the ones Taylor and Adam had heard.

*Could he have killed Adam?*

The thought is there before I can stop it. This place turns us against each other. I don't want to imagine that Hudson is a killer, but the thought won't go away. I hate that I can't trust anyone.

"What about Abigail?" Cole asks. "Where is she?"

I push aside jealous thoughts of Abigail. It would be great to find her, but the odds that someone like her is still alive are pretty minimal.

"No sign of her," Hudson says. "Like I said, I've been alone this whole time. I ran into that one girl, Grace, but she didn't want anything to do with me. And then there was that drunk kid, Dominic. He tried to latch onto me in Zone Beta, but he's on a one-way track to getting himself killed. I can't bother myself with that. The goal is to stay alive, right?"

"We saw Dominic," Cole says. "Back in the forest zone. He said he hadn't been to any other zones."

"Then he's lying," Hudson says. "Because I definitely saw him in Zone Beta."

"Why's it so dark in here anyway?" Taylor asks.

"No clue," Hudson says.

I walk to the perimeter of the light but there is nothing beyond it. Just blackness. "How long have you been here?" I ask.

"Hours," Hudson says. "I can't find the exit."

"You tried the binoculars?" Cole asks.

"Of course I tried the binoculars," Hudson says. "All they show is black."

I try my own binoculars, but Hudson's right. They're not working.

"That's not very helpful," I say.

Cole stomps on the ground, and where his foot hits, white lines extend outward like a giant grid, like the room where we started.

"None of this is real," Cole says.

"Except we can die here," Taylor says.

"Maybe this zone's offline," I say. The snippet of computer code I saw in Zachary Gomez's lab mentioned `cur_zone` being equal to `PI`. `cur_zone` must be the current zone, we're in Zone Pi, and the exit is not working.

"Offline?" Hudson says.

"We're in a giant computer game," I say. "But all computer code has bugs in it. So maybe this is a bug. But they needed the labyrinth online. There was no time to fix the bugs."

"Which means what?" Taylor asks. "We're all trapped here?"

"Not trapped," I say. "We need a way to reboot the zone. It's probably gotten into some funky state. Happens with electronics all the time. If we can restart it, then maybe everything will work like it should."

"And how do we do that?" Taylor says.

I run my hand through my bushy hair. "I'm working on it."

"So we do what?" Taylor says. "Stand around here picking our asses."

I put up my hand. "Just give me a second."

Think computers. If this place is one big computer simulation, then each zone is going to have some way to be controlled not only from the outside, but from whoever tested this system—on the inside. Beta testers. I'd beta tested enough games to know the small cheats designers put in place to make testing easier. Zachary Gomez is the epitome of computer geek. He absolutely would have put controls on the inside. But it's a simulation, and there is nothing around, so I'm betting that it's not a physical control, like a button we need to push or anything like that.

Maybe it's a vocal command, like the name of the zone.

"Pi," I say.

Nothing happens.

"Debug," I say.

Again, nothing.

Zachary Gomez is a nerd. Fine, I'm a nerd, too. And what nerds like most is to feel clever and for their cleverness to be recognized and appreciated. And who better to appreciate Zachary's nerd skills than a fellow nerd—like me.

"Klam Soup," I say.

The room remains in darkness.

"What are you talking about?" Taylor says. The frustration on her face has shifted to annoyance, at me.

I ignore her. It wasn't klam soup. That's not quite right.

"Klam stew," I say, and the grid lines around the room illuminate and a whooshing of a computer coming to life fills the silence around us.

"How'd you do that?" Hudson asks.

"Not now," I say. If I brought the system to life, then the most important thing is to get out of here before whatever deadly forces are in play come after us.

My binoculars are at my face before I can blink, but Hudson is even faster.

"Over there," he says, pointing at a glowing Pi only visible through the binoculars.

"Debug exit engaged for thirty seconds," the computerized voice of Iva says.

Thirty seconds!

We take off, running for the exit. I grab Cole's hand and drag him toward the opening. I'm not willing to risk him falling behind in this zone; the exit could close at any second.

"Exit," Hudson says, and the glowing arched doorway appears. But before we're even halfway through, it begins to fade. The white grid lines of Zone Pi flicker off and on. Hudson is through first followed by me and Cole, but Taylor isn't going to make it.

"Hurry!" I scream and reach my hand out through the door. But she turns at the wrong time, and the arrow she's holding nicks my palm. I wince as pain shoots through me, traveling up my arm. I try to ignore it, and I grab her wrist, pulling her through just as the door slides closed.

## XXXVII

**"SOMETHING'S WRONG WITH EDIE," COLE**
says. He drops to the ground next to me, supporting my head. I can hardly hear him, and his face keeps moving in and out of focus.

"How did she know about that debug stuff?" Hudson says.

"Who cares right now?" Cole says. "She needs help."

Hudson retreats a few steps, like he doesn't want whatever happened to me to happen to him. "What makes you think I can help?"

"He never said you could," Taylor says. She squats down next to me, on the opposite side of Cole, and presses a hand to my forehead. I don't need the worried look on her face to tell me that it's burning up. My hand throbs. My arm aches. Each beat of my heart is like vials of poison running through me.

"I can't help her," Hudson says. His hand goes to his water bottle, not like he wants a drink, but protectively.

Taylor stands and takes a step toward him.

"What are you hiding?" she says.

"Nothing."

But he is hiding something. Even in my delirious state, I can see that. I open my mouth to say so, but the words won't come out. I'm slipping with each second that goes by, and my arm has become nothing but a throbbing nightmare.

In one second flat Cole has hold of Hudson by the front of his shirt and gets right in his face. "If you can do something to help her then you better. Because if not, I am going to kill you right here, right now."

Hudson doesn't move. He may be fast, but Cole is strong.

Cole presses his face forward, closer to Hudson. "Now."

Silence fills the pod, so intense that I can hear the beating of my heart. One beat. Two beats. Three. Four. Ten beats of my heart pass before Hudson shoulders past Cole and kneels down beside me.

"It's poison," he says after a single glance.

"From somebody's arrow tip," Cole says.

Taylor puts her hands up. "It's not my fault she touched it."

"She was trying to help you," Cole says.

"I don't need her help." Taylor puts the arrow back in the quiver and crosses her arms.

"If I do heal her," Hudson says, "and I'm not making any promises—then she better tell me what she did. She made the exit appear out of nowhere. And if she can do that, then why are we having to search the zones trying to find the exits? Why not do that every time?"

"Not now," Cole says. "Help her."

Their words float around in the air, fighting back and forth over my head. I try to call Cole's name, to ask him to come sit near me. But I can't speak. I can't move.

If I die, then what will happen to my parents? What will happen to Thomas? What will happen to the world? My logic, normally so solid, falls apart.

"Hold on, Edie," Cole says. He's somehow right next to me, across from Hudson. He takes my unhurt hand and holds it. And I have to wonder what Pia would say if she saw him at this moment. Or what he would do if she were here with us.

Hudson uncorks his water bottle and dribbles some of the liquid into my mouth.

"What are you doing?" Cole says.

Hudson doesn't answer. Once I've swallowed the liquid, he gives me more. After three large sips, he re-caps the water bottle and stands. "Guess we'll find out if it really works."

I focus on my throbbing arm. Try to count the heartbeats. When I hit twenty, my vision begins to clear. The pod stops spinning. I can't feel my heartbeat pounding in my arm any longer. I flex my fingers and clasp them into a fist. Cole squeezes my other hand, bringing me back to the present.

"How are you feeling?" he asks.

I turn so I can see him, and the worry lines that were present only minutes before are gone.

"Your water bottle is filled with healing potion?" I say, meeting Hudson's eyes which are not pleased.

"Was filled with healing potion," Hudson says. "I just used up half of it on you. Now tell me how you did that thing with the exit. Klam Stew. What does that even mean?"

I prop myself on my hands, looking around the circular pod. Cole lets go of my hand at my movement. Taylor stands about ten feet back, pretending she's looking around, but she's listening to every word we say.

"It's the trigger word to start debug mode," I say. "I saw it in the prep room. The guy there had written it on the board. There was computer code. Bug fixes."

*Thank you, Zachary Gomez,* I think in my head. Without the code, we could have been stuck in Zone Pi forever.

"Any more debug stuff you're not telling us about?" Hudson says.

"That's the only thing," I say. "But, if it worked here—"

"Then it might work in future zones," Cole says. Even though he's not a gamer, he can follow along with the logic.

"It's kind of cheating, isn't it?" Taylor says.

"Not if winning is all you care about," I say. I don't cheat at video games. Never have. But here, so many things are at stake. My life. My parents' lives. My escape from this labyrinth. The future of the world.

"It's not all I care about," Taylor says.

Right. There is revenge. Taylor's revenge, not mine. I'd rather trap Owen in the labyrinth forever. That's enough revenge for me, because when I do that, Owen will never hurt anyone again.

"Whatever our motivations, let's move," Hudson says. He runs up and down in place and if the mere action of standing still is too much for him.

I stand but wobble as my head spins.

"You're okay?" Cole asks, edging closer to me without making it obvious. Or maybe he is making it obvious. I can't get past the mixed signals he's sending.

"Fine," I say. He's probably thinking about Pia right at this very moment.

"I can't believe you have healing potion," Taylor says, and instantly I know what she's wondering: if Adam could have been healed. Maybe if she'd filled her bottle with something to heal rather than something to kill, she could have saved his life.

"No more wasting it," Hudson says.

"I do appreciate it," I say.

"Yeah, whatever." He steps to the pedestal in the center of the room.

"Pi."

"Zeta."

"Nu."

"Three choices," he says. "Except Pi doesn't light up because you can't—"

Taylor cuts him off. "Can't return to a zone you just came from. We know. Just like you can't leave a zone through the pod that brought you there."

"Nothing like keeping things simple," Hudson says. "It's why I went so quickly from one zone to the next. I'm trying to get a layout of the place in my mind. But so far, it's not making much sense."

"So Zeta or Nu?" Taylor says.

Cole looks to me. "Edie?"

"I don't know," I say. "Nu?"

"Why Nu?" Taylor asks.

"Why not?" I have zero clue what to pick. I walk to the center of the room to join Hudson.

"Which zone do you want to go to this time?" Iva's voice says.

"Nu," I say. May it bring only good things. The thought is laughable.

"Zone Nu. You're sure?" her voice says.

"We're sure," Hudson and I say at the same time.

The outline glows. The door slides open. We step through.

# xxxviii

**THE SECOND WE'RE INSIDE ZONE NU,**
Hudson says, "Klam Stew."

No grid lines appear, but Hudson doesn't give up.

"Exit," he says.

"Debug mode disabled," the computerized voice of Iva says. "Unauthorized access."

"Shit," Taylor says.

"How come it's not working?" Hudson asks.

"Probably because we're not supposed to use it," I say. "What? You don't think Iva's watching our every move? It worked once and she must've flipped a switch and turned it off so we wouldn't be able to use it again."

Hudson kicks that ground. "Well, that's stupid."

"We're not beta testers," I say, not that I think anyone will understand my reference.

Hudson scowls at me—I don't think it's personal—then he's off and running.

"So much for working together," I say.

"Can you shoot him between the eyes?" Cole asks Taylor. I'm pretty sure he's joking. Or maybe not. The tension between Cole and Hudson is palpable.

"I never miss," Taylor says. "But he'd just heal himself."

"Are all your arrows poisoned?" I ask. I'm recovered but still feel weak.

"Of course," Taylor says. "I'm not planning on shooting anyone I don't want to kill."

It explains why she'd snapped her arrow in half before using it to cut her face. Her blood has since crusted and turned nearly brown.

"Well, that's comforting," Cole says. "Remind me to walk behind you."

This actually gets a grin out of Taylor. Maybe the first one since we've met her.

We stand on a dusty road next to what might have been a playground at one point but is now a rusty pile of safety hazards. The slide has gaping holes where the metal has deteriorated, the monkey bars are missing rungs, and of the three swings, only one still hangs by both sides. Links have broken on the other chains, leaving the dilapidated rubber swaying like corpses at the gallows. Grackles speckle the tops of the rusty pieces of metal, filling the air with their haunting calls. Their sound is so harsh compared to the comforting hoot of my owl. How much I'd love to have her here, flying silently in the sky above.

"Looks like the playground where I grew up," Cole says. "A rusty death trap. When I was seven, this kid and I were playing, daring each other to do stupid things like jump from the top of the slide or see who could make the other launch higher into the air on the see-saw."

"See-saws are banned where I live," I say. My parents talked about them from when they were little, but when they tried to find one for me, I found out that I would never share in that childhood memory.

"That's because they're death traps," Cole says. "We nearly killed each other."

"Was that before or after you lost the leg?" Taylor says.

Cole studies her, maybe trying to figure out why she wants to know. I want to know, too.

"Before," he finally says.

Taylor nods but doesn't say any more about it.

"We shouldn't let Hudson go off alone," Taylor says. "I don't trust him."

"You gonna stop him?" Cole asks.

Taylor looks off in the direction Hudson went, sniffs the air, then turns back to us. "Yeah, I am." And before I can tell her to stop, she takes off, hopping the rusty slide and venturing farther into the playground.

A low giggle follows her departure, so faint that I'm not convinced I really heard it.

"What was that?" Cole says.

"Creepy giggle?" I say, zipping my jacket to keep the chilly breeze out.

"So I'm not going crazy?"

"Maybe we both are." It's comforting if unsettling.

"At least I'm in good company," Cole says.

Now that Taylor's gone, I bring it back up. "How did you lose your leg? Was it an accident?"

"Not really," Cole says. "It was a stupid thing. One of those things you think about forever. Wonder if you could have done something different. Something to change it."

"What happened?"

Cole grabs the rusty metal links of the swing set chain, running it through his fingers. The ancient metal squeaks, joining the call of the grackles.

"I was out playing with friends," he finally says. "It was summer, so it was crazy hot outside, and we lived in the shittiest part of town. This one kid, his name was Conner; he was a total ass. He shoved me, you know, how kids do. Maybe harder than he needed to. We were down near the bayou, sorting through this enormous pile of junk, looking for some kind of treasures or something. I fell. It didn't hurt, but when I got back up, my leg was covered in blood. I washed it off in the water, and I see this giant rusty nail sticking into me. But I didn't want to look like a wuss because Conner would have been all over that. So I pulled it out. Just like that."

"Didn't it hurt?" I ask.

"Hell yeah, it hurt," Cole says. "I was about to pass out. So I told Conner I had to go home. That my stepmom would be furious if I didn't get there in time for dinner, not like she ever gave a shit where I was. And my dad was always drunk. I think he forgot about me most of the time."

The difference between Cole's family life and mine is enormous. And yet here we both are.

"I didn't let my stepmom see it because I knew she'd get mad. The next day I started feeling really bad. I still didn't tell her. Stayed in bed. The day after that things went blurry, like a nightmare. And when I woke up a few days later, the leg was gone."

I can't even respond. Cole seems so vulnerable as he tells me, so small, like he's gone back to his childhood and is reliving the moment all over again. He couldn't have been much older than Thomas is now when it happened.

"Is that what you have your visions about?" I ask barely in a whisper. I don't want him to stop talking. I need him to tell me. Because maybe if I know his visions aren't real, then I'll know that mine aren't either.

"In my visions the same thing happens. I get really sick. My stepmom tells me that she's going to do something about it. But we're dirt poor. We can't afford doctors. So she takes me to some sort of tent. There's dirt and rats everywhere. I can't stand because it hurts too bad. Everything kept moving in and out of focus. Some guy lifts me up onto a table. Before I can do anything, he grabs an ax, raises it over his head, and cuts off my leg. Except that's not real, Edie. That's not what really happened. My step-mom told me they amputated it in a hospital. And even though I know that must be the truth, this other scenario keeps playing over and over in my mind, like I'm living some kind of nightmare. And I can't make it stop."

"It's not real," I say. My stomach twists at his words.

"How do I know that?" Cole says. "She said the infection was the devil and it had to be removed. Maybe there was a hospital. Maybe there wasn't. The visions cloud everything. And then there's the scar."

"She did it to you?"

He angles his face away, probably not even realizing he does so. "She said it was an accident. That I was screwing around in the kitchen and fell. Sliced open my face on the corner of the stove. But in the visions I see her holding a knife to my face, punishing me for dropping a plate. A stupid plate. I don't know what I can believe."

I don't know what I can believe either. Maybe voicing what my visions are about won't make them more real. Maybe it will help.

"It's like there's no difference between what's real and what's imaginary," Cole says. "The line is gone."

Taylor's visions had come true. Cole's may or may not be true. And mine?

No. They're a trick, designed to make me weak. But I'm not weak.

"What are your visions about, Edie?" Cole asks.

Almost by habit, my head begins to pound. Except here Cole is. He's told me what his visions are about. How can I not tell him about mine?

Owen's fingers paw at me even as I think about it.

"I don't really want to talk about them," I say.

"Why not?"

"Because . . ." My words drift off.

"Because why?" Cole says.

Deep breath. "Because I don't want to believe that I'm the person in those visions. I don't want to give any spirit to the thought that they could be real."

"You can tell me, Edie," Cole says. "I won't judge."

He will. He'll think I let Owen do those things to me. It will change the way he sees me. Change everything.

"They're just about really bad things," I say. Owen's face looms at the edges of my mind.

Hurt? Betrayal? A range of emotions crosses Cole's face. "You don't trust me."

"It's not that at all," I say. Cole may be the only person in the world I can trust. It's just that keeping the bad things silent will help keep them from becoming real.

"Never mind," Cole says. "You can tell me or not tell me. I don't really care."

I push aside the hurt that his comment elicits within me. It's my own fault.

We start across the dilapidated playground, picking our steps between broken glass and rusty nails sticking out of broken boards. "I'm trying to remember everything I can about this drawing I saw in the prep room. The inner circles had numbers, but the outer circles were unmarked, like maybe they were the zones. We've been to Eta, Kappa, Pi, and now Nu, right?"

"Right," Cole says. "So maybe if we never repeat those, we'll eventually find the final zone."

"Unless the only way to the final zone is through a pod we've already been in," I say. "It's freaking impossible. How are we supposed to know?"

"Was there anything else in the drawing?" Cole asks.

I concentrate on the drawing, but nothing comes.

"I'll keep thinking about it," I say. "Maybe I'll remember something else."

Through our journey across the playground, the sky overhead has been cloudy, as if there is a sun above, but it's obscured by layers upon layers of film, but once we're through the playground, whatever sun is above sneaks lower in the sky, casting us into dusk. Our long shadows stretch before us, leading our way to whatever waits for us ahead.

The binoculars show nothing but a dull gray that matches the sky. No Greek letters. Nothing. Wherever the exit is, we need to keep looking for it. Except for the grackles, the world around us is dead, with no living trees or plants, no animals. No sign of Taylor or Hudson. Only the dirt ground we walk on. The shadows lengthen as dusk continues to fall. And maybe I'm not thinking straight, but I reach for Cole's hand, touching the tips of my fingers to his, intertwining them. And we walk on, hand in hand.

Wherever Pia is, she'll just have to deal with it for now. I'm not trying to move in on her boyfriend at all, but the comfort our small amount of contact gives me fuels my courage.

From out of the shadows ahead, a shack appears, made of red wood and a shingled roof. Three short steps lead up to the front door which, in contradiction to the rest of the decrepit shack, is solidly hung on bright gold hinges. Embedded in the wood is one of Taylor's arrows.

"Who do you think she was shooting at?" I ask Cole in a whisper.

"Whoever lives here?" Cole whispers back, still holding my hand.

"Who would live in a place like this?" I squeeze his hand tightly with no intention of letting go. "You think Taylor and Hudson are inside?"

A scream rings out, the voice of a girl, piercing the quiet of the world around us, then another giggle, but both evaporate, leaving us in silence once again.

Cole and I exchange one quick look and run in the direction of the scream, up the steps and to the door.

"That didn't sound like Taylor," I say, not quite finding the courage to open the door but knowing I should. My heart pounds. My legs feel like Jell-O.

Cole reaches forward and pushes the door. It swings easily and silently on the hinges as if they've been oiled. And I'm struck with a horrible, horrible thought. Like what if it is Pia inside and Cole saves her and then I have to watch as they're reunited? I'm an awful person for even thinking or worrying about something like that right now.

Cole releases my hand, and we stand there as the blackness of inside stretches before us. Then, as if our presence is known, lights begin to illuminate, growing from nearly nothing until they settle at the brightness of a dim bulb.

It's not Pia inside, and even if it were, of course we would save her.

"On three?" Cole says.

I nod.

"One. Two. Three."

We step across the threshold together.

## XXXIX

**AHEAD OF US STRETCH ROWS AND ROWS**
of shelves, laid out in long aisles, spanning a distance far greater than the width of the shack. I turn and the door is gone, replaced by a solid brick wall that matches the walls on either side of us.

"Are those dolls?" Cole asks, stepping forward, entering the aisle ahead of us.

*Dolls* is an understatement. The shelves are lined with them, starting at the bottom and stacked six rows high. They're in perfect formation next to each other, as if someone has placed them with precision. They're missing arms, legs, eyes, hair. Many have no clothing. Others have gouges so deep, their faces are completely disfigured.

"Remind you of anyone you know?" Cole asks, point to a nearby doll. It's a guy doll, and half its face is torn off, as if someone took a knife and flayed the plastic from it. One leg is missing.

"Don't say stuff like that," I say.

"Why?" Cole says. "It's true. It's just like my face. You can't deny it."

"I can deny it." I try to reach up to his face, but he shrugs away. My heart aches for Cole. The scar is what every single person sees first when they look at him . . . unless they're looking at his missing leg.

But the thing is that the doll does remind me of Cole. It's not just the scarred face and missing leg. It's his shaggy dark hair. The way its hands are balled into fists. The Green Lantern T-shirt it wears. And next to it . . .

I look away because it can't be real.

"This one looks like you, Edie," Cole says, walking closer to the dolls.

"It doesn't," I say, not wanting confirmation of what I've just seen.

"No, really," he says. "Look at it."

So I turn and face the doll. Her hair is a wild mess of brown curls that looks like it's been shocked with electricity. Mascara smears half her face. And the dress she wears is identical to the brown silky one I'd worn to Homecoming. It's ripped at the shoulders and torn far enough down so that one of her breasts nearly shows. Her eyes are closed, as if she doesn't want to look me in the face any more than I want to look at her.

"That's not me," I say. "And the other one isn't you."

"Why are they here?" Cole asks, reaching out to touch the doll that looks like him.

I grab his arm and pull it back. "It's the labyrinth, trying to screw with our minds. Just walk away."

Cole takes a step back but can't seem to pull his eyes away from the dolls.

I take his head in my hands and swivel it so it's looking at me instead. "Leave them alone, Cole. They're a trick, just like the tapestries in the den of the spider."

He blinks and snaps out of whatever trance the dolls had caught him in. "Yeah, you're right."

We continue down the aisle, and the dolls only get freakier. Some wear dresses stained red with what looks like blood. Others have sticks driven through their eyes. There's one that looks like Adam, lying with a knife in its back. Another made of china that is identical to Abigail, standing in front of a mirror. Still more hold weapons like axes and spears. They're posed around tables, on sofas, pushing doll baby carriages.

A giggle comes from somewhere on my left. I turn, but there is no movement. Nothing. Another giggle from the right. Nothing there.

"I hate dolls," Cole says.

Tiny footsteps come from the next aisle, punctuated by the giggling again.

"I used to like them, but I've changed my mind," I say. These dolls are nothing like Mom's collection. They're freaky and creepy and hit way too close to home.

The scream comes again, this time much closer than before. But there's no one around. Another scream. Then another, as if whoever is screaming is in horrible pain. We run forward, down the long aisle of mutilated dolls. And when we reach the end, there is the tiny Asian girl from the room where we all started. She's spiked to the ground, with her arms and legs spread eagle, stuck with knives through her palms and her calves. Her long dark hair spreads out around her head and is tied to different implements that hold it in place. She shrieks when she sees us, but her eyes don't focus, like she can't even process the fact that we are here.

I run toward her but am stopped as a doll who looks exactly like the girl lands in front of me, holding a butcher's knife, as if she's ready to throw it if I dare interrupt.

I freeze.

"They're going to kill Grace!" Hudson says, pointing at the girl on the ground. He and Taylor are here, too, also being held back by psychotic dolls with weapons. Amid the dolls, I see one with a bow and arrows and scars on her face, just like Taylor. Another wears running clothes like Hudson. As I watch, a doll that looks exactly like my best friend Emily, dressed in an elaborate blue velvet gown with a matching blue derby hat, raises a spear above Grace.

The dolls chant, a spine-chilling jumble of words that dredges up images of voodoo rituals. Human sacrifice.

"No!" I cry out, but my plea does no good. The Emily doll in the blue gown lowers her hand and stabs Grace directly in the chest, over and over again as blood spurts out from her heart, spraying everywhere. The dolls are covered. We are covered. And Grace is dead.

Cole's face echoes the horror I feel. As we watch, her body fades the same way Adam's had, until it vanishes completely. Grace got here before us, making her the first victim, though I'm certain by the way the dolls turn their heads toward us that we'll be next if we don't get out of here. One at a time, they will take us down.

"We have to find the exit!" I scream, and we all raise our binoculars.

Through the augmented reality layer the binoculars create, I spot it immediately, there behind another doll with cropped brown hair who's dressed in a golden gown, her ghostly white face decorated with gold glitter. She's a third my size, but the spear she points at me could skewer me.

"Come closer," she hisses. "You know you want to."

The Greek letter Nu is behind her. We have to get past her.

Hudson grabs for her spear. It nicks his arm as he catches it below the deadly point. He uses it to lift the doll from the ground, tossing her flat on her tiny back in front of us. Cole kicks at the golden glittery doll as Hudson wrestles the spear from her hands. I stomp on her, again and again until there is no sign of movement from her. But no sooner is she subdued then ten more dolls take her place, aiming weapons our way. Our doppelgänger dolls are among them. The fact that there are four of us to fight is the only thing going for us. Grace had no one. Or if she did, they are now dead, too.

"Exit!" Taylor screams, as we battle the hoard of dolls.

"Are you sure you want to leave?" the voice of Iva says.

"Yes!" we cry in unison as the dolls trip over their fallen comrades in their effort to get to us.

The arched doorway illuminates. The dolls come faster, trying to stop our escape. We jump through the exit just in time, leaving the dolls and their psychotic world behind.

## NO ONE SPEAKS. THAT'S THREE PEOPLE

confirmed dead. Three kids just like us. Unspoken is that what just happened to the girl could have happened to any of us, especially if we had been on our own.

We pick Zone Phi next, and scan for the exit the second we pass through the entryway. The binoculars show nothing.

"Catch you all later," Hudson says, and takes off. So much for team work. Had he not just seen what happened to the girl with the dolls? Does he not understand that we need to stay together?

We're in a junkyard like none I have ever seen before. Stacked cars make up towers that stretch high into the infinite sky, but not cars like I'm used to seeing. These cars are five times as big and equally as wide. The cars of titans.

Beyond the stacked cars are enormous houses fallen into ruin with only their steel skeletons showing. Bones of the past.

"Did you guys see this?" Taylor asks.

She stands by a pile of junk holding a scimitar aloft. The blade is as long as she is tall and curves around like the crescent moon.

"It's a whole pile of weapons," she says.

Weapons are something with increasing value every second that ticks by. People are trying to kill us. The labyrinth is trying to exterminate us. I move to join her, but she swings the blade around just then. It makes a whooshing sound as it slices through the air, inches from me.

"Careful," Cole says, taking the weapon from her and replacing it in the pile. "This one's too big for you."

Taylor doesn't want to admit it, but Cole is right.

"I can handle it," Taylor says, reaching for it again.

Cole grabs it before her hand is halfway there. "It's not just the size," he says, and in a swift movement, he slams the scimitar down onto the ground, showing every single muscle in his arms as he does so. The blade cracks into four separate pieces, leaving Cole with only the hilt and a jagged piece of curved metal at the end. He tosses it aside.

"The metal had too many impurities," Cole says. "You would have noticed it yourself if you looked more closely. Plus, it was too big for you."

Taylor looks like she's going to argue with him, but he winks at her, and she amazingly keeps her mouth shut.

"Throwing knives," I say.

"What?" Taylor says.

"With your aim, you'd be the master of throwing knives. You could strap two to your legs and two to your arms." Not like I'm some expert, but it would be cool.

Taylor actually seems to consider this. She digs through the pile to see what else she can find. Me? I have no clue. My weapons have always been computer code. I used to think I wanted to be a hacker, back when I was eight. I wrote a program on Dad's computer that made it do all sorts of flipped out things like flicker the screen and have the mouse jump around from corner to corner. Needless to say, Dad was not thrilled.

I push things around in the pile with the toe of my combat boot, looking for something that might work. There are a bunch of shiny swords and knives, but they all seem too specialized. I do plenty of fighting in video games, but it's not like I've had sword training or anything in real life.

Cole digs into the stack and pulls out an ax that looks like it was discarded centuries ago. "Try this."

The wooden handle may have been polished in another life but now is splinted and dull. The metal doesn't come close to shining. But the second my fingers grasp it, I'm back in my family room, pulling the ax from the wall where Thomas accidentally threw it. It's the same ax that my parents had. The *exact* same ax, down to the split in the wood along the right side.

I balance the ax on my finger, watching its weight settle perfectly. Next, I use the edge of my jacket to wipe the blade, prepared to put in extra effort since it's so discolored that it doesn't even look like metal anymore, but when I rub the cloth of my jacket across it, it wipes clean. Shiny. Brand new.

"The metal's strong," Cole says. "It's going to last forever."

"My parents had this ax," I say. "And now it's here. What does that mean?"

"It means you need to keep it with you," Cole says. "For protection."

He's right. It's a part of my parents. A part of me.

I clip it on my belt where my knife was before I lost it in the den of the spider. I'm ready to face enemies. Which is good because in that moment, something flies through the open air, lands on the ground near the pile of weapons, and explodes.

## xli

**I'M THROWN BACKWARD, LANDING**
hard on my butt. Cole is next to me in a second, covering me.

"Watch out!" he yells.

There's no use being quiet. Whoever attacked us already knows we're here.

I shift around, trying to break free from under him, to fight, because otherwise we're all going to die. But Cole's not letting me up.

"Are you okay, Edie?" His eyes are filled with concern.

I do a quick check. Nothing feels broken or cracked. Maybe a few cuts here or there, but nothing serious.

"I'm fine," I say.

"You're sure?" he says, and his voice is filled with panic. His hands trace along my face. My neck. My sides and hips, as if he needs to feel it for himself.

"I swear."

Next to me, Taylor lets out a scream. I risk a quick glance. Blood pours from her leg.

"Oh, god, Taylor," I say.

"We need to get behind something," Cole says. He's off me and pulling Taylor to safety in what I hope is the direction opposite our attacker. I shimmy down the pile of weapons until I'm next to him.

"Get it out!" Taylor screams. "Now."

Embedded in Taylor's calf is a piece of cracked metal.

"Oh, Taylor," I say.

"Get. It. Out."

I clench my teeth and reach for the jagged piece of metal. It's slippery from her blood so I use the sleeve of my jacket to get a better hold of it, and I yank it out of her.

Her scream could wake cadavers. Blood gushes from the wound, but Cole is ready. He's taken off his shirt, and he quickly wraps the wound, round and round, staunching what he can of the blood. Tears stream down Taylor's face, and her breathing is coming hard, fast. I've never seen anyone hurt so badly before . . . at least not someone who's still alive.

Oh, god, Taylor can't die.

It'll be okay, I tell myself. She'll be fine. The bleeding will stop and everything will be fine. But I'm not very convincing. Taylor's face is pale, and the blood pours from her calf. So much blood.

"Show yourselves," someone calls from across the distance of the junkyard. A male voice. A voice I know well.

I clasp my ax tightly and dare to peek over the pile of weapons. Ahead of me is a battlefield. The ground smokes from where the explosion struck, leaving a crater in the ground. Far across the field of junk, leaning against a stack of scrap cars, is Owen.

He stands so confidently, back straight and head held high, sure no one will attack him. If Taylor wasn't hurt, she could put an arrow through his brain right now. I would welcome his death, as Homecoming and the visions blend together in my mind. Hatred burns in my belly, filling me so intensely that it takes my breath away. I've never known such hatred. The power behind it consumes me.

"Don't ask for—" I start, but I'm not fast enough in my words.

"Truce," Cole calls, interrupting me.

Truce is the last thing I want with Owen. Truce will block the path I have to follow.

Owen's response is laughter. Cold, harsh laughter.

"Forget truce," Owen calls. "Truce is for the weak."

He shifts so he's not leaning against the cars anymore, and he walks out into the open. Abigail comes around from behind the stack of cars to join him, and then they're locked in a kiss so unfitting the situation that I can't stop watching. The world seems to glow around them. When they finally separate, he licks his lips and smiles.

It's then that I see Hudson. My already tense body tightens to the point of snapping, because what if he's sided with Owen, too? He's staying hidden, off to the side, but when our eyes meet, he gives me a quick nod.

Relief. We may not be completely on the same side, but we have a common enemy.

Owen must hear something because he glances quickly to where Hudson hides, but when I look, Hudson is gone.

"Show yourself, coward!" Owen calls in the general direction of Hudson.

Hudson's only reply is something sailing in the air, toward Owen.

Owen laughs and dodges it easily. Some sort of spiked tire rim that must weigh a ton hits the ground exactly where he'd been. I look to where it came from.

No Hudson.

"I see," Owen says. "It's a game. Bring it on. You and I can play while your friends die."

One glance at Taylor tells me that Owen is not far from being correct. She bites her lip, but her face is so pale that I worry she's lost too much blood. I yank my jacket off and wrap it over the wound which has already soaked through Cole's shirt. My jacket is thicker and seems to hold back the blood better.

"It's Hudson," I whisper to Cole and Taylor.

Taylor's eyes can hardly focus. Her hand still grips the handle of her bow which lies at her side. She's not going to last much longer. Hudson continues to taunt Owen. Each time Owen gets angrier.

I place a hand on her cheek but flinch because it's like ice. "Just hold on a little bit longer."

Taylor grips her bow even harder in reply.

Another tire rim lands at Owen's feet. This time he barely jumps out of the way in time. It's like Hudson is screwing with him. Abigail has slinked back behind the stack of cars. Her eyes are wide as she watches the scene unfold in front of her. And yet, through it all, she looks amazing.

"I'm going to sneak over to Owen while he's distracted," I whisper to Cole.

"No you're not," Cole says.

"Yes, I am." I give him a look that tells him that I don't need protecting. That if anything, I am more up to this than he is. But I don't want to say this because it will only hurt his feelings.

"I'll go instead," Cole says.

"I'm going."

We listen to the battle, Hudson continuing to throw things, and Owen continuing to taunt him. They're both so competitive, but we're not talking baseball or track here. The game they play now is deadly.

"Fine, but we go together," Cole finally says.

Taylor's not going anywhere; she's nearly dead. Owen won't waste time on her.

"You need your jacket though," Cole says, and he reaches to

**247**

pull it from Taylor's leg.

I stop him with my hand. "She needs it more than me right now."

"But he has some kind of explosives. If he hits you . . . ," Cole says.

"I'm not afraid of Owen," I say, but my voice wavers. Stupid visions. They make me feel so weak. "My visions aren't real."

"So your visions are about him?" Cole says.

They build up inside me. They threaten to spill over. I have to keep them contained. Letting them out is showing my fear. I can't give in to things that aren't real. It's ironic given that I'm living in a virtual reality world right now.

"My visions—" I start, but our conversation is cut short as another spiked tire rim flies through the air. This one slams into the car Abigail hides behind. She lets out a shriek and runs to Owen. He looks pissed off, but she clings to his arm like he's going to save her from the world.

"Ugh, Edie. You drive me crazy," Cole says, but there's no time to talk about anything else right now.

We creep around the stacks of junk so we're ninety degrees from where we started. I catch glimpses of Hudson's shadow as he skirts around, throwing the wheel rims at both Owen and Abigail. We're silent, everything goes perfectly, until Cole's prosthetic catches on a rusty metal chain that's hooked on something. It causes a domino effect. The metal pile of junk begins to move, like a giant landslide. Metal scrapes on metal, and sparks fly.

Owen's face breaks into a grin, and then he sees me. His eyes meet mine. I am completely exposed and fear grips me. The ax at my side is forgotten. Owen reaches for a knife from the pile in front of him, almost lazy-like. Filled with a confidence he deserves in every manner. I'm back on the beach, asking him to stop and he's not listening. The visions paralyze me. Visions I hate as much as I hate Owen.

Cole lunges for me at the same time Owen releases the knife. It sails through the air, coming right for my chest. My legs won't move. I tense up, prepared to fall. Prepared for the knife to tear into me.

## xlii

**COLE KNOCKS ME OUT OF THE WAY JUST** as Owen falls to the ground.

"Is he dead?" Taylor says. She's dragged herself halfway to where we are and sits up with her bow clasped tightly in her left hand.

Across the clearing, Abigail kneels at Owen's side. She's ugly crying, and yet she still looks amazing. Her hands are clasped near her chest, as if she's holding her cross necklace. She can't have picked that to bring into the labyrinth. It's so useless. Yet her lips move in prayer, the same way they had on our journey.

Owen is flat on his back with an arrow protruding from his left thigh.

I hurry over to Taylor. "You shot him."

She nods and collapses onto her side. "He moved at the last second. Otherwise it would have gone through his heart. But the poison . . . it should kill him." She looks disappointed, and I realize then that she feels like she needs to make an excuse for her missed accuracy.

"You did good," Cole says, thinking the same thing I am. "Really good."

Hudson runs over to us. "I leave you guys alone for two seconds and you almost get yourselves killed."

"Can you help her?" I ask. Taylor isn't going to last much longer at this rate, especially given her recent exertion.

Taylor shakes her head. "Make sure he's dead first."

Abigail is trying to get Owen to his feet. He's reaching for his water bottle. But before he gets a chance, Cole takes off, picking his way through the carnage of junk. He kicks the water bottle out of the way and grabs a giant hammer, holding it over his head, aimed straight down at Owen.

"Don't move," Cole says.

Taylor lets out a gasp of pain, and worry creases Hudson's face. Then without another word, he uncorks his water bottle and holds it to Taylor's lips, forcing her to drink deeply.

Healing. Taylor will be okay. But if we can't get out of this labyrinth, the rest of us may not be.

"Is he dead yet?" Taylor asks as color returns to her face. Hudson gives her another sip, the last of his water bottle, then tosses it away. It clatters on the metal scraps behind him.

Cole is still holding Owen off with the hammer, but the blood has stopped flowing from the wound in his leg. He reaches down and in one single movement, he yanks the arrow from his thigh. I expect blood to spurt out or him to cry out in pain, but either of these things would make Owen almost seem human, which he's not. He's a monster.

There is no blood, no cry of pain. Owen snaps the arrow in half and tosses it to the side.

"Your poison didn't work," he shouts, and he kicks out at Cole's prosthetic, knocking him off his feet.

Maybe Cole's expecting it, because he's only down for a second, but it's one second too long. Cole and Owen square off, pacing.

**251**

Taylor must be getting her strength back. She grabs another arrow and nocks it, readying to take Owen out.

"Why didn't the poison work?" I ask her.

She sights down the arrow. "I won't need poison if I hit him in the head."

I'm not sure that will work if Owen has something to make himself invincible.

"I found the exit," Hudson whispers so only Taylor and I can hear. His binoculars are in his hand, but he holds them discreetly so Owen and Abigail won't see. "We should go now."

"I'm not leaving Cole," I say. Hudson can't possibly think I would.

"You have to," Hudson says. "He'll catch up with us later."

"No," I say.

Cole and Owen pace warily around each other while Abigail stands back. And in one quick, completely unexpected, movement, Cole swings the giant hammer forward.

He catches Owen totally off guard, and the hammer slams into Owen's head. Owen drops before the hammer even comes to a stop.

Abigail shrieks and runs to Owen. "You killed him!" she cries, and she grabs her cross again.

I only hope she's right, but I'm not going to wait around to find out.

"Come on, Cole," I yell.

Cole tosses the hammer down and runs across the field of junk to join us.

"What about Abigail?" Taylor says, nocking another arrow.

Abigail may have been traveling with Owen, she may have sided with him, but that doesn't make it right for us to kill her.

"Don't," I say, pushing her bow down.

Taylor raises it again. "Why shouldn't I?"

It's a good question. There needs to be a reason.

"Truce!" I yell across the battle field to Abigail.

She stops her prayers long enough to repeat the word. "Truce," she says. Abigail isn't stupid.

"Damn it," Taylor says, still holding her bow. "Why did you do that?"

"Because you're not a killer," I say, standing in front of the arrow.

She levels the arrow at my chest, just barely keeping the tip of the arrow from touching me. "Don't pretend you know anything about me."

I hold my ground. "Don't pretend you know anything about me either."

## xliii

**WE DON'T TALK. THE UNSPOKEN THREAT**
that Owen isn't dead looms. Taylor's poison arrow did nothing to
stop him. It wouldn't surprise me if a solid hit to the head won't
either. We exit Zone Phi and wind up in a pod identical to all
the others. Even as the doorway seals, I still clench my ax. Owen
and Abigail could be right behind us. And though Abigail has
accepted truce, Owen never will.

My head pounds, but I close my eyes and force the oncoming
vision away. I imagine my owl there with me, and even her imaginary presence comforts me. I imagine she glides through the air
and calls out to me, pulling me from the horrible visions. When I
reopen my eyes, Cole studies me but doesn't say a word.

"Eta."

"Kappa."

"Lambda."

"Phi."

The impassivity of Iva's voice mocks our near death.

"A circle," I say. "We've gone in a freaking circle."

Cole and I have been in this pod before. Futility threatens to bubble over inside me. What if we never get out of this place?

The Phi isn't lit because we just came from there. Eta is where the spider lives. If I go back there, she will kill me the second I pass through the door. Kappa is the forest zone, but we could survive again if we had to, I think. Not that there's much point in repeating the zone. It will only make our circle feel more futile.

"Eta, Kappa, or Lambda," Cole says.

Kappa or Lambda. K or L.

KL.

The second I hear them together like that, it clicks for me.

"Klam Stew," I say aloud.

"I thought it was disabled," Taylor says.

I shake my head and piece it through. KLAM STEW. None of the letters repeat. It's not only a debug code. It's a cheat code. That's what Zachary Gomez had told me. And in gaming, cheat codes give players a huge advantage. They can win games.

My eyes settle on each of my opponents. Or is it teammates? Cole, whom I trust completely. Taylor, who is a valuable ally even if her motivation is skewed. And Hudson, whom I hesitate to trust though he's saved both my life and Taylor's.

"KLAM STEW," I say, sharing what may be my most valuable card in getting out of the labyrinth first. "It's the way out. Kappa would be the first zone we'd take, but since we're between it and Lambda, we take Lambda."

"What? Like there's a pattern?" Hudson asks.

"Exactly. A pattern. A code that will lead to the end. It was written on the board in my prep room. My guy told me it was a cheat code."

"Your guy?" Cole says.

I shake my head. "The guy who was in charge of making sure I was ready. One of the designers. He told me it was a cheat code."

"Why would he tell you that?" Cole asks.

"Yeah, nobody told me anything," Hudson says.

"I don't know why he told me," I say, though truthfully I think he told me because he has a crush on me. "Does there have to be a reason? Maybe he wanted me to get to the end first. Who knows? But the fact of the matter is that this code could totally get us out. And if we don't hurry, that door is going to open and Owen is going to walk through. So do you want to stand around bickering about it, or can we just trust me here?"

All I can think about is getting to the end. Finding the power. And saving my parents.

I wave my hand over the circular pedestal, and the Eta, Kappa, and Lambda take turns lighting up. Three options. One ahead or two behind. If we choose the Kappa, we can't come back this way. We'll have to go around again, pass through everything: the dolls, the forest, the junkyard. Not to mention Zone Pi may not be back online.

"Which zone are you picking this time?" Iva's voice asks.

I hold my hand over the Lambda. The second letter of our KLAM STEW.

"Zone Lambda. Are you sure?"

"I'm sure," I say.

The door lights up and opens.

I don't check to make sure the others are following. I step through. This is the way I am going, and they are welcome to join me if they want.

## xliv

**ZONE LAMBDA IS FREEZING. I REACH**
to pull my jacket around me, but it's gone, left by Taylor in the
junkyard world in our hurry to escape. The weather is brutal,
making it feel like ice shards are digging into my skin. But I'm
not going to complain. I am alive.

We're in the middle of an endless landscape of snow and ice.
Wind blows against us, making the already chilly climate seem
even colder, fighting our every step. But we have to keep ahead of
Owen. We have to reach the end.

The labyrinth seems to sense our approach as we near the end
and begins throwing more at us, blocking our way. White boul-
ders come to life as ice monsters, tearing at our heels. Snow an-
gels innocently etched in the snow manifest and fly through the
air, chasing us with wings and teeth made of sharp ice. Bright
blood stains mark the snow as if others have made it this far and
then been killed.

We try to scan for the exit as we run, but slowing down at all is
deadly. We finally stumble into an icy cave, hoping to escape the

terrors of the outside. We're rewarded with the exit along with a thick layer of ice that covers it.

Cole uses up nearly all of his fire melting it as Hudson, Taylor, and I fight off the creatures that threaten us.

We make it through. And Owen has not caught up to us yet.

Zone Alpha is nothing but dark water. Things bite at our feet as we swim and dive, looking for the exit. Zone Mu is a giant hurricane that worsens with each step we take. I keep looking back, thinking I hear something. Someone. But each time, there is nothing I can see. Still, my skin prickles with Owen's presence.

He's not here, I tell myself. The only problem is that I don't believe myself.

In Zone Sigma, everything changes.

Cole and I stick to the back of the group. I can't believe I'd frozen up so much when confronted by Owen. It's so weak. Next time I won't make the same mistake. I keep my eyes forward so I won't have to look at Cole, because he must think I'm the biggest coward in the world. But even as I walk, I'm sure Owen is creeping up behind me. I jump at the smallest sound.

Cole grabs my shoulder and stops me. "Tell me what's going on."

I shrug his hand off my shoulder. "Nothing is going on." I can't make the visions real.

I glance back. I can't help it.

"He's not there, Edie," Cole says.

I look again. No Owen.

"He could be," I whisper.

"I'll protect you," Cole says.

"I don't need protecting."

"What did he do to you, Edie?"

"Nothing," I say. "End of story." But each time I close my eyes, rest for even a second, the visions are there. Owen hurts me, and he enjoys it.

"Tell me," Cole says. "Please."

I look into his eyes—one perfect, one misshapen from the scar his own stepmother may have given him—and I think that if I can't trust him, then I can never trust anyone again in this entire world. And that thought frightens me more than anything. It frightens me more than not reaching the power. It frightens me more than finding out the visions are real.

I bite my lip. Pick my words. "After Homecoming, Owen tried to force himself on me. I bit him and he stopped. But in my visions, he goes through with it. He rapes me and beats me, and if I try to fight, he kills me. And even though I know the visions are layered with lies, everything about them feels so real. Feels like it could have happened exactly that way and maybe I forgot. Blocked it out."

Cole's eyes harden. His hands ball into fists, and he opens his mouth like he's going to say something, but I can't stop now.

"I hate him so much. I want to kill him. I can't believe they're real, but what if they are? What if he did rape me and I've pushed it aside as a way to cope with it?"

Cole's eyes mirror the hatred I feel. "I'll kill him. I swear I'll kill him. If he comes near you. If he even speaks to you—"

Taylor and Hudson's arguing stops Cole mid-sentence.

"You are not skipping out on us," Taylor says, and she levels an arrow at Hudson's head.

Hudson backs up and puts his hands in the air. "And here I thought we were getting along."

I'd thought so, too. I'd actually entertained the notion that they were even flirting with each other, in some sort of competitive camaraderie, but obviously I am very wrong.

"Maybe we are," Taylor says, keeping her aim steady. "But that doesn't mean you should have an advantage. If Edie is right and this *KLAM STEW* thing is right, then we're only three zones away from the end. And when we get to the end, whatever alliance you think we have is gone. The truce will be broken. I intend to be the one who reaches the power first. And once I get it, I'm bringing Adam back."

We all have people we want to bring back from the dead.

At Taylor's words, Hudson laughs. "You may have great aim, but you'll never beat me there."

She pulls back on the string. "I will if you're dead."

"Whoa," Cole says, walking forward so he's between the two. Taylor's arrow now points directly at him. I want to yank him out of there, to tell him to get out of the way, but he's not a child. Cole can take care of himself. And Taylor would never slip up accidentally and let the arrow fly. But what if she let it go, not as an accident? What if, now that we are getting close, she's decided to eliminate whoever she can?

"Get out of the way, Cole," Taylor says.

He puts his hands out to either side. "Put the arrow down."

"No."

"Do it, Taylor."

"He's going to ditch us and make a run for it," she says. "I know he is."

"He's not," I say, though I don't fully believe my own words. Hudson's speed gives him a huge advantage.

"I'm not going to ditch you guys," Hudson says.

"Right. We take your word for that?" Taylor says.

"Trust him, Taylor," I say. "Hudson won't leave." I glare at him, telling him that if he does betray my trust, I will kill him myself.

Hudson gulps. Taylor is frightening. And vengeful.

"What Edie said. I'm not leaving."

The tension doesn't even come close to dissipating, but Taylor lowers her arrow.

"I'll kill you if you do," Taylor says. "Remember that."

I doubt Hudson will forget.

We decide to split up, to look for the exit. The plan is to meet back here in fifteen minutes. Taylor refuses to be paired with Hudson, so even though Cole is reluctant to leave me after what I've told him, he and Taylor take off in one direction while Hudson and I head in the other. We mark the ground with an X before we leave.

"Fifteen minutes," Taylor says, leveling her eyes at Hudson.

He ignores her and we set out. The terrain is hard packed dirt with a lot of nothing, reminding me of Texas when we drove across it. Hudson bounces back and forth on his feet, like he is dying to run but holding himself back. Taylor's arrow must've scared him.

"What does she think?" he asks. "That I'd just walk away? We do have a group. A truce. Right? And I may not be as noble as your boyfriend, but I'm not going to ditch."

"He's not my boyfriend," I say.

"Right," Hudson says. "Does he know that?"

I let out a laugh. "Cole hardly likes me. He has a girlfriend. It's the whole reason he's here."

"Look, I know you're smart, Edie. We all know that. But I also think you must be kind of stupid if you can't tell. It's painful how obvious it is."

I let it go at that. Hudson is just plain wrong, but I'm not going to argue with him now, especially given the fact that right then, something slithers over my foot.

"Snakes!" I say, jumping back. When I turn, there are more snakes behind us. They're everywhere.

Hudson stands his ground, letting the snakes slither over his boots and across his pant legs. "If you jump around, it's only going to upset them."

"I can't help it," I say, jumping again as a snake as thick as my arm twists up my leg. "Where are they coming from?" Before the snakes showed up, this zone was a barren wasteland.

Hudson raises his binoculars, somehow ignoring the snakes.

Then he points at a large boulder ahead. "They're coming from the exit," he says.

I lift my own binoculars to my eyes. Through the binoculars, the seemingly plain stone is intricately carved with orderly rows of designs and a thick seam around the middle. Light escapes from the seam, illuminating the Sigma symbol carved at the top of the stone. Curled around the base of the stone, and also only visible with the binoculars, is a snake so large, it makes an anaconda look like a baby. Its body is easily three meters in diameter, but it's hard to tell how long it is because it twists around on itself multiple times.

"A titan snake," I whisper, hoping the thing doesn't wake and see us here. I scoot closer to Hudson, taking tiny steps so my movement won't disturb the snake.

"You got any special snake tricks?" Hudson says.

"No snake tricks," I say, fighting the urge to fling the snakes away from me. Another climbs my legs, twisting around. "Get it off," I say between gritted teeth. It's almost at my waist. Two seconds pass then suddenly it's gone.

"Did you see that?" Hudson says.

"You got it?"

"I didn't do anything," Hudson says. "It vanished the second it touched your belt."

Another crawls up, then another, and each time, the snakes disappear. It's like my jacket is keeping them away except I don't have my jacket anymore.

"Whatever it is, keep doing what you're doing," Hudson says.

"We should go back and get Cole and Taylor," I say, still trying not to freak out.

I take a step backward into the mass of snakes. They slither everywhere, snapping as they crawl, curling back and forth, keeping me from leaving. If anything, they drive me forward, closer to the titan snake. They cover the lower half of my body, but they all vanish at the touch of my belt. I try not to think about them. I attempt to step backwards again. I lower my binoculars, but the snake is still visible.

The titan snake's eyes fly open.

I jump back, but the snakes behind me bar me.

*"What do you come for?"* the giant snake asks. But it's not talking with its mouth. It's using telepathy. Its words enter my mind.

*"The exit,"* I think.

"Be careful, Edie," Hudson calls from far behind me. How is he not up here with me? Why did the snakes not block his way?

*"Come closer so I can smell your fear,"* the titan snake says.

Its words pull me forward. Instead of terrifying me, they erase my fear. I am a worthy opponent to this creature. I shouldn't fear it. It should fear me.

*"Come closer so I can smell your fear,"* I say as I approach the snake.

The snake laughs in my mind. *"Good, Eden. You wear your bravery well. And for that, I will offer you something more than the exit."*

*"And what is that?"*

*"A prophecy,"* it says. *"Iva isn't the only one who knows the future. I can also show you what will happen."*

*"Will I reach the end first?"* I ask.

*"No,"* the titan snake says.

One simple word, but a word with the ability to destroy my hopes.

*"Don't be disappointed, Eden,"* the snakes says. *"Know that your sacrifice can mean saving everything."*

*"Which means what?"* I ask.

*"It means that you have to go with him, or everyone will die, including those you love,"* the snake says.

My parents.

*"I'm not going to let anything happen to my parents,"* I say.

*"Then remember what I said,"* the snake tells me. *"Also, know that*

*he is my enemy, too."*

"Who is your enemy?" I ask.

The snake hisses in reply. *"The fruit tastes delicious,"* it says. *"Now return to your friends. They need you."*

The titan snake doesn't need to tell me twice. I turn to leave. But before I do, on impulse, I reach out and touch the titan snake on the head. A flash of an image flows through my mind. An image where I'm opening my water bottle. I don't know what it means because my water bottle is empty. I lift my hand and the titan snake fades away.

When Hudson and I return to the others, Owen has found us.

xlv

## COLE AND TAYLOR KNEEL SIDE BY SIDE.

Taylor's bow lies on the ground in front of Owen, snapped in half. Owen has two swords, one strapped to his side where his knife should be and the other held in both hands, aimed at Taylor's neck. Abigail stands behind him, her gold and ruby cross clearly visible over her gray tank top. Her full red lips move in silent prayer. I'm pretty sure her prayers aren't for us.

We haven't been fast enough. Or somehow they've been following us.

"Stay where you are," Owen calls as soon as Hudson and I come into view.

"Run, Edie," Cole calls. "Keep going. Taylor and I can hold him off."

Given the fact that they're on the ground about to get their heads cut off, I'm not sure about that.

"Run and I kill Cole," Owen says, and he shifts the sword to Cole's neck. Cole flinches, and it's obvious that, with his missing leg and the prosthetic, he's miserable on his knees. The hatred on his face is palpable.

Just then a doorway opens, and someone else plunges into our world. He's holding a bottle and stumbles as he stands.

"Dominic," I whisper.

"You left me," Dominic says. But he's not talking to us. He's talking to Owen. "You drank all my wine, and then you left."

Owen rolls his eyes. "There is not 'all my wine.' Your bottle keeps refilling."

"That's not the point," Dominic says. "It's rude. That's the point. Everywhere I go, people ditch me. Leave me to fend for myself. I may take offense if it doesn't stop."

"Kill him, Edie," Taylor says. "Kill him for Adam."

"I hated Adam," Dominic says.

"Is that why you killed him?" Taylor says.

"Killed him?" Dominic says, taking a long sip from his bottle.

Owen looks from Taylor to Dominic and back again. Then he begins to laugh.

"What's so funny?" I ask, eyeing the sword in Owen's hand. I'm not fast enough to get it before he hurts Cole, but Hudson may be. I look to Hudson who seems to be thinking the same thing. His eyes are locked on the sword.

"Yeah, I'm curious, too," Dominic says. "Why are you laughing?"

"Nothing," Owen says, but his face disagrees. He's highly amused.

"I'm always the easy person to blame," Dominic says.

"That's what happens when you're a drunk," Owen says. He narrows his eyes and looks my way. "Edie, I've been having the craziest visions about you."

I shoot venom at him with my eyes, but my body begins to shake.

"I mean, they feel so real," he says. "And even though I know that what I'm doing is wrong, I can't stop myself. You drive me crazy."

Oh god. It's bad enough that I've been having the visions. Knowing that I share them with Owen makes me want to retch.

"They're not real, Owen," I say.

"So you've been having them, too?" Owen says. "I knew it! Tell me, when I'm about to kill you, are you relieved? Does it feel like I'm setting you free? Because that's what I imagine it feels like for you. Escape from this screwed up world. Like I'm doing you a favor."

Words cannot form past the rage inside me. How dare Owen taunt me? How dare he? I want to throw my fury at him, but I'm afraid if I open my mouth, all I will do is scream.

"Shut up or I'll kill you," Cole says.

Owen smacks him on the scarred side of his face with the sword, making Cole fall forward. When he rights himself, blood trickles down from a cut.

"Oh, did I cut you?" Owen says. "Better be careful or it might leave a scar."

He busts out laughing as does Dominic. But Abigail's eyes flick my way, almost as if she's apologizing for Owen.

There is no apology for him. He becomes more of a monster every hour he lives, as if something were born inside him and is only now manifesting. We're all changing in here, Owen not for the better.

"Tell me how to get out of here, Edie," Owen says. "Or I kill your boyfriend."

"He's not my boyfriend."

"So you won't care if I kill him then," Owen says.

I bite my lip, trying to buy time. Trying to figure out how to save Cole—save everyone—and get us out of here.

"Don't tell him, Edie," Cole says.

Does he think I'm going to watch Owen kill him?

"Put the sword down," I say.

"Not a chance," Owen says. "Tell me first."

**267**

Cole will die if I don't. But if I do tell him, then Owen could reach the exit first. This entire thing has turned into a mess beyond control. All I know is that I don't want Cole dead.

"*KLAM STEW*," I say. "It's a code. It leads the way we need to go." I spell it out for him slowly. "K-L-A-M-S-T-E-W."

"And the exit is at the end?" Owen says.

"Back away from Cole and Taylor."

Owen looks to his sword then lifts it from Cole's neck, taking a step backward, and then another.

"We should check it out," Dominic says. "But we should bring Edie with us."

The snake's words come back to me. *You have to go with him, or everyone will die, including those you love.* This is what the snake was talking about.

"Edie's not going anywhere with you," Cole says, then he's up and standing. But Owen still has the upper hand. He could throw the sword and stick Cole through.

"Very sweet of you to offer to come along," Owen says. "But all I need is Edie, thanks."

My skin crawls at the thought of joining Owen. I can't do it. I can't be with him. But if going with Owen will keep everyone safe, then I have to.

"I'll come along if you promise not to hurt the others," I say.

Cole looks at me like I've flipped. "No, Edie," he says, stepping forward. But Owen pushes him back with the point of the sword.

There is no other choice. The titan snake had told me.

"I'll be fine." I only hope my words are true.

*Find me,* I think to Cole. It's not hard to know where we're going. After Zone Sigma will be the T, then the E. We have the pattern.

It kills me to leave him, Taylor, and Hudson. But it's what I have to do.

Owen unclips his water bottle from his belt and holds it out.

"Mine's filled with explosives. If I see you in another zone, Edie swallows it. You understand?"

Cole looks ready to kill Owen on the spot, but the threat of the explosives keeps him back.

"Yeah, we understand," Taylor says. *Kill him if you get half a chance*, her eyes seem to say. Or maybe those are just my internal thoughts.

Dominic has chosen sides. He's coming with Owen, Abigail, and me. I lead them to the carved stone, wishing the titan snake were here now to devour them, but it's nowhere to be found. The doorway slides open, and we're into the next pod.

## I PRETEND OWEN IS SOMEONE I DON'T

know. I fight the headache every time the visions threaten to come my way. I don't look at him. I don't talk to him. I focus on getting away from him.

"You know what's funny, Edie?" Owen says.

I don't respond. Abigail hovers nearby but keeps her distance. Nothing is funny, and I don't want to talk to Owen.

"What's funny is that I really liked you," Owen says. "I mean sure, it started out as me trying to get help in class. You were like a genius and I was going to fail. And you were so willing to do my work for me. But then I started to think you were pretty cool."

"Whatever," I say.

"It's true," Owen says. "The more I liked you, the more I wanted to be with you. I started having these fantasies about you. About the things I wanted to do with you. And then at Homecoming . . . well, it's like some dark part of me took over and I couldn't control myself. Except I knew exactly what I was doing, and I didn't want to stop. In my visions I don't stop."

I bite my tongue to keep from speaking.

"And the thing is, when I texted you on Monday, you know, to talk about it because I couldn't freaking stop thinking about it, I was all set to meet you. I couldn't get you out of my mind. But then I went up to my room. And I swear I don't know how it happened but I really did fall asleep. I woke up four hours later."

"You are such a liar," I say. "How can you do that so easily?"

He gives me the puppy-dog look I used to think was so cute. It makes me want to vomit.

"It's not a lie," he says. "Something happened. Something made me fall asleep."

I don't believe him. It's just one more lie on top of the others.

"It doesn't matter," I say. "You're not the person I thought you were."

"Later that night, I had the first vision about you," Owen says. "I was up all night thinking about it. I wanted that kind of power all the time. It's addictive, you know. I lose myself in it every time the visions come. That power . . . it's why I have to be the one to reach the end first. I was meant to wield it. I know I was. It can't be anyone else."

"You make me sick," I say, stepping back. I want this conversation over. I want to be back with my friends. I want Owen dead.

Owen looks directly into my eyes and grabs my hands. I try to pull back, but he's holding too tightly. "I have to win, Edie. I've known it from the second we came to this place. Winning is the only thing that matters. I'll do whatever I have to in order to win. When I win, I'll have the power to do anything."

"What will you do?" I ask.

"I'll rule the world," Owen says.

He'll destroy the world. He has to be stopped. By me. By Cole or Hudson or Taylor. It almost doesn't matter at this point as long as someone stops him.

Owen releases my hands, and I step out of his reach. Dominic already has the pedestal active, and the arched doorway appears.

## xlvi

**ZONE TAU IS A MISHMASH OF SILVER**
metal. It stretches on forever, with nothing else visible.

"You're kidding, right?" Owen says.

"It's kind of pretty," Abigail says. "So shiny . . ." Her words
trail off. Abigail acts like she's almost drunk, but she hasn't been
drinking from Dominic's bottle, not that he hasn't tried. He's been
offering it to Owen and Abigail non-stop. He doesn't ask me.

"Pretty?" Owen says. "This place blows. It's like a fun house."

He's right. These aren't sheets of silver. We're in a world of
mirrors.

Owen and Dominic trail ahead, leaving me next to Abigail in
the rear.

"Why are you even with him, Abigail?" I ask once they're out
of earshot.

Abigail's eyes widen as they meet mine. "I have to be with him,
Edie. He's my soulmate."

I force myself not to laugh. "Owen's not anyone's soulmate. He
doesn't care about anyone but himself. How could you even think

that he does?"

"Because God told me," she says with enviable faith. To believe in something so completely must be comforting. "He told me it was my duty to stay with Owen. To help him get the power."

"You don't want to reach the power for yourself?" I figured that each of us wanted the same thing. That Abigail was just like the rest of us, trying to find the power to change the world.

Abigail shakes her head, making her long blond hair move in gentle waves. "Look at me, Edie. I never had a chance of getting to the end first. You know that. I'm not a survivor like you."

I hope I'm a survivor like Abigail thinks, because I have every intention of getting to the end.

"So what?" I say. "You just blindingly do whatever god tells you do to? You don't question it? Or ignore it?"

Abigail bites her lip, and tears form in her eyes. "I'm not a nice person like you think I am," she says. "I'm actually a really, really horrible person. Mother always told me I was, and I proved her right."

"You're not horrible," I say. Abigail may be vain, but she's not a bad person. And what kind of mother tells her kid she's bad anyway?

"I am. I did something awful."

"What?" I ask.

"I . . . Mother hated me. She always had, from the time I was a little girl. She despised the attention Daddy gave me, even though . . . it doesn't matter. She just couldn't stand to be in the same room as me. Never looked at me. I used to want her attention so badly. I would try so hard, dressing like her, talking like her. Sometimes I'd think things were going to change. We'd go out to lunch with the church ladies group. Her eyes would shine when she'd look at me and talk about me. She'd act like she was so proud of me. And no sooner than we'd get home, she'd tell me I was ugly. That I would never be good enough to be like her. So I'd just try harder. I used to think that maybe if I didn't spend special time with Daddy, she'd learn to love me, or maybe even like me a little. But Daddy never let that happen. Once I started going out more during the day with my friends, he'd visit me at nighttime, and even though Mother never said anything about it, I know she knew. And instead of being angry at him, she was jealous of me."

Oh, god. Is Abigail saying what I think she's saying? I look for other logic in her words, but there is none.

She goes on, almost like she's forgotten I'm here. "Mother got sick at church one day. Died right there near the altar with the entire congregation watching. We buried her a couple days later. Then it was just Daddy and me. And I . . ." Her voice trails off.

"You what?"

Deep breath. "I prayed for Daddy to die. I prayed so hard. Took all those prayers Daddy had forced me to memorize from the time I was a little girl, and I prayed and prayed. And one day, after Daddy left my room, I heard God's voice. God said he would kill Daddy for me if I helped him. I said yes without hesitation, and God killed Daddy that day. He tripped over an extension cord and fell from a balcony. I never regretted it. So when God told me to help Owen, I didn't even consider not doing it. God helped me, and I'm helping him by praying for Owen's survival. It's why the arrow didn't kill him. Why Cole's hammer only knocked him out. My prayers are keeping Owen alive."

Holy wow. I'm speechless.

"You think I'm awful, don't you?" Abigail says.

"You're not awful at all." I wish I could comfort Abigail, but the whole thing is a freaking mess.

She shakes her head. "It doesn't matter anyway. I know I'm doing the right thing. Otherwise God wouldn't be talking to me."

I'm not sure who Abigail's been talking to, if there is some god that is listening to her or if she's one hundred percent delusional. But I know she believes in this god, and maybe that's enough.

"I had no idea, Abigail," I say.

"No one did. Or they all pretended it wasn't happening."

If Abigail's god is real, then Abigail is a killer. Maybe not in the same way Owen is, and maybe for a better reason, but a killer nonetheless.

"Hurry up back there," Owen calls. He and Dominic have stopped walking about twenty yards ahead and wait for us.

Abigail's face softens and returns to the confident façade it was only minutes ago. "Coming," she says and runs toward him.

I take my time, trying to piece out my thoughts, as I join them.

"We need to get moving," Owen says.

Abigail releases the cross necklace that she's been holding constantly, like she's praying for him even now.

"Hey, Abigail," Dominic says. "You can look at yourself forever."

This fact is not lost on Abigail. She glances at herself constantly in the mirrored world, then bends down so she can study her face, which is of course flawless. "It's amazing," she says. "It looks just like me."

"That's because it is you," Owen says.

She shakes her head. "No. I mean like more than any other reflection I've ever seen. It's like another me is inside the mirror."

I can't resist glancing in a nearby mirror myself, and I'm met by my own face, looking back at me. But unlike any reflection, Abigail is right. There is another me in there. An Edie who is the girl I was before this all started. I still have a mom and a dad. I drive Thomas to and from school each day. I eat lunch with Emily and think about where I'm going to go to college.

But then the Edie in the mirror changes. Her face clouds over and her eyes darken and fill with disgust. *How could you have let him do those things to you?* she asks. *How could you have been so weak?*

*I'm not weak,* I tell her. *I'm not the person in the visions. They're in my head, but they aren't me. They will never be me. I will fight Owen until I can prove to this girl in the mirror and to myself that I am strong. That I am a survivor.*

I snap my head away from the Edie in the mirror, just as Abigail screams.

"Help me!" she shrieks.

Other than not being able to stand, nothing seems to be wrong with her. But Abigail is freaking out, twisting and turning like there's something on her and she can't get it off.

Owen grabs for her, but his hands pass right through her.

"What the hell?" he says.

"It's taking me," Abigail cries.

Dominic clips his bottle to his belt and joins Owen, tugging on Abigail, but the same thing happens. It's like she's no longer there. She manages to scramble to her feet, but connecting her to the mirror is a trail of white dust. It travels from her to the mirror, flowing like a river. Her cries grow quieter until there is nothing left but a whisper, and then even that is gone. And the place where Abigail once stood is vacant.

"What happened?" Dominic asks. His hands shake as he reaches for his bottle, but he stops himself short.

"I was looking in a mirror," Owen says. "I didn't see."

I was looking in a mirror, too. We all were. It had drawn each of us, and Abigail it had kept.

"She's in there," I say, staring down at the spot where Abigail once stood. Abigail's face stares up from the mirror, panic etched in her expression. Her hands press upward on the glass, but she is trapped below. Owen kicks at the glass with the heel of his boot, but it doesn't shatter. He hits it with the hilt of his sword, but it makes no difference. The glass is not breaking.

*Look away,* I think. The reflection has captured Abigail. If I look again, see more of myself, it will do the same to me.

Again, Dominic reaches for his water bottle but stops before he unclips it, as if something in the mirror has made him want to stop. Something he has seen about himself.

"We need to find the exit," Owen says.

"You're just going to leave her here?" I say, hardening my voice as I speak to him. I am strong. I am not the person in the visions.

Owen turns away from the mirror. I guess he's smart enough to have figured out to not look in it, too. "I tried to break it. You saw me. What else am I supposed to do?"

"But she's trapped in there," I say.

"And I can't waste time trying to get her out," Owen says. "I have to get to the end first."

"But she saved your life," I say. "She helped you."

"And now her job is done. I'm alive," Owen says. "And the only thing that matters is getting the power. Abigail knows that. She'd want me to leave her here and keep going."

Owen is seriously psychotic. Iva's visions of the future almost pale in comparison to what Owen would really do with the power. But the worst part about what he says is that I think he's right. Abigail would want him to leave her here and keep going. It makes me sick to think about.

"What do you think happens to her in the real world?" Dominic says. "I mean she's not dead. Not really. Which means she must still be alive in the real world, too."

Alive, maybe, but trapped in this virtual world forever.

"Maybe," Owen says, but the tone of his voice says that he doesn't really care one way or the other. He begins to walk away.

"So that's your answer?" I say. "We're leaving her here?"

"That's my answer," Owen says. "It's her own fault for looking at herself so much. It's just a shame she won't be there to pray for me anymore. Now I just have to be careful not to die."

It gives me a small amount of hope to know that, in the wake of Abigail's demise, Owen has lost his advantage.

"You see the exit anywhere?" Owen asks, scanning the horizon with his binoculars. He's moved away from Abigail who's still clawing at the mirror that traps her. She opens her mouth as if she's screaming, but we hear nothing.

"All I see are mirrors," Dominic says.

"Edie?" Owen says.

*Ignore him,* I think.

No, that's the weak Edie talking. I am better than Owen.

"Edie," Owen says again. "You see the exit?"

I look through my own binoculars. "Nope."

This place is its own maze of mirrors. And if Abigail is trapped inside one, then maybe the exit is, too, because there is nowhere else for it to be.

We continue onward until, through my binoculars, I see a change in the landscape. A small shift in the reflection that fills the unending mirror world. I give a small start before I catch myself.

"What do you see?" Owen asks.

"Nothing."

With his free hand, Owen grabs my arm, squeezing until his fingers press the bones of my arm. "Tell me what you see."

"No." I'm not sure why I'm bothering being obstinate about the whole thing. It's Owen and Dominic against me. If I was smart, I would pretend to cooperate.

"Really, Edie?" Owen says.

The smart side of my brain takes over. The side that tells me to play along. Bide my time. And constantly look for an advantage. "About fifty yards ahead. Do you see how the reflection shifts?"

Owen takes his eyes off me enough to look through his binoculars to where I'm pointing. I could try to overwhelm him. Take him by surprise and grab his bottle of explosives. And then what? Have him fight me to get it back?

He squints but must not see it because he nudges me with the end of the sword. "Lead the way."

I keep the reflection in the edge of my vision because if I look

**277**

at it full on, it blends into the mirrors all around. But in my pe-
riphery, it bends differently in the light. It's only when we're about
ten feet away that I can actually see it face-on: a giant T in the
concave mirror. Across from it, there is nothing being reflected.
Like Abigail.

"Exit," Owen says, like he need to prove he's the one in charge.
Like he already has the power.

"Are you sure you want to leave?" Iva asks.

"We're sure," Owen says without another glance back in Abigail's direction. The door slides open.

## xlvii

**ZONE EPSILON . . .**

Fog fills the air, blanketing everything. Cole, Hudson, and Taylor are waiting. I have no idea how they've managed to get ahead of us, but whatever magic they pulled may save all our lives.

Hudson catches Owen off guard and grabs Owen's water bottle. One hard yank, and the entire belt comes loose. Hudson tosses it far across the foggy expanse. When it lands, there's a giant explosion that shakes every bone inside me. The fog is so thick that all I see is the orange glow of a fireball.

"Gotta love shot put," Hudson says once the echoes from the explosion have settled down. "Did I mention that I won first in state in that, too?"

I could hug Hudson in this moment. Him with all his bragging about how great he is at track and field. I'll happily take that bragging if it means Owen is now at a disadvantage.

Owen regains his composure quickly and grabs me around the neck. He twists one of my arms behind my back. I scream out from the pain, sure he's going to dislocate my shoulder, but he holds it steady.

"Where's your knife, Owen?" Taylor asks, clutching the hilt of hers. I'm willing to bet that, though it may not be her weapon of choice, she's still pretty deadly with it.

"I lost it," Owen says.

"You killed my brother," she says. "You threw your knife into his back."

Owen laughs. "I thought you said Dominic did it."

She narrows her eyes. "I was wrong."

"You don't know that," Owen says.

"I do," Taylor says. "I saw it in a vision. I couldn't see who it was for the longest time, but this last time, there you were. You killed him."

"You're going to believe some stupid vision from a crazy little girl?" Owen says.

Isn't that what we're supposed to do? What Iva wants us to do? She makes them real. Taylor's vision had come true. Cole's may be true also. And mine . . .

"Why would you think it was me?" Dominic says. "We had a truce."

Taylor scowls at him. "Because you drink too much."

"So you thought I killed your brother? Because I like a drink here or there?"

"Yeah, I did."

"Funny," Dominic says. "Because you're right. When you got yourself captured by the trees, Adam blamed me. He came after me. And I may be a coward. I may even be a drunk. But I'm not going to stand around and let anyone talk to me the way he did."

Taylor's eyes widen. It's like she can't believe the words. "You actually did it?"

Taylor's visions are laced with untruths.

"So what?" Dominic says. "It's one less person in this screwed up place to worry about getting to the end."

With no warning Taylor lunges for Dominic, clasping her knife tightly. But Dominic isn't as slow and unaware as he looks. He darts to the side and begins to run. Cole takes the chance and raises his left leg, kicking Owen in the knee with the hard metal of his prosthetic. Owen loses his balance, and I elbow him in the side then the mouth. He spits blood and a string of curse words.

"No, Taylor!" Hudson yells, drawing all our attention.

Dominic is flat on his back, and Taylor straddles him. Her right arm is lifted, the knife pointing downward. She ignores Hudson and plunges the blade into Dominic's chest. Again and again, in horrific imitation of the Emily doll in the blue dress, until she's covered in his blood and Dominic stops fighting. As she stands, his body fades away.

Even Owen is speechless. Taylor turns to face us, still clenching the dripping knife, covered in Dominic's blood. She points the knife at Owen. "Don't you dare cross me. And from this point forward, there is no such thing as truce. Truce means nothing. What matters is finding the power and getting the hell out of here, everyone for themselves."

It's a horrible idea. Calling off our truce means that no one can be trusted. I trust Cole, but disbanding our truce means that I can no longer trust Taylor or Hudson.

"But don't you guys get it?" I say. "We have to work together. The last level is always the hardest. If we think spiders and mirrors are tough, then what do you think the final zone will throw our way? Monsters? Demons?"

"I'm not scared of monsters," Owen says. "And as far as I'm concerned, we can split up now. It's everyone for his or herself." He gets to his feet and brushes himself off, limping slightly. Cole's kick was hard. Owen will definitely have a bruise.

We face off in the circle, Cole and I together, Taylor, Hudson, and Owen alone. We're all that's left. One of us will get to the end first. Get the power. The others will be left to wander this place for eternity.

Hudson puts up his hand. "If you'll excuse me," he says, and he's off and running through the fog. In two seconds, I can no longer see him. Owen growls in his direction, but he's no match for Hudson's speed, especially given that the fog makes visibility nothing but a pipe dream.

Taylor's face is drawn tight. Her eyes don't focus. Blood drips down her arms. I worry that she's gone over the edge. That her sanity has slipped away with the death of her brother though she's gotten the revenge she so desperately craved.

Owen reaches for his binoculars before remembering that his belt is gone. "Shit," he says, and takes off, maybe hoping to find Hudson.

Taylor is gone next, not bothering with a goodbye. This leaves only Cole and me.

"I'm glad you're okay," Cole says, then he shifts the tiniest bit forward, like he's going to kiss me.

I freeze, not daring to move, wondering if I should lean forward to meet him, wanting to, but not wanting to risk rejection. Wondering if he's thinking about Pia now that we're so close to the end. So I don't move, and the moment slips away.

"God, I was worried about you," Cole finally says. "After what you told me . . . I couldn't think straight."

I squeeze his hand, wishing the moment would return, knowing it won't.

"I'm glad you were worried," I say.

Reality drifts back to us and with it the painful reminder that our challenge is far from over. I unclip my binoculars and scan the fog, and though the others have run off, we walk hand in hand, searching for the exit. Growls and screams come from all around us, making the fact that we can't see anything that much more horrible. Anything could be beyond the fog. But whatever is out there keeps its distance, letting us pass, as if the true enemies in this zone are each other.

"You think we'll get through this okay?" I ask when we finally spot the exit through the mist. It drifts and moves but stays together.

"We'll get through it," Cole says. "I can tell these things."

His confidence is infectious. I want to believe. The two of us being together has to be more than a coincidence. We are a team. We've kept the truce. That means something.

"Exit," I say, and the glowing outline of the exit door appears in the mist.

When we step through, into the pod, everyone is there waiting. And I can't understand why they haven't gone on without us.

"It's a dead end," Hudson says, holding his hand over the panel. "Epsilon is the only choice, and it's not active since we just came from there."

"It can't be a dead end," I say, releasing Cole's hand and walking over to join Hudson.

"Can't be, but it is," Hudson says.

Owen narrows his eyes at me. "How do we get out of here?"

I don't know.

## xlviii

**THINK COMPUTER GAME. IT KEEPS GO-**
ing through my mind as I try to puzzle out the solution. We're
trapped in the pod. There is no other way out. And yet there has
to be.

I press every spot on the pedestal looking for more letters. I
walk the perimeter of the pod, feeling along the wall. I can't even
feel the door we came through, so my hopes of finding a second
door, if there is one, are pretty much nil. But I have to try. My
parents are so close.

"What's the Greek letter for W anyway?" Taylor says. "Why
isn't Iva telling us?" Dominic's blood has dried on her face, mingling with the lines from her own blood.

I go over all the Greek letters I know. All the ones Mom used
to scribble around the house. *The Greek alphabet doesn't have as
many letters as our alphabet, Edie,* she used to say. *We have silly
letters that we don't need. The Greeks got smart and got rid of them.*

"What are we looking for, Edie?" Hudson says.

I don't answer him because Hudson is no longer on the same

team as me.

Owen says nothing. He's waiting for us to find a way into the next zone.

I try the pedestal again. There is only Epsilon. Iva repeats it over and over. But this computer game has to follow rules like other games. It's the nature of programming. And what had Zachary Gomez said? That the game was made up of twenty-eight zones but that five of them were hidden. Maybe the letters the Greeks got rid of make up the hidden zones. Maybe Zachary had been hinting at that.

*You have to find it on your own, where everyone else has forgotten,* Mom had said on the voicemail. *You have to remember.*

She'd always gone out of her way to tell me about those discarded letters. They had funny names, mixed up names of other letters. Like Sampi. And Koppa. And . . . what was the W letter? I remember it because it looked nothing like a W. It was more like a quirky F. She used to write it when she wrote Dad's name in Greek. It's right on the tip of my tongue.

*You have to remember.*

"Which zone are you going to pick this time?" Iva's voice says as my hand hovers over the console.

"Like there's a choice," Hudson says to her.

But there is a choice. We just can't see it. Then it comes to me. Mom had the letter tattooed on the inside of her wrist. I remember.

"Digamma," I say. The Greek W. Discarded.

No sooner are the words out of my mouth, than the circular pod slips away. The labyrinth dissolves. And in its place are the grid lines, surrounded by blackness.

"Zone Digamma," Iva says. "Are you sure?"

We found it. I found it. The final zone. It's all come down to this moment.

"We're sure," I say.

The black grid lines get replaced by a world of musty brick. Less than a second later, something hits me on the side of the head, and everything goes black.

# xlix

**I WAKE SITTING AT A LONG WOODEN**
table. Cole is next to me, hands bound and tied to spikes that
have been embedded into the thick wood. Across from me are
Hudson, Taylor, and Owen, bound the same way as Cole and I.

A low growl comes from the head of the table, but it's cloaked
in blackness, as if a monster is here with us yet hidden from view.
The growl is visceral. It evokes in me such fear that I'm not sure I
can stand it. My vision darkens, and in its place comes an image
of my younger brother, Thomas, tied to a large wagon wheel, arms
and legs spread. The wheel rotates slowly. Knives spin through the
air, barely missing him. And Cole is the one doing the throwing.

"Let him go!" I scream, but the words won't come out. I try to
run to him, but my legs won't move. My chest won't contract. I
stand still, unmoving, as I watch my brother being tortured. I'm
helpless to stop it.

The image shifts away as the fog is lifted from my mind. But
the growl remains. Then a sound, like a claw tracing along the
wood of the table, scraping until I have to cover my ears, except I

can't since my hands are bound to the table.

"Stop!" Cole screams next to me. His head thrashes around, and underneath the table, his leg and prosthetic kick, like he's desperately trying to flee whatever horrors he's facing.

"Let her go!" he screams, and I know he's talking about Pia.

Owen, Taylor, and Hudson move and scream the same way we do, and though, maybe it should bring me satisfaction to see Owen humbled like the rest of us, if I could cut him free in this moment, I would.

From the darkness, another growl builds. I press my eyes closed, preparing for the worst, but I'm not prepared at all. I'm surrounded by fire. Flames lick at my boots. My pants. The heat is unbearable. Standing outside the ring of fire is Cole, fueling the fire, burning me alive.

I shriek until my throat is raw, but it does nothing to stop the flames.

"Stop screaming," someone says, except I can't stop screaming. I have no control of myself. The flames continue to consume me. The pain is everything.

Then, like the image of Thomas, the flames are gone.

I collapse back in my chair, gasping from the effort of it. It had been so real. Death was so certain. Once my breath settles, I risk glancing down. I am completely unharmed. No sign of flames or fire. But Cole is still screaming. He twists and begs for mercy. His cries join Hudson's. Owen and Taylor, like me, have collapsed.

Another wave of pain and torture hits. All thoughts are erased from my mind. And when it is over, I fall head first onto the table and pass out.

## WHEN I WAKE, I SIT ON WET GROUND

in the middle of a forest, leaning against a hard tree. Across from me, collapsed on the ground in a heap, is Cole.

I rush over and help him sit upright.

"Make it stop," he moans.

"It's over," I say.

"Make it stop."

I hug him close to me, giving him whatever comfort I can. "I'm here, Cole. It's Edie."

"She cut it off," he says, shaking his head back and forth. "I didn't think she really would. She threatened to. But I never thought she would really cut it off."

"She didn't cut it off," I say.

Cole doesn't seem to hear my words, like the visions have consumed him.

"It's not real," I say. "And neither is what Owen did to me. Those things never happened. We can't give in to them."

At the mention of Owen, Cole's eyes regain clarity. "Where is he? Has he been here? Did he hurt you?"

I shake my head. "I haven't seen him."

"I swear to god, if he comes near you again, I will tear him apart with my bare hands," Cole says.

"Just don't leave me, okay?" I say. And I lean forward, closing the distance between us, and press my lips on his, not letting the moment slip away one more time. My hand is still on his face, and I trace my fingers over the scar, testing his reaction, which doesn't disappoint. Cole's mouth joins mine and we're kissing. We're already close, but I cross my leg overtop him and press myself closer, letting my lips part, wanting this moment to last forever, knowing that this moment is real, even in this virtual world.

His arms pull me to him hungrily, and his fingers comb through my tangled hair and trace along the back of my ears. Shivers travel everywhere in my body. Thoughts of Pia vanish from my mind in this kiss. She may be part of his past. Maybe even part of his future. But right here, right now, it's about the two of us, and nothing is going to intrude. Not a girlfriend. Not false visions.

Cole rolls me onto my back and wraps his arms around me. I

trail my fingers across his back, loving the way his muscles harden and shift at my touch. Knowing that everything is right about this moment. All I want is for this to last for eternity.

"Don't you dare tell me this is a mistake," I say between kisses.

"Not a mistake," Cole says, breathless. "I've been wanting to do this forever. Since the first time I saw you."

"Then why didn't you?" I ask.

Cole kisses my neck, below my ears. It makes every part of me feel alive. "I didn't want you to say no."

"I wouldn't have," I say.

"My own stepmom rejected me," Cole says. "Why wouldn't you? To this point, there's only been one other person in the world I could trust."

"Pia."

He nods.

"You're in love with her," I say, not wanting to hear his answer but needing to.

"I was. She was perfect in so many ways. She saw through the scars. Saw past the ugliness."

I fight the jealousy that runs through me. I will not be jealous of this girl. She's had a hard enough time as it is.

Maybe my face gives away more than I want it to.

"But then I met you," Cole says. "And maybe I thought I loved Pia, but I was wrong. You made everything change for me. You're all I can think about. All I want, ever."

His words are the sweetest music I have ever heard. He leans down and kisses me again. And that kiss is the only true moment of perfection I can imagine. I can erase the labyrinth—maybe erase the entire world—and lose myself in the kiss forever.

"You lied to me," a voice says, disrupting us from the moment.

We both look, and Cole rolls off me. A girl with cropped brown hair that frames her face like a pixie watches us from about ten meters away.

"Pia?" Cole says.

This is Cole's girlfriend. Oh my god, she's here.

Her eyes narrow at the two of us together. "It doesn't look like you've missed me very much. In fact, it looks like you've forgotten about me."

"I did miss you," Cole says, getting to his feet. "I came all this way for you."

"I trusted you, Cole," she says. "You were all I had. After middle school, after those horrible girls were so mean to me, you let me think I could believe in you. You told me you'd always be there for me. I thought we had something so special. Something that would last. And now I can't believe it. I find you here, with her."

I want to shrink and hide, but I hold steady at Cole's side. Something is way wrong. This can't be Pia.

Cole raises his hands in offering. "I'm here to save you, Pia. I swear."

"All you're doing is killing me," Pia says, and she pulls her hand from behind her back, exposing a broken mirror shard clenched between her fingers. Before Cole or I can move, she draws it across her wrist, cutting deep.

Blood gushes everywhere, copious amounts. Pia switches hands and cuts the other wrist. "You killed me, Cole," she says. "You did this to me. You are no better than the girls who tormented me. I hate you."

Her face whitens and the blood drains from her body.

Cole starts to run for her, but I grab his arm, holding him back. "No, Cole. Look."

Pia's blood is nearly drained, making her skin paler with each second that passes. And when the blood stops flowing, Pia begins to morph. No longer alive, she shifts into a life-sized version of the doll in the golden dress from Zone Nu, her doll doppelgänger. Like the doll, Pia's face is ghostly white and decorated with golden glitter. She opens her mouth, exposing teeth that have been sharpened into points. She curls her hands, flexing fingers with nails filed into razors.

Then she lunges for us.

## I

**WE TAKE OFF, RUNNING THROUGH THE**
forest. The doll who was Pia is right behind us.

"Faster!" I yell to Cole though he's going as fast as he can with
the prosthetic. She's gaining on us with every second. Or at least
I think she is. My legs pound. I run until I feel like I'll drop if
I take one more step, and only then do I dare to glance over my
shoulder.

There's no sign of her.

"Do you see her?" I ask.

"That wasn't Pia," Cole says, breathing hard next to me. It's like
he has to convince himself by saying it.

"It was another trick," I say. "We need to stay alert."

Ahead, the forest path widens and the brick walls return. Along
the path, there are signs of a monster everywhere. Gouges in the
bricks as if made by claws. A pile of stinking feces, still warm with
flies buzzing around it. Human fingers, bleeding, freshly cut, but
from whom I'm not sure. Who is left besides the five of us? Each
sign we find sends a fresh wave of fear rolling through me. Images

of my family burning. Of Thomas drowning. Of the world dying. Each image is worse than the one that came before it. Each brings death to those I love.

Cole shudders as the waves of fear roll through him. Knowing what his visions are makes my heart ache for him. How are we supposed to distinguish the lines between reality and fantasy?

*"Come to me."* The monster speaks in my head.

A quick glance to Cole tells me that he's heard the same thing. This zone is ruled by a monster who taunts us, hunts us, feeds our minds with horrors.

Cole gives my hand a quick squeeze. "We're in this together."

"Together," I say.

Yet as much as I want to believe this, if only one of us can get the power, what will happen when we reach the end?

*"Closer,"* the monster says. Its words are slippery, flitting around my mind with echoes and images of the very fear it breeds. "Let me see you."

I will not let this monster feel my fear. I will conquer it.

We turn the corner, and the dark, enclosed brick corridor spills into a brightly lit English garden, exactly what I would expect to find at the center of a garden maze. The sun shines down, instantly warming my skin and lighting the world. The center of the garden has a fountain, and at the center of the fountain is a tree, twice as tall as I am, with golden leaves that flutter in the gentle breeze. A single golden apple hangs from the lowest branch, shriveled as if it's at the point of dying.

*You have until the fruit dies,* Iva's voice echoes in my mind.

This is the power.

This is what I've come all this way for. So close, and yet unattainable, because next to the tree is a monster, and clasped in its enormous arms is Hudson, slumped over like he's dead.

The reality of the monster is worse than anything I could have imagined. Its shoulders reach over fifteen feet in the air, and it has a gargantuan neck that supports its hideous head. Two horns like a bull sprout from the head of the beast, dripping with thick mucus as if they've impaled victims for centuries and never been cleaned. It has fangs the size of fingers, fingers the size of footballs, and thick skin like leather armor covered in dark bristly hair. Its legs are packed with muscles bulging out of its thighs and calves, and where its feet should be are two cloven hooves instead.

Owen and Taylor stand together, beyond the edge of the fountain, outside of the monster's grasp. The fountain, rather than being filled with sparkling blue water, is piled high with bodies. Bodies I begin to recognize. Tattoos. Red hair. Thick dreadlocks.

It's the bodies of our dead. The monster has dragged them back here, to its lair.

"Not good," Cole says.

The monster is unstoppable. Hudson must've gotten to the tree first, but this time, his speed is his undoing. The monster tosses him aside like a discarded toy, knocking him into the stones that make up the fountain of bones. If he is still alive, it's a blessing that he's passed out.

*"Who's next?"* the monster speaks in my mind. Then it roars, so loudly that behind me, bricks fall from the walls of the pathway we just came from, raining down on the hard ground below.

The monster reaches for the fountain and begins pulling pieces of bodies out, tossing them at us. I duck as an arm flies over. A sword, snapped in two. Boots identical to the ones I wear. When it reaches for short bleached hair and lifts Adam's head into the air, Taylor loses it.

"Put my brother down!" she screams. Rage fills her face, so thick it ripples off her. Owen backs away, but Taylor doesn't seem to notice. She steps forward, solid on her two feet. She has no weapons left. Nothing to fight this monster with except her anger. But maybe it's enough.

The monster turns its hideous face to her, still clasping Adam's head in its thick fingers. It holds the head forward, taunting her, and it opens its mouth into a grin, exposing sharp white fangs covered in gore.

*Come and get me,* it seems to say, and then it lets out a low growl, filling the air with the sound of its awesomeness.

Taylor takes another step forward. Then another. And in response the monster brings its arm around in a giant circle to gain momentum and tosses the head.

Adam's head lands on the ground, rolling until it comes to a stop when it touches Taylor's feet. She doesn't even look down. In a single motion, she leaps over the head of her twin brother and begins to run, straight for the monster. It's going to kill her with one swipe.

My fingers dig into Cole's arm. "We need to help her."

He unhooks his water bottle and opens it, and a fireball bursts from it, straight toward the monster. It's a solid hit, but it doesn't even darken the thick leather, and it doesn't draw the monster's attention. The monster has its sights set on Taylor.

When she reaches the stone of the fountain, she jumps onto it and uses her momentum to propel herself up and over the top of the monster. She lands on its broad shoulders, grasping its massive horns with her hands. The monster flails its head, back and forth, trying to throw Taylor. It reaches its arms around in an attempt to grasp her, but its thick arms aren't long enough. It can't get to her.

She twists at the horns, as if she's trying to break them off, but also like she is trying to not die.

I'm a horrible person, because in that moment, I have a thought. A single thought I can't get rid of. Now that the monster is distracted, I could make a run for it. I could make it to the tree. The power of the gods is in my grasp.

No.

But the thought persists.

I won't follow through on it. Never. What I'll do is help Taylor.

Owen has the same thought I do, and apparently no guilt about it, because he's already edging forward, trying not to draw the attention of the monster. He skirts along the edge of the fountain, even as Taylor and the monster stay locked in battle.

I can't let Owen get to it first. Everything that is still right in the world will be ruined. He'll destroy everything.

"I'll take care of Taylor and the monster," Cole says. "You get to Owen."

One look, and I know we are in agreement. We can do this, together.

I take off running. I risk a quick glace back to see Cole moving toward the monster and Taylor. It's a mistake. He is defenseless. Unarmed. Unshielded. But I can't help him now.

Owen pulls my thoughts back to what I need to do. He's only a few feet away from the tree. I leap through the air, falling against his chest and knocking him to the ground onto his back. Then we're locked in battle. He reaches for my face, my eyes. I twist my head enough that his thumbs miss my eyes, but they press into the bones of my cheeks, while the rest of his fingers pull my ears forward.

"I'm going to get it!" he screams between gritted teeth. "You can't stop me. You've never been able to stop me. Don't you see that?"

The truth behind his words hits me. It's the visions all over again. He's on top of me, forcing himself on me. I'm helpless to do anything about it, and he violates me even as I beg him not to. I fight and kick and punch, but he never stops. The vision is like a memory that will never go away. In the memory I am completely helpless.

I am not helpless here.

I knee Owen hard in the crotch, trying to drive my knee up through his torso and out his mouth. Owen's confident words fall away and he crumples into a ball, rolling off me, releasing my head and face. I scramble around, trying to find something to fight him with. The fountain is filled with bodies and bones. I wrap my fingers around something and bring it down hard on Owen's head, catching him while he's still weak.

But I'm not giving Owen enough credit. Adrenaline fuels his battle. He's on me in seconds, pressing my back into the hard stone ground, grinding my head into the bricks until I'm sure the hair is being torn from my scalp. I hear screaming and realize it's coming from me, which is attracting the monster's attention. A fist slams into my face and then another as Owen is caught in his bloodlust, unaware of anything else going on around him. My head spins. He hits me again. And again. I bring my arm up to block my face. I can't let him hurt me anymore. I twist under him, fast, using his own mania as a distraction. He raises his arm, ready to strike again, but I'm ready. I pull my binoculars from my belt and hit him upside the head.

I don't wait for the stars in my head to clear. While he's stunned, I roll out from under him. I try to get up, but nearly fall over as my head spins. I have to get to the golden apple before Owen.

Cole's running for me, leaving the limp body of Taylor at the monster's feet. I try to open my mouth and call his name. To tell him to run for the tree instead of me. To make this end. I stagger to my feet because he's not listening, but Owen punches me in the stomach, knocking the wind from me. I fall to the ground, still at least ten feet from the tree. So close, but I can't move. And yet I have to.

Something digs into my back, but I don't have the energy to move. Cole reaches me, leaning down and lifting me from the ground so I'm sitting up. Blood fills my mouth. My vision swims. His face moves in and out of focus.

"Too late!" Owen screams, and he staggers towards the tree. He's going to get the power. It's all going to be over.

That can't happen. My hand travels to my belt. I unhook my ax and throw it as hard as I can. My hands shake. My aim is off. It's never going to hit. The ax spins through the air, end over end, until the blade lands solidly in the center of the golden apple.

The apple splits clean down the middle. Both halves drop. One half rolls to a stop at my feet, the other at Cole's. We bend down at the same time and pick up the pieces.

omega

li

## ZONE DIGAMMA DISSIPATES.

The fountain and English garden fade. Taylor and Hudson and Owen slip away. The monster vanishes. Time lapses in that moment. I am disconnected from the world.

lii

# REALITY BEGINS TO SEEP IN AT THE

edges of my mind. I'm back in the stasis pod where I started. Fluid drains around me. The tubes pull from my flesh. The force field dissolves.

I fall to the ground, landing hard on my hip. Clothes like the ones I wore in the virtual reality world are folded neatly in a pile on the ground next to me. My missing jacket is there, returned to me now that I'm back in the real world. On top of the pile is half of the golden apple, no longer withered but juicy. Immediately I want to sink my teeth into it, to feel the power. But I have to find Cole first.

I dress quickly, hooking my belt around my waist, and I run to find him. His pod is right where I remember. The fluid has already drained, and the tubes pull from his skin as I watch. I catch him as he falls, easing him to the ground next to his prosthetic. The other half of the apple rests on his clothes. I don't touch the apple. It is rightfully his just as my half is rightfully mine.

No words are enough, so I simply wrap my arms around Cole,

and we stay like that until I feel strong enough to face the world.

Once we're both dressed and as ready as we'll ever be, we turn away from our stasis pods forever. We walk by the other pods where our friends still drift in their stasis gel. Abigail, Taylor, Hudson, even Owen . . . they're all there, floating, alive. Kevin, the guy with the bear tattoo, is not so lucky. His hands are pressed outward on the force field that holds him, his eyes are wide. A scream is frozen on his open mouth. Dominic and Adam are the same, as are both the tall red-headed girl and Grace.

I tap the side of Taylor's pod, but nothing happens. She looks so peaceful, floating in the thick gel. Only moments ago she was battling the monster. She may still be for all I know.

"They're still alive, right?" I ask.

"They have to be," Cole says.

We have to believe we can help them.

A bark sounds through the darkness followed immediately by the hoot of an owl. Nails runs up to Cole and places her front paws on his chest as my owl swoops down, landing on my forearm. Relief floods me. My owl has come back.

In that moment, it seems like everything will be all right. We can figure this all out. Find a way to save our friends. Save my parents and Pia. Everything will be okay.

I turn to Cole, and without a word, my lips find his. I run my hands over his face, through his hair, needing to feel him and know that he's real. His fingers trace my shoulders, sending chills to every part of my body.

"I was so worried about you," he murmurs as he kisses my cheek. His tongue traces my ear, drifts down to my neck. I lean into him. Pull him closer. I could stay like this forever.

"Just don't leave me, okay? No matter what happens." My fingers trail along his back, his stomach. His muscles tense at my touch. He lets out a small groan.

"Never," he says.

I raise his face to mine one more time and allow myself one more kiss. It's hard and fierce and filled with everything I need. Then I back away, panting.

"We need to go," I say, trying to catch my breath. Every part of me wants to stay here, with him, forever. To forget about the rest of the world. But I can't.

He slowly nods, then reaches for my hand. "Together," he says.

The grid lines lead us through the dark to an arched door just like the ones in the labyrinth. Overhead is the last letter of the Greek alphabet. Omega. The end. We started at the beginning, when we set out on our journey, and now we've reached the finale.

Hand in hand, we pass through the door.

On the other side is a throne room. At the top of a set of steps is the large golden throne from my fleeting moments with the power, the same throne from the tapestries in the den of the spider. An old man sits in the throne, so weak he can hardly hold his head up. His long gray hair is unruly, and his beard rests on his stomach which rises and falls as he breathes. His skin is so pale, it's almost translucent. Next to him stands Zachary Gomez who has one hand placed on the old man's head. My eyes immediately try to meet his, but Zachary won't look at me. It's like he's trying to pretend he doesn't know me.

Nails runs to the base of the steps and begins to bark. My owl flies circles, swooping low to the throne but not touching it.

Iva steps forward, on level ground with us. I hadn't noticed her at first, but she's here in her sequin blue shirt and matching blue and white checked Vans. *There will be Drama,* her shirt reads. It's so fitting.

"You survived," she says, almost as if she's surprised. She ignores Nails and my owl.

My stomach is still weak from where Owen knocked the wind out of me. My face aches from where his punches landed. Two teeth wiggle when I push them with my tongue.

"You didn't think we would," I say.

Her eyes drift to Cole, still at my side, each of us clasping half of the golden apple.

"Nobody has so far," she says. "And now, to see two of you here before me . . . it's—"

"He says it's unheard of," Zachary Gomez says.

"It happened," Iva says, addressing the old man, not Zachary, as if Zachary is only there to speak for the old man because maybe he's too weak to speak on his own.

"He says they cheated," Zachary Gomez says. "They had help."

Of course we had help. Zachary's the one who gave me the code. He told me about the hidden zones. Without the information we would have wandered around in the labyrinth until the power was cut to our virtual reality cells. But why would he act like he hadn't helped . . . unless he wasn't supposed to?

"We didn't have help," Cole says, standing straight.

"We worked together. We had a truce," I say, hoping my face doesn't give away the truth. But in addition to Zachary giving me the cheat code, there was other help. The ax from my real house was planted there in the virtual junkyard. Zachary could have been behind that, too, programming it into the game. Mom had spoken to me from the dead, telling me not to eat the fruit. My parents had left me the compass. And then there's the jacket. Someone had planted it for me here in the real world, in Florida.

"He says they are liars!" Zachary Gomez screams, and his voice echoes around the chamber, amplifying the old man's feelings.

This seems to exhaust the old man. Each breath he takes rasps in his chest. His eyes don't blink for long periods of time, and when they do, they remain closed for seconds. His head hangs forward as if strength slips away with every second that passes. He looks like he could die any moment.

"He says that you should come forward and bestow the power upon him," Zachary Gomez says, but he winces as he says it, as if the Zachary from the lab is in there somewhere and does not want me to ever give away the power.

I grasp my half of the golden apple more tightly. The power is ours to keep. I have no plans to deliver it to anyone. I don't know who this old man is. He's most likely one of the dying gods Iva had mentioned.

Iva addresses the old man, hands on hips as if to assert herself. "It is theirs to keep. Those were the rules. That was the game."

"There are no rules," Zachary Gomez says for the old man. "The power is only for him. It has always been his. It will always be his. He will destroy the world if it isn't delivered." Zachary's voice falters, and his eyes finally meet mine. They seem to say, *Don't do it. Don't give in to him.*

My owl hoots, in warning, as if she can sense the same deception that I can.

"We're not giving it to anyone," Cole says, speaking for both of us.

"And you shouldn't," Iva says. "It is yours to keep. You won the game."

"The game is irrelevant!" Zachary Gomez screams for the old man. "You will give him the power, or he will take it from you."

Thankfully this old man doesn't look capable of breathing, not to mention stealing the power from Cole and me. I take a step back, searching for an exit. The Omega door we came through has been sealed. The other walls are solid, giving me no clue how Cole and I can get out of here.

Iva walks up the steps until she's directly in front of the old man. "This won't be like the other times. Your time is done. You will fade away and let others take your place."

"He won't!" Zachary Gomez says.

The old man's hand flies out, grabbing Iva by the wrist. She drops to the ground, writhing in pain as the old man's hand tightens. Then, though no part of me wants to be near the old man, I take a step toward him, and then another, as if something is drawing me forward, forcing me. I can't stop myself. I grab onto Cole, but he's moving forward also. Cole's face is creased with worry, and from the top of the steps, the old man laughs. His withered face breaks into a smile.

*Run away, Eden Monk,* Zachary seems to say. *Take the power and run.*

If I could, I would, but I'm no longer in control of my own body.

"Release me!" Iva yells. She twists and kicks, but the old man is having no part of it. His hand secures her, and he uses his mind to continue drawing us forward.

I pull against the invisible bonds that hold me. I try to drop to the ground. My owl swoops for me, just as Nails runs for Cole, but the animals can't get near us. Panic builds with each second that passes. I can't let this old man get the power.

"What do we do?" Cole says as he fights to keep his ground. But his efforts are as ineffective as mine. One step after another, we get closer. We're at the bottom of the steps. I continue to struggle. When we're halfway up, I think to take the apple and throw it, far away from this old man. But my body won't let me. I clench it in my fist.

Zachary Gomez watches me. Begs me to do something. But there is no way out of this. We are only steps away from losing what we worked so hard to gain. I can't let that happen. I will not be a pawn in this old man's game.

The old man's withered lips crack as his smile grows. His eyes widen as he sees us coming, almost as if he can smell the power coming toward him. I'm forced to take another step. My mind spins, working to figure out what I can do. How I can keep this old man from ruining everything. After fighting so hard, I'm not going to turn the power over to someone who would destroy the very world he is supposed to protect. I may as well have let Owen have it. Iva continues to twist and cry out, and Zachary's hand seems as unwillingly planted on the old man's head as my and Cole's movement forward. As we get closer, the old man lifts a hand out, beckoning us.

Another step, then another. And then Cole and I are directly in front of the old man. His hand brushes against my arm, and my skin crawls, almost as if bugs run across it. No, not like bugs. More like . . . little electrical pulses. Invisible grid lines, like this is all part of some simulation. It all clicks together then. The clothes we wear are the same. The belts are still slung around our waists. We thought we left the VR world when we were freed from the pods, but we're still here, in the final zone. Zone Omega. The end.

An image comes back to me then, of me opening my water bottle, releasing what is inside.

With my free hand, I yank the water bottle from my belt and flip open the cap. Snakes pour from it, falling to the ground, falling on the old man's lap. They slither and move and hiss, free from their captivity.

The smile falls from the old man's face, and where his skin had cracked, blood begins to drip across his lips. Zachary Gomez jerks his hand away from the old man's head, now released from the bonds that held him. He dashes down the steps, but I don't give him another thought and neither do the snakes. Instead they climb the old man's throne, twisting around him. They bite his arms. He claws at them with his decrepit hands, trying to get to the pieces of apple, but Cole and I hold the apple far from his reach.

The old man opens his mouth to speak, but the snakes are too fast. They slither inside, down his throat, gagging him. He thrashes and flails, but the snakes show him no mercy. Then he stops moving.

I think that, if there is a god, then I've killed him.

## LIII

**THE OLD MAN BEGINS TO SHRIVEL. HIS**
hair falls from his head in thick clumps, and skin peels from his
face and body until there's nothing left but a skeleton that looks
like it's smiling but isn't at all. Its jaw opens, as if it's still trying
to command me. Still trying to control the world. But the teeth
fall out. The bones crack and fall apart. When they hit the ground,
they are dust. The snakes sink into the ground and vanish.

*Thank you,* I think to the titan snake.

*Know that he is my enemy, too,* the titan snake says in my mind,
and I know now that this old man is who the snake had been
talking about. But that still leaves the question of who put the
titan snake in the labyrinth in the first place.

No sooner has the old man turned completely to dust, Iva
blinks out of existence next to the throne. I want to scream her
name. To bring her back because she's left me with more questions than answers, but it's no use. She's gone. I'm left standing at
the top of the steps in front of the throne with Cole at my side.
We hold the two pieces of golden apple.

I lift a shaking hand to Cole's face. He catches my hand with his and leans in to kiss me, pressing his lips softly against mine, trying to still my tremors. I wrap my arms around him, pulling him close because I have to believe that something is real. That this may still be the virtual reality world—we may have never left it—but we're both still here.

"You destroyed him," Zachary Gomez says.

I pull away from Cole, away from the kiss that I want to last forever. Zachary watches us from the bottom of the steps. He smiles when my eyes meet his, but just as quickly frowns when his eyes move to Cole. I release Cole's hand and walk down the stairs to confront Zachary.

"Should I be sorry?" I say. "Because I'm not."

Zachary shakes his head. "No. It's good. Great in fact. It makes everything so much simpler."

"Everything like what?" Cole asks, coming up beside me.

Zachary doesn't even look at Cole. He keeps his eyes locked on me. "Everything like what to do now. With him gone, there's a clear path for the power."

"We have the power," I say. "We escaped the labyrinth. The power is ours." The piece of apple feels like a part of me. Like I would die without it. Even now, the energy licks off it, tempting me.

Zachary steps back and puts his hands up. "Don't worry. I'm not going to take it. I don't have the abilities for that. That's why I came up with the idea for the labyrinth. It was a way for the power to be passed on to someone worthy."

"It was your idea?" I ask.

He nods. "Well, mine and the others. Minors gods I guess you can think of us. We knew the old gods had to be destroyed; they were killing the earth. So slowly, bit by bit, we stole the power away from them. Stored it in the apple. And when we had it all, we designed the labyrinth to protect it."

"You're not just a glorified janitor, are you?" I say. "That's what the programming team is. You and your other . . ." I can't bring myself to say it.

"Minor gods," Zachary says. He runs a hand through his hair, like he's trying to straighten it and look respectable, but it's futile. His hair is messier than Cole's.

Zachary Gomez is a god? He'd been watching me. He'd helped me win. He wanted me to defeat the old man. This is all some giant conspiracy between the gods, and we're caught in the middle.

"You designed the whole thing," I say, trying to make sense of his words.

"Pretty much," Zachary says. "Iva became the manifestation of the power. She helped us find all of you. Helped bring you here. And then the game was played."

The game that we just escaped from. Except we haven't really escaped from it at all.

"We're still inside the labyrinth, aren't we?" I ask.

"Not exactly," Zachary says.

I piece through the logic. *IF-THEN.* If we came out of our stasis chambers, then we can no longer be in the labyrinth. It's not possible. But . . .

"The labyrinth was a VR world inside another VR world," I say. "We've been in stasis longer than we realized."

"There you go," Zachary says, grinning at me in his own nerdy way. "I knew you'd figure it out."

"How long?" Cole asks.

Zachary actually looks annoyed that Cole has spoken instead of me, because even though Cole is right here next to me, Zachary definitely hasn't included him in the conversation.

"Eden Monk, how long have you been here?" he asks, like he expects me to have the answer.

I trace back everything that has happened. Before entering the labyrinth, I was in Zachary's lab. And before that I was on the

**313**

beach, talking to Iva. Is that when it all started? I remember so well the gel of the VR stasis chamber surrounding me. The tubes inserting themselves into me. I was sure I was going to die. And now Zachary is telling me that none of that was even real.

"In your lab," I say.

"Earlier."

"When we entered the volcano," Cole says.

Zachary frowns at Cole. "Not quite."

Earlier. I continue tracing my steps backward, thinking of the world of the sirens. Their world doesn't fit with ours.

"When we reached the garden," I say. "This whole place doesn't exist."

Zachary seems to consider this. "It exists. Not in a flesh and bone form. But you have to think beyond that. This is the power of the gods we're talking about."

"So it was when we reached the garden," Cole says.

"Maybe," Zachary says, finally looking to Cole, resigning himself to the fact that Cole is here, too. "Or maybe even earlier."

Earlier than when we entered the garden? That means it would have happened on our journey, while we were trying to reach this place.

"You're telling me we've been in a virtual reality world when we thought we were back in the real world?" I say. "That's impossible."

"Oh, come on, Eden Monk. You know it's not impossible. You adore this kind of thing. Why can't this be a giant VR world?"

"Because it's not," I say, knowing it sounds weak, but I'm grasping at straws. "Because I remember things. My family. Thomas. School. Nothing changed."

"Really?" Zachary says.

Things had changed. There are things that can't be explained. The letters of the Target sign shifting before my eyes. The jacket which protected me from harm. Nobody being able to see me. The dead walking the earth. It would have been impossible. Should

**314**

have been impossible. Unless it was all part of some simulation.

As these unexplained moments pass through my mind, panic begins to rise. If Zachary is telling the truth, then maybe nothing is real.

"Where are my parents? Where is Thomas?" I ask. "I want to see them now."

"Are you sure they're real?" Zachary asks. "How do you know they weren't part of some great computer program, developed specifically for you? A program you could have been living in for weeks? Years? Your whole life?"

His words hit me like a shock wave, but I refuse to be pushed under.

"I know my family is real," I say. "I can feel it."

Zachary Gomez steps forward and takes my face in his hands, looking me directly in the eyes. "Don't assume you know anything, Eden. Assumptions will only get you killed."

My head pounds with anger. "What is real?" I demand. Then the vision comes.

*Cole and I exit the volcano. The sulfur smell is thick in the air, and the steam makes for poor visibility, but the staircase we came up is there, carved into the stone of the volcano. Lava flows around us on both sides but doesn't block our path as we walk down. I count the steps, one after another, until we reach the bottom. We're in the garden, and through the gates is a road that leads off into the distance.*

*We take the road, walking hand in hand, until we come to a dome. This is what I've come for. I feel it deep inside me.*

*We push open the heavy doors and enter. And I'm sure my parents are inside.*

My owl hoots, and the vision slips away.

"Where is the dome?" I ask. "Where are my parents?"

Zachary plants a very gentle kiss on my forehead then releases my face. "I don't have all the answers, Eden. Because the thing is that we were all working on this together. The whole programming team. But things haven't been going as planned. The zone that wasn't working. Abigail praying to save Owen. The old man almost getting the power back from you. Those things weren't supposed to be happening."

"So why did they happen?" I ask.

"I don't know," Zachary says.

"There's a lot you don't know, isn't there?" Cole says, eyeing Zachary warily. I'm not sure why, but there is some sort of invisible animosity between the two of them.

"Unfortunately, yes," Zachary says. He reaches in to his lab coat and pulls out the golden compass. The owl gleams on the cover. He hands it to me.

I take it, running my thumb over the engraving, feeling the connection to my parents all over again. And in that moment, I know this is the secret to seeing them again. To finding them.

"The old man was right," Zachary says. "You did have help."

Before I can say anything, before I can ask him why he would help me, before I can ask him what we should do next, he winks at me then vanishes, leaving Cole and me alone in the throne room.

liv

## "WHAT'S YOUR FAVORITE CHILDHOOD

memory?" I ask Cole, knowing that his childhood is not filled
with many favorites. But it has to be asked. The illusion has to be
broken.

"Edie . . . ," he begins.

"Just tell me," I say. "What the best thing you remember from
when you were a kid?"

"Mardi Gras," he says. "My dad worked on a float one year in
his spare time, and as a reward, he and I got to stand on the float
during a parade. It was before everything changed. Back when I
still had my leg. When my face looked normal. And the funniest
thing about it is that I had this mask on. Everyone wore a mask.
It was part of the whole Mardi Gras thing. But my mask was like
*Phantom of the Opera*. It only covered half my face."

"What was fun about it?" I ask, pressing him past the sad part
of his memory.

"The beads," Cole says. "The float had them by the thousands,
and they were letting everyone throw them, even me. I wasn't

strong enough to get them to the sidewalk. I was that young. But my dad kept handing me more and more to throw. Why do you ask?"

"I remember the day Thomas was born," I say, tucking his question aside for the moment. "My mom went nearly two weeks over her delivery date. Every morning she'd wake up and say, 'It's a great day for a baby,' and every day the baby wouldn't come. She didn't know it was going to be a boy ahead of time. She wanted to be surprised. And then in the middle of the night, my dad ran into my room. Said the baby was coming. I demanded to go along with them to the hospital. I was not going to miss it for anything. I fell asleep in the waiting room, but my dad woke me up. He had tears in his eyes. 'It's a boy,' he said. 'What should we call him?' And I'd just read this biography of Thomas E. Kurtz, one of the creators of the computer language BASIC. I idolized the guy; wanted to be just like him. 'Can we call him Thomas?' I'd asked, and my dad said it was a great name."

"Why are you talking about this now?" Cole asks.

"Because my memory is real," I say. "And if I believe it strongly enough, no one will be able to convince me any differently. My family is real. Pia is real. And I know how to get back to them."

"Break out of virtual reality?" Cole says.

I nod. "All the signs were there, from nobody being able to see us to the dead people crawling out of the ground. None of it was real. It still isn't."

"Then how do we get out?" Cole asks.

I scan the room, thinking there must be an exit. Some portal we walk through that will release us from the virtual world and bring us back to the real world. But I don't see an exit. The Omega door we came through is sealed. The walls are blank.

I reach my hands to my neck, to my ears and eyes, feeling for sensors. Given that we are still in a virtual world, there have to be connectors linking us from one world to the other. A way to make this all seem real. But I can't feel anything different from I would expect.

I reach for Cole, running my hands along his face and chest, reaching under his shirt.

"Where are they?" I want to claw my eyes out with frustration.

"Where are what?"

"The sensors. They have to be here."

I try again, this time going slower. I blink, pressing my fingers into my tear ducts. I shake my head, probe my fingers into my ears. Then I feel something, in the canal of my right ear. It's small but it might be enough to break the illusion. Without thinking about what I'm doing, I yank it first from Cole's ear then from my own.

The world shatters around us. Everything—the throne, Nails, my owl—flickers and blinks away.

Everything except the compass and the pieces of golden apple. They're still there, held in our hands. We risked our lives for this apple. We watched friends die for it. We've rightfully earned it. It is the power of the gods, and it's ours to use.

Together we lift the pieces of the apple up, a symbol of our victory. A future that we control. We tap them together, a sign of our truce. Unbroken. It may be the only way we survived. Then we devour them.

**Don't miss Book 2 in the *Game of the Gods* Series**

# A RUINED LAND